ROGER ZELAZNY

TO DIE IN ITALBAR
A DARK TRAVELLING

ROGER ZELAZNY authored many science fiction and fantasy classics, and won three Nebula Awards and six Hugo Awards over the course of his long and distinguished career. While he is best known for his ten-volume *Chronicles of Amber* series of novels (beginning with 1970's *Nine Princes in Amber*), Zelazny also wrote many other novels, short stories, and novellas, including *Psychoshop* (with Alfred Bester), *Damnation Alley*, the award-winning *The Doors of His Face, The Lamps of His Mouth* and *Lord of Light*, and the stories "24 Views of Mount Fuji, by Hokusai," "Permafrost," and "Home is the Hangman." Zelazny died in Santa Fe, New Mexico, in June 1995.

D1799393

TO DIE IN ITALBAR

A DARK TRAVELLING

ROGER ZELAZNY

ibooks
new york
www.ibooks.net

DISTRIBUTED THROUGH SIMON & SCHUSTER, INC

TO DIE
IN ITALBAR

To Janie and Dan Armel,
with pleasant memories
of crustacea craft,
artillery practice,
slushes, bicycles,
lots of Crocketts,
roads that went nowhere
and never on Sunday.

CHAPTER 1

On the night he had chosen months before, Malacar Miles crossed the street numbered seven, passing beneath the glow-globe he had damaged during the day.

All three of Blanchen's moons were below the horizon. The sky was slightly overcast, the few visible stars tiny and weak.

Glancing up and down the street, inhaling another puff of lung-conditioner, he moved forward. He wore a black garment with slit pockets, stat-sealed up the front. While crossing, he tested his pockets for access to the side-pacs. Having dyed his entire body black three days before, he was near-invisible as he moved among shadows.

Atop the building across the street numbered seven, Shind sat, a two-foot ball of fur, unmoving, unblinking.

Before proceeding to Employee Entrance Four, he located three key points in the durrilide wall and deactivated their alarm devices without breaking the circuits. The door at Entrance Four took him longer, but within another fifteen minutes he stood inside the building. The darkness was complete.

Donning goggles and lighting his special torch, he moved ahead, passing through aisles containing identical pieces of machinery. In recent months, he had practiced dismantling and reassembling the proper sections of this particular piece of equipment.

A human guard is passing in front of the building.

Thanks, Shind.

After a time, *He is turning up the street you took.*

Let me know if he does anything that seems unusual.

He is just walking, shining his light into shadows.

Tell me if he stops at any of the places I stopped before I came in.

He has passed the first.

Good.

He has gone by the second one.

Capital.

Malacar opened the housing of one of the machines and removed a component the size of a pair of fists.

He has stopped by the entrance. He is testing the door.

He commenced the installation of a similar-appearing component he had carried in with him, stopping only for occasional whiffs from his aerosol.

He is moving away now.

Good.

Finishing the installation, he replaced and affixed the console cover.

Advise me when he is out of sight.

I will.

He returned to Employee Entrance Four.

He is gone.

Malacar Miles departed then, halting only at key points to remove all traces of his visit.

After three blocks, he paused at an intersection and looked in all directions. A sudden splash of red across the sky indicated the arrival of another transport vessel. He could go no farther.

Blanchen was no ordinary world. So long as he remained within the twelve-by-twelve complex of blocks and did not trip an alarm-device on any of its windowless buildings of durrilide, he was moderately safe from detection. There were, however, several living watchmen assigned to each complex, along with rolling patrols of robots covering a larger area. This is the reason he stood within shadow. He avoided as best he could the glow-globes on each building, the lights which guided low-flying nightcraft and served to orient watchmen.

Seeing nothing at the intersection, he reentered the complex and scouted the rendezvous point.

To your right. One block over and two ahead. A mechanical car. It is turning a corner. Go right.

Thanks.

He moved to the right, keeping track of the turns he made.

The vehicle is well off in the distance now.

Good.

He retreated from a watchman, retraced a block, turned at right angles to his course, proceeded three blocks. He froze when he heard the sound of a flying machine.

Where is it?

Stay where you are. You are out of their line of sight.

What is it?

A small skimmer. It came in quickly from the north. It

has slowed. Now it is hovering above the street of your recent activities.

Oh God!

It is descending.

Malacar checked the chrono on his left wrist and suppressed a groan. He patted at the bulges of various weapons that he bore.

It has landed.

He waited.

After a time, *Two men have emerged from the vehicle. They appear to have been its only occupants. A watchman is coming to meet them.*

Where did he come from? Not the building?

No. From the opposite street. It is as if he had been waiting for them. They are talking now. Now the watchman is shrugging his shoulders.

Malacar felt the pounding of his heart and sought to control his breathing, so as not to hyperventilate himself in the unusual atmosphere of Blanchen. He inhaled more mist from his aerosol. He started then, as two transports cut the sky in rapid succession—one headed toward the southeast, one west.

The two men are reentering their vehicle.

What of the watchman?

He is just standing there—watching.

He counted twenty-three heartbeats.

Now the vehicle is beginning to rise, very slowly. Now it is drifting toward the face of the building.

Though the night was chill, Malacar felt perspiration across his high, dark brow. He brushed it away with the edge of his forefinger.

They are hovering. Now there is some activity. I cannot determine what it is. It is too dark—There! Now it is light.

They have replaced the globe you damaged. Now they are rising again. The watchman is waving. They are heading back in the direction from which they came.

Malacar's great frame shook. He laughed.

Then he began working his way, slowly, back in the direction of the rendezvous point—a point he had chosen carefully, as Blanchen was no ordinary world.

In addition to the watchmen and the alarms, there were air-surveillance networks at various altitudes. On the previous evening, his vehicle had blocked them effectively on the way down, and presumably had done the same on the way back out. He checked his chrono and whiffed more of the lung-cleaning vapors. He had not taken the trouble to have himself conditioned for the airs of Blanchen, in the fashion of the watchmen, laborers and technicians who dwelled there.

Less than forty minutes . . .

Blanchen had no oceans, lakes, rivers, streams. Not a trace of indigenous life remained—only an atmosphere to testify that something had once dwelled there. At one point in its more recent history, the notion had been entertained of retaining a worldscaper to beat it into livable shape. It was rejected on two grounds, however: expense, and the fact that an alternative to habitation had been proposed. A combine of manufacturers and shippers had recommended that its dry lands and preservative atmosphere would provide ideal conditions for making use of the entire planet as a warehouse. They offered the discoverers full partnership in the venture, and for their own part wanted to undertake the development and staffing of the world. These terms were acceptable, accepted and accomplished.

Now Blanchen lay like a durrilitic pineapple with millions of eyes. Thousands of interstellar freighters circled constantly, and between them and the hundreds of thousands of landing docks plied the transport vessels, bringing and taking. The three moons of Blanchen served as traffic control centers and rest havens. The ground crews, working out of area centers, moving between docks and warehouses, bringing and taking. Depending upon the output of industry and the demands of the consumer worlds, a particular dock, area or complex might be constantly busy, occasionally busy or seldom used. Ground crews were shifted according to the flows of activity. The men's pay was good, with living conditions comparable to those of the peacetime military. Unlike a warehouse which serves the world it occupies, however, while storage space means money and prolonged storage a loss thereof, transportation across interstellar distances is extremely costly.

Accordingly, goods in small demand may remain in storage for years, centuries, even. The building which Malacar had visited had remained undisturbed for almost two Earth months. Knowing this, he had expected small difficulty; that is, unless the impending deal of which he had become aware had been concluded ahead of schedule.

Considering the overworked traffic control centers, and the monitor and avoidance system programmed into his tiny, personal vessel, *The Perseus*, he did not feel that he would be taking too great a personal risk in leaving the DYNAB and entering into the territory of the Combined Leagues, in coming to Blanchen. If they found him and killed him, he would be proven incorrect. If they found him and captured him or accepted his ready surrender, they would have no choice but to send him home. But they would probably question him first, under drugs, find out what he had done and then undo it.

But if they did not find him, inside, in time . . .

He chuckled, softly.

... The bird would have struck once more, halving another small worm.

His chrono gave him fifteen to twenty minutes.

Where are you, Shind?

Above you, keeping watch.

This one, Shind, should be a good one.

It seemed so, from the way you described it.

Three transports flashed above them, heading east. Malacar followed them with his eyes until they were out of sight.

You are tired, Commander, said Shind, reverting to a bygone formality.

Nervous fatigue. That is all, Lieutenant. What of yourself?

There is some of that. My main concern, of course, is for my brother . . .

He is safe.

I know that. But he will not recall our assurances. He will grow lonely, then afraid.

He will come to no harm, and we will be united soon.

There was no reply, so Malacar sniffed his vapors and waited.

Half-dozing (for how long?), he was alerted:

She comes! Now! She comes!

Smiling, he stretched his muscles and looked upward, knowing that for a few moments he would be unable to see that which the eyes of Shind had already detected.

It dropped like a spider and hung like a grim festival float. For a moment it hovered above him, while Shind boarded it. Another moment, and it had lowered itself farther and extended the drop-bar. Seizing it, he put his weight upon it and was taken up into the belly of *The Perseus*, passing by that mask of Medusa with the smile of the Mona Lisa which he had painted there himself. He longed for a serpent, but would settle for worms.

He spat out of the hatch just before it closed, striking the side of the building below him.

Heidel von Hymack, on the way to Italbar, watched his companions die. There had been nine of them—volunteers all—who had set out to accompany him through the rain forest of Cleech to the mountain town Italbar where he was needed; Italbar, a thousand miles distant from the space port. He had taken an air car to reach it. Forced down, he had told his story to the villagers by the River Bart, who had come upon him walking westward. Now five remained of the nine who had accompanied him against his protestations. Now one of the five was sweating, and another coughed periodically.

Heidel ran his hand through his sandy beard and continued to kick his black boots through the growth that covered what was supposed to be a trail. He perspired and his shirt stuck to him. He had warned them that it was dangerous to accompany him, he reflected. It was not as if he had not warned them.

They had heard of him, heard that he was a holy man, heard that he was on an errand of mercy.

"The last part is correct," he had told them, "but you will not score any heavenly merit points because of me."

They had laughed. No, he would need someone to protect him from the animals and show him the trail.

"Ridiculous! Point me in the right direction and I will get there," he had said. "You will be in more danger in my company than you would be out there alone."

But they had laughed again and refused to show him the way unless he permitted an escort to accompany him.

"But it can be death to be with me for too long a period of time!" he had protested.

They were adamant.

He had sighed.

"Very well, then. Give me a place where I may be completely alone and undisturbed for a day or so. It will be an expenditure of valuable time, time that should not really be lost at this point. But I must try to protect you if there is no other way that you will assist me."

They did this, and then they danced about one another and laughed at their part in a great adventure. Heidel von Hymack, the green-eyed saint from the stars, was obviously going to pray, to arrange things for their safety and the success of the trip.

Two or three days, walking, they had told him. So he had tried forcing the catharsis in order to get under way. A child lay dying in Italbar, and he had come to measure the minutes in terms of her breathing.

The Blue Lady had told him to wait, but he thought of that breathing and of the contractions of a large heart that had once been tiny. He had started out after fifteen hours and it had been a mistake.

The fevers of two of his companions had gone undetected, because of fatigue and the excessive heat of the forest. They had expired on the afternoon of the second day. He was unable to identify which of the many possible diseases it was. This was because he did not try very hard. Once a man is dead, he considered the means an academic point. In addition, his desire for urgency was such that he begrudged the others even the brief funeral ceremony and burial in which they indulged. He felt this doubly on the following morning, when two of the remaining seven did not awaken and he was compelled to witness the same rite repeated. He cursed in other languages as he helped prepare the graves.

The faceless, laughing ones—for so he had come to consider them—now possessed expressions and lacked laughter. Their ruby eyes were wide and darted at every sound. The six digits of their hands shook, writhed, snapped. Now they were beginning to understand. Now it was too late.

But two or three days . . . This was the third day, and the mountains were nowhere in sight.

"Glay, where are the mountains?" he asked the coughing one. "Where is Italbar?"

Glay shrugged and pointed ahead.

The sun, a giant yellow ball, was all but invisible from their trail. Its light leaked through the starfish leaves, but in every place that it missed there was moisture or fungus. Small animals or large insects—he did not know which—darted from their path, scurried behind them, rattled the bushes and moved along the branches. The larger creatures of which he had been warned never appeared, though he heard their hisses, their whistles, their barks often in the distance; and occasionally there was the sound of something huge crashing through the forest near at hand.

He was taken by the irony of it. He had come to save a life and the effort had already cost four. "Lady, you were right," he muttered, thinking of his dream.

It was perhaps an hour later that Glay collapsed, racked with coughing, his normally olive complexion the color of the leaves about them. Heidel moved to his side, recognizing the condition. Given several days' preparation, he might have been able to save the man. He had failed when he had tried with the others because his own catharsis had not been complete. The necessary balance had been lacking. At that moment—as he had looked upon the first of the fallen—he had known that all nine of them were going to die before very long. He helped to make Glay comfortable, back against a tree trunk, his pack for a pillow, gulping water. He glanced at his chrono. Anywhere from ten minutes to an hour and a half, he guessed.

He sighed and lit a cigar. It tasted foul. The moisture had long before gotten to it, and it was obvious that the fungi of Cleech had nothing against nicotine. The little green mound of it that flared momentarily smelled something like sulfur.

Glay looked up at him. A glare of accusation seemed to be in order.

Instead, "Thank you, Heidel," he said, "that we may share with you in this thing," and then he smiled.

Heidel wiped the man's brow. It took him another half hour to die.

This time he did not mumble to himself during the burial, but studied the faces of the remaining four. The same expression was present. They had started out with him as though on a lark. Then the situation had changed and they had accepted it. It did not seem a matter of resignation either. There were expressions of happiness on their dark faces. Yet they all knew it, he could tell. They all knew they were going to die before Italbar.

He appreciated stories of noble sacrifices as well as any man. But futile deaths—! To do it for no reason . . . He knew—and they knew, he was certain—that he could have made it to Italbar alone. All along, they had done nothing but walk with him. There had been no menacing beasts to fend off; the trail had been clear enough once he had set foot upon it. It would be pleasant simply to be a geologist, as he had been on that day . . .

Two died after a lunch during which they ate little. Mercifully, it was mawl fever, previously unknown on Cleech, which makes for a sudden cardiac arrest and twists the victim's face into a smile.

Both men's eyes remained open after death. Heidel closed them himself.

They set about the business again, and Heidel did not interrupt when he saw that they were digging four graves. He assisted, and afterward he waited with them. Nor did he have long to wait.

Finishing, he shouldered his pack once more and continued on his way. He did not look back, but in his mind's eye he could see the mounds he had left behind. The obvious, grisly analogy could not be suppressed. His life was the trail. The graves were symbolic of the hundreds—no, probably thousands—of dead that he had left behind. At his touch men died. His breath withered cities. Where his shadow touched sometimes nothing remained.

Yet it was within his power to undo ills. Even now he trudged uphill with this intention. For this he was often known, though the name was only H.

The day seemed to brighten, though he knew it was well into the afternoon. Seeking the answer, he saw that the trees were smaller, the gaps between their leaves greater. The sunlight fell in more places and there were even flowers—red and purple, bearded and haloed with gold and pale yellow—drifting on the vines the breezes pushed about him. His way grew steeper, but the grasses that had snatched at his ankles were shorter now and fewer small things rushed chittering about him.

After perhaps half an hour's time, he could see farther ahead than at any previous point on his journey. For a hundred meters the way lay clear and bright. When he had traversed this distance he met with the first full gap in the living roof and saw there a huge, pale, green pool, the sky. Within ten minutes, he was walking in the open and was able to look back upon the shifting sea of boughs beneath which he had passed. A quarter mile ahead and above lay what seemed the summit of the hill he now realized himself to be climbing. Small, pale-jade clouds hung above it. Avoiding rocks, he approached.

Attaining this vantage, he was able to see what he guessed to be the final leg of his route. There was a descent of several dozen meters, an hour's walk across a fairly level valley, sloping upward at its far end, and then a steep ascent of high hill or low mountain. He rested, chewed some rations, drank water, moved on.

The crossing proved uneventful, but he cut himself a staff before he reached its end.

The air grew more chilly as he climbed the far trail, and the day began to wane. By the time he had reached the halfway mark on his ascent, he felt a certain shortness of breath and his muscles were aching from this as well as the previous days' exertions. He was able to look back over a great distance now, where treetops were like a vast plain beneath a darkening sky and a few birds circled.

He paused to rest more frequently as he neared the summit, and after a time he saw the first star of evening.

He pushed himself until he stood upon the broad ridge that was the top of this long, gray line of rocky prominence; by then, the night had come down around him. Cleech had no moons, but the great stars all shone with the brilliance of torches through crystal, and behind them the lesser stars foamed and bubbled in seeming millions. The night sky was a blue and illuminated place.

He crossed the remaining distance, following the trail with his eyes, and there were lights, lights, lights, and many dark forms that could only be houses, buildings, ground vehicles in motion. Two hours, he guessed, and he could be walking those streets, passing among the inhabitants of peaceful Italbar, stopping at some friendly inn perhaps, for a meal, a drink, passing the time of day with some fellow diner. Then he looked away and thought upon the trail he had walked, knowing that he could not, yet, venture this thing. The vision of Italbar at that moment of time, however, would remain with him all the days of his life.

Moving back away from the trail, he found a level place to spread his bedroll. He forced himself to eat as much as he could and to drink as much water as his stomach would hold, in preparation for what was to come.

He combed his hair and beard, relieved himself, undressed, buried his clothing and crawled into the bedroll.

He stretched his not quite six-foot frame full length, clamped his arms tightly to his sides, clenched his teeth, regarded the stars for a moment, closed his eyes.

After a time, the lines went out of his face and his jaw sagged. His head rolled toward his left shoulder. His breathing deepened, slowed, seemed to stop altogether, resumed much later, very slowly.

When he rolled his head to the right, it appeared as if his face had been shellacked, or as if a perfectly fitting mask of glass had been laid upon it. Then the perspiration ran and the droplets glittered like jewels in his beard. His face began to darken. It grew red, then purple, and his mouth opened and his tongue protruded and his breath came into him in great paroxysmic gasps, while saliva dribbled from the corner of his mouth.

His body shuddered, and he curled himself into a ball and began to shake steadily. Twice his eyes snapped open, unseeing, closing again only slowly. He foamed at the mouth and groaned. Blood trickled from his nose and dried upon his mustache. Periodically, he mumbled. Then his body stiffened for a long while, loosened finally and was still until the next seizure.

The blue-touched mists hid his feet, billowed about him, as though he were walking through snow ten times lighter than any he had ever known. Curving lines of it twisted, drifted, broke, recombined. It was neither warm nor cold. There were no stars overhead, only a pale blue moon that hung motionless in that place of perpetual twilight. Banks of indigo roses lay to his left and there were blue rocks to his right.

Turning, beyond the rocks, he came upon the shallow flight of stairs that led upward. Narrow at first, they widened until he could no longer see their limits at either hand. He mounted, moving through blue nothingness.

He came into the garden.

There were shrubs of all shades and textures of blue, and vines that climbed what might have been walls—though they grew too densely for him to be certain—and stone benches of seeming random situation.

Wisps of mist drifted here also, slowly, seeming almost to hover. He heard birdsongs above him and from within the vines.

He advanced into the place, passing at irregular intervals large chunks of stone that glittered like polished quartz. Little rainbows danced about them and hordes of large blue butterflies seemed attracted by the shining. They swarmed, pirouetted, lighted a moment, returned to the air.

Far ahead, he saw a barely distinct shape, so vast as to be unbelievable, did he possess that critical faculty which gives rise to disbelief.

It was the form of a woman that he saw, half-hid amid bewilderments of blue, a woman whose hair, blue-black, swept the skies to the farthest horizons, whose eyes he could not see, but only feel, as though she watched from all directions, while her aura and partly glimpsed lineaments were, he knew, the anima of the world. Then came to him a feeling of immense power and immense restraint.

As he drew nearer to that place in the garden, she vanished. The feeling of her presence persisted.

He became aware of a blue stone summerhouse, situated behind a high stand of shrubbery.

The light faded as he neared it until, when he entered, he felt once again the sorry realization that he would only glimpse a smile, a fluttering eyelid, an earlobe, a strand of hair, the sheen of blue moonbeams upon a restless forearm or shoulder. Never had he, nor would he—he felt—look her full in the face, describe with his eyes her entire form.

"Heidel von Hymack," came the words—not voiced, but in a whisper that carried far better than ordinary speech.

"Lady—"

"You did not heed my warning. You started out too soon."

"I know. I know . . . When I am awake you seem unreal, just as now that other place seems but a dream."

He heard her soft laughter.

"You have the best of both worlds, you know," she said, "a thing that is seldom given to a man. While you are here with me in this pleasant bower, your body writhes with the extreme symptoms of terrible diseases. When you awaken there, you will be refreshed and whole once again."

"For a time," he said, seating himself on a stone bench that ran along a wall, resting his back against the wall's cool roughness.

"... And when that fresh time has passed, you may return here at will—" (Was that a trick of moonlight or a glimpse of her dark, dark eyes? he wondered) "—to be renewed."

"Yes," he said. "What happens here when I am there?"

He felt her fingertips brush against his cheek. There came a whelming of delight within him.

"Are you not happiest when you are here?" she asked.

"Yes, Myra-o-arym," and he turned his head and kissed her fingertips. "But other things than disease seem to remain behind when I come here—things that should be in my mind. I—I cannot remember."

"This is as it must be, Dra von Hymack.—Now, you must remain with me this time until you are fully refreshed, for the fluids of your body must be in perfect balance for you to do what must be done upon your return. You may depart this place at will, as well you know. But this time I recommend that you await my advice."

"This time I shall, Lady.—Tell me things."

"What things, my child?"

"I—I am trying to think of them. I—"

"Do not try too hard. It will be of no avail—"

"Deiba! That is one of the things I sought! Tell me of Deiba."

"There is nothing to tell, Dra. It is a small world in an insignificant portion of the galaxy. There is nothing special about it."

"But there is. I am certain. A shrine...? Yes. On a high plateau. There is a ruined city all about it. The shrine is underground—is it not?"

"There are many such places in the universe."

"But this one is special. Isn't it?"

"Yes, in a strange, sad way it is, offspring of Terra. Only

*one man of your race ever came to proper terms with what
you met there."*

"What was it?"

"No," she said; and she touched him once more.

*Then he heard music, soft and simple, and she began to
sing to him. He did not hear—or if he heard, did not understand—any of the words she sang; but the blue mists swirled
about him and there were perfumes, breezes, a kind of quiet
ecstasy; and when he looked again there were no questions
at all.*

Dr. Larmon Pels orbited the world Lavona and transmit-
ted a message to Medical Central, a message to Immigration
and Naturalization Central and a message to Vital Statistics
Central. Then he folded his hands and waited.

There was nothing else for him to do but fold his hands.
He did not eat, drink, smoke, breathe, sleep, excrete, feel
pain or indulge in any of the other common expressions of
the flesh. In fact, he possessed no heartbeat. Various powerful chemical agents with which he had been invested were
all that stood between Dr. Pels and putrefaction. There were
several things which kept him going, however.

One was a tiny power system implanted within his body.
This allowed him to move about without expending his own
energy (though he never descended to the surface of a
world, for his mini-powered movements would be overcome
immediately, transforming him into a living statue cap-
tioned, perhaps, "Collapse"). This system, feeding as it did
into his brain, also provided sufficient neural stimulation
for his higher cerebral processes to function at all times.

Totally spacebound and continually thinking, therefore,
was Dr. Pels, an exile from the worlds of life, a wanderer, a

man who sought, a man who waited—by normal standards, a moving dead man.

The other thing which kept him going was not so tangible as his physical support system. His body frozen seconds before the onset of clinical death, it was not until days later that his Disposition of Assets Statement was read. Since a frozen man "does not enjoy the same status as a dead man" (*Herms* v. *Herms*, 18,777 C., Civil No. 187-3424), he may "exercise authority over his possessions by means of earlier demonstrations of intention, in precisely the same fashion as a sleeping man" (*Nyes et al.* v. *Nyes*, 794 C., Civil No. 14-187-B). Accordingly, despite the protestations of several generations of well-meaning offspring, all of Dr. Pels' assets were converted to cash, which was used to purchase a bubble ship of interstellar capability with full medical laboratory, and to transform Dr. Pels himself from a state of cold inanimation to one of chilly mobility. All of this because, rather than await, dreamless, the hoped-for-but-maybe-never treatment of and recovery from his own condition, he had decided that he would not be especially troubled by dwelling indefinitely at a point perhaps ten seconds removed from death, so long as he could continue with his research. "After all," he had once said, "think of all the persons who at this moment are but ten seconds removed from death and are not even aware of the fact, so that they might attempt that which they most love."

That which Dr. Pels most loved was pathology, of the most exotic sort. He had been known to trace a new disease halfway across the galaxy. Over the decades he had published brilliant papers, had developed major remedies, had written textbooks, had lectured medical classes from his orbiting laboratory, had been considered for both the

Dyarchic Nations and Allied Bodies and Combined Leagues Medical Awards (each, it was rumored, rejecting him for fear that the other might award him) and was granted full access to the general medical information banks of virtually any civilized planet he visited. Just about any other information he desired was relayed to him also.

Hovering above his laboratory tables—gaunt, hairless, six and a half feet in height and pale as bone—his long, thin fingers adjusting a flame or tilting a squeeze-bulb toward a vacuum-sphere, Dr. Pels seemed uniquely appropriate for the investigation of the many-splendored forms of death. Now, while it was true that he was not liable to the common exercises of living things, there was one pleasure which he possessed in addition to his work. He had music wherever he went. Light music, profound music; there was music about him constantly. His numbed body could feel it, whether he listened or ignored it. It may be that in some way it substituted for the heartbeat and the breathing and all the other little bodily sounds and feelings most men take for granted. Whatever the reason, it had been years since he had been without music.

Amid music and with folded hands, therefore, he waited. Once he glanced at Lavona, in its black and tawny beauty above him, a tiger in the night. Then he turned his mind to other matters.

For two decades he had wrestled with a particular disease. Realizing then that he was only a little further along than when he had begun, he decided upon a different avenue of attack: locate the one man who survived it and find out why.

With this in mind, he had set out in a roundabout fashion for the hub of the Combined Leagues—Solon, Elizabeth and Lincoln, the three artificial worlds designed by Sandow himself, orbiting Kwale's Star—where he might consult the Panopath computer for information as to the whereabouts of the man called H, whose identity he had recently ascertained. The information should be there, though few would know the proper questions to put to the machine.

Dr. Pels stopped along the way, however, to make inquiry at various worlds. It would be worth the extra time, should he locate his man in this fashion. Once he reached SEL he might wait over a year before obtaining access to Panopath, as major public health projects had automatic priority.

So he beat a circuitous route toward SEL, hub of the Combined Leagues, concerts streaming about him, death-analysis gear at the ready. He doubted that he would ever reach SEL, or need to. From the little that he had learned in his two decades' struggle against *mwalakharan khurr*, the Deiban fever, he was certain that he would recognize as clues items that another man would dismiss as isolated phenomena. He was also certain that from these clues he would locate the man he sought, and that he would be able to extract from him the weapon which would lay another shade of the Reaper.

Ten seconds away from eternity, Dr. Pels bared his teeth in a white, white grin above his bony knuckles, as the tempo of the music increased. Soon he would have his answer from the tiger in the night.

When he awakened, his chrono told him that two and a half days had passed. He propped himself up, seized one of the canteens and began to drink water. He was always terribly thirsty after the catharsis-coma. Once he had slaked his thirst, however, he felt perfect; he was vibrant and in tune with everything about him. This balance achieved, it generally stayed strong for several days.

It was only after minutes of drinking that he noticed it to be a pleasant, cloudless morning.

Hurriedly, he cleaned his body by means of canteen and handkerchief. Then he donned fresh garments, re-rolled his pack, located his staff, moved toward the trail.

The downhill way was easy, and he whistled as he went. The trek through the forest seemed a thing that had happened to another person, years ago. In less than an hour he reached level ground. Shortly, he began to pass dwelling places. As he advanced, they became more common. Almost before he realized it, he was walking along the main street of the small town.

He stopped the first man he met and asked directions to the hospital. When he tried the second major language of the planet, he received an answer rather than a shrug. Ten blocks. No trouble.

As he neared the eight-story building, he withdrew a narrow sliver of crystal from a case he carried. Fed into their med-bank, it would tell the doctors all they needed to know about Heidel von Hymack.

However, when he entered the smoky, periodical-strewn lobby, he found that he did not need to present immediate identification. The receptionist, a middle-aged brunette in a silver, sleeveless thing, belted at the waist, was on her feet and moving toward him. She wore an exotic native amulet on a chain about her neck.

"Mr. H!" she said. "We've been so worried! There were reports—"

He leaned his staff against the coat rack.

"The little girl . . . ?"

"Luci's still holding on, thank the gods. We heard that you were flying up here, and then they lost radio contact; and—"

"Take me to see her doctor at once."

The three other inhabitants of the lobby—two men and a woman—stared at him.

"Just a moment."

She returned to her desk, touched controls behind it and spoke into a communications unit.

"Please send someone to the front desk to fetch Mr. H," she said; and to him, "Won't you be seated while you wait?"

"I'll stand, thank you."

Then she regarded him again, through blue eyes which for some reason made him feel uncomfortable.

"What happened?" she asked.

"Power failure in several systems," he said, looking away. "I had to belly-land it and walk."

"How far?"

"Quite a distance."

"After all this time and no report, we thought that—"

"I had to take certain medical precautions before I could enter your town."

"I see," she said. "We are so relieved that you made it. I hope that—"

"So do I," he said, seeing for a moment the nine graves he had helped to fill.

Then a door beside her desk opened. An old man dressed in white emerged, saw him, moved toward him.

"Helman," he said, extending his hand. "I'm treating the Dorn girl."

"You'll want this then," said Heidel, and handed him the gleaming sliver.

The doctor was about five and a half feet in height and very pink. What remained of his hair stood out in wisps from his temples. Like all doctors he had known, Heidel noted that his hands and fingernails seemed the cleanest things in the entire room. The right hand, bearing a slim ring with a twisted design, moved now to clutch his biceps, steered him through the door.

"Let's find an office where we can discuss the case," he was saying.

"I'm not a doctor of medicine, you know."

"I did not know. But I guess it doesn't really matter, if you are H."

"I am H. I would not like to have it widely known, of course. I—"

"I understand," said Helman, leading him along a wide corridor. "We will naturally cooperate in the fullest."

He stopped another man in white.

"Run this through the med-bank," he told him, "and send me the results in Room 17.

"In here, please," he said to Heidel. "Have a seat."

They seated themselves beside a large conference table and Heidel hooked an ashtray toward him and withdrew a moldy cigar from his jacket. He stared out the window at the green sky. On a pedestal in the corner beside it crouched a native deity—exquisitely carved from some yellow-white substance—about eighteen inches in height.

"Your condition fascinates me," said the doctor. "It has been written up so many times that I almost feel I know you personally. A walking antibody, a living pool of remedies—"

"Well," said Heidel, "I suppose you could put it that way. But it is oversimplifying. With proper preparation I can effect the cure of almost any disease, if the patient is not too far gone. On the other hand, my own condition is not a completely one-sided thing. It might be more appropriate to say that I am a living pool of diseases which I can bring into a sort of balance. When that balance is achieved, I can act as a remedy. Only then, though. The rest of the time, I can be very dangerous."

Dr. Helman plucked a dark string from his sleeve and deposited it in the ashtray. Heidel smiled at this, wondering how he must look to the doctor.

"But there is no indication as to the mechanism involved?"

"Nobody seems to be certain," Heidel said, finally lighting the cigar. "I seem to find diseases wherever I go. I contract them, then some sort of natural immunity seems to stave off the worst of the symptoms and I recover. Thereafter, under the proper circumstances, a serum made from my blood is effective against the same condition in someone else."

"What, specifically, are the preparations, the circumstances you speak of?"

"I go into a coma," Heidel began, "which I can induce at will. During this time, my body does something which seems to purify it. This takes anywhere from a day and a half to several days. I am told—" He paused here, quickly drawing upon his cigar. "I am told that during this time my body undergoes frightful symptoms from all the diseases I carry. I don't know. I never have any memory of this. And I have to be alone at such times, as my diseases then become quite contagious."

"Your clothing—"

"I disrobe first. My body carries nothing when I awaken. I change clothes afterward."

"How long does this—balance—last?"

"Usually a couple days, and then I revert—slowly. Once the balance is destroyed I become progressively dangerous again. I become a disease-bearer until the next catharsis-coma."

"When did you last undergo this coma?"

"I just woke up a few hours ago. I haven't eaten anything since. That sometimes seems to prolong the safe period."

"You are not hungry, after all that time?"

"No. In fact, I feel very strong—powerful, you might even say. But I do get quite thirsty. I am just now, in fact."

"There is a water cooler in the next room," said Helman, rising. "I'll show you."

Heidel placed his cigar in the ashtray and stood.

As they were passing through the side door, the man Helman had spoken with earlier entered the room, holding a sheaf of crystal-extrusion reports and a small envelope which Heidel judged to contain his med-ident crystal. Dr. Helman gestured toward the water cooler and, when Heidel nodded, turned back into the room they had departed.

Heidel began filling and draining a small paper cup. As he did this, he noted the tiny green Strantrian good luck mark painted on the side of the cooler.

Somewhere between the fifteenth and twentieth cup, Dr. Helman entered the room. He held the papers in one hand. Passing Heidel the envelope, he said, "We had better take your blood right now. If you will come with me to the laboratory, please . . ."

Heidel nodded, disposed of the cup, returned his crystal to its case.

He followed the doctor out of the room and walked with him to an old-fashioned lift. "Six," said the doctor to the wall, and the lift closed its door and began its ascent.

"The reports are strange," he said, after a time, gesturing with the papers he held.

"Yes, I know."

"There is something here to the effect that your mere proximity after a coma will often result in arrest and reversal of disease."

Heidel tugged his ear and regarded his boot tops.

"That is correct," he said, finally. "I didn't mention it because it smacked of faith healing or something of that sort, but it seems to be the case. The use of my blood at least provides a somewhat scientifically acceptable explanation. I can't explain the other."

"Well, we'll stick to the serum for the Dorn girl," said Helman. "But I wonder if you would be willing to participate in an experiment afterward?"

"What sort of experiment?"

"Visit all my terminal patients with me. I shall introduce you as a colleague. Then you speak with them briefly. About anything."

"All right. I'll be glad to."

"Do you know what will happen?"

"It will depend upon the conditions from which they are suffering. If it is a disease I've had, it may go away. If it is something involving major anatomical damage, the condition will probably remain unchanged."

"You have done this before?"

"Yes, many times."

"How many diseases have you been exposed to?"

"I don't know. I'm not always aware of taking one. I don't know what I'm carrying around inside me.—You being willing to try me on them this way," said Heidel, as the lift halted and the door opened, "that's interesting. Why not use my serum on everybody, now that you have me here?"

Helman shook his head.

"These reports only tell me what it has proven specific

against in the past. So I'll trust it—well, try it, I should say—
on the Dorn girl. None of my other terminals fit your list,
though. I would not risk it."

"Yet you would try the other?"

Helman shrugged.

"I am quite open-minded about these things," he said,
"and there would be no risk. It certainly can't do them any
harm, at this point.—The lab's at the end of this hall."

As he waited for his blood to be drawn, Heidel stared
out the window. In the late morning light of that giant sun,
he saw no fewer than four churches of as many different
religions, as well as a flat-roofed wooden building, the face
of which was covered with ribbons and tacked-on devo-
tions, much on the order of one he had seen in the village
beside the River Bart. Squinting, turning his head, leaning
far forward, he could also make out the aboveground structure which indicated a Pei'an shrine below, far up the road
to his right. He grimaced and turned away from the window.

"Roll up your sleeve, please."

John Morwin played God.

He manipulated the controls and prepared the birth of a
world. Carefully . . . The rosy road from the rock to the star
goes *there*. Yes. Hold. Not yet.

The youth stirred on the couch at his side but did not
awaken. Morwin gave him another whiff of the gas and
concentrated on the work at hand. He ran his forefinger
beneath the front edge of the basket which covered his
head, to remove perspiration and the latest attack of a
recurring itch in the vicinity of his right temple. He stroked
his red beard and meditated.

It was not yet perfect, not yet the thing the boy had
described. Closing his eyes, he looked farther into the

dreaming mind beside him. It was drifting in what he took to be the proper direction, but the feeling he sought was not there.

Waiting, he opened his eyes and turned his head, studying the fragile, sleeping form—the expensive garments, the thin, almost feminine face—that wore the mate of his basket, connected to his own by a maze of electrical leads, the narcotic-bearing airjet fluttering the jacket's lacy collar. He pursed his lips and frowned, not so much with disapproval as with envy. One of his great regrets in life was that he had not grown up in the midst of wealth, been indulged, spoiled, turned into a fop. He had always wanted to be a fop, and now that he could afford it, he discovered that he lacked the proper upbringing to carry the thing successfully.

He turned to stare at the empty crystal globe before him—a meter in diameter, nozzles penetrating it at various points.

Push the proper button and it will be filled with swirling motes. Transfer the proper sequence and it will be frozen there forever...

He reentered the boy's dreaming mind. It was wandering once again. The time had come to introduce stronger stimuli than the suggestions he had employed.

He threw a switch. Softly, then, the boy heard his own recorded voice, as he had spoken earlier in describing the dream. Then the images shifted and from within the dreaming mind he felt the click of *déjà vu*, the sensation of the appropriate, the feeling of desire achieved.

He depressed the button and the nozzles hissed. At the same moment, he threw the switch which severed the connection between his mind and that of his client's son.

Then, with his powerful visual memory and the telekinetic ability which only he among those few creatures possessing it could employ in this fashion, he laid his mind upon the swarming particles within the crystal. There he hurled the key instant of the dream he had snatched from the mind of its dreamer, its form and its color—the dream of a sleeper still informed with something of a child's exuberance and wonder—and there, within the crystal, with the mashing of another button, he froze it forever. Another, and the nozzles were withdrawn. Another, and the crystal was sealed—never to be broached again without destroying the dream. A switch, and the recorded voice was stilled. As always, he found then that he was shaking.

He had done it again.

He activated the air cushion and withdrew the supports, so that the crystal floated before them. He lowered the black velvet backdrop and turned on concealed lights, adjusting them so that they struck the thing perfectly.

It was a somewhat frightening tableau: something part man was twisted snakelike about orange rocks which were also a part of itself, and it looked back upon itself to where it was joined with the ground; above it, the sky was partly contained in the arc of an upflung arm; a rosy road led from a rock to a star; there was a moistness like tears upon the arm; blue forms were in flight below.

John Morwin studied it. He had seen it by means of assisted telepathy, sculpted it telekinetically, preserved it mechanically. Whatever adolescent fantasy it might have represented, he did not know. Nor did he care. It was there. That was enough. The psychic drain that he felt, the feeling of elation that he felt, the pleasure that he felt in contemplating his creation—these were sufficient to tell him that it was good.

Occasionally, he was troubled by doubts as to whether what he did was really art, in the mere representation of

another man's fantasies. True, he possessed the unique combination of talent and equipment to capture a dream, as well
as a large fee for his troubles. But he liked to think of himself as an artist. If he could not be a fop, then this was his
second choice. An artist, he had decided, possessed as much
ego and eccentricity, but because of the added dimension of
empathy could not behave toward his fellows with the same
insouciance. But if he were not even a true artist . . .

He shook his head to clear it and removed the basket. He
scratched at his right temple.

He had done sexual fantasies, dreamscapes of peace,
nightmares for mad kings, psychoses for analysts. No one
ever had anything but praise for his work. He hoped that the
fact that these were externalizations of their own feelings
was not the only . . . No, he decided. Portraiture was valid
art. But he wondered what would happen if one day he
could do his own dream.

Rising, he shut down and removed the equipment from
the boy Abse. Then, from his workstand, he picked up the
pipe with the old insignia carved into the side of the bowl,
ran his thumb over it, packed it, lit it.

He seated himself behind the boy, after activating the
servomechanisms which slowly moved the sleeper's couch
into a semi-recline position. The stage was set. He smiled
through his smoke and listened to the sounds of breathing.

Showmanship. He had become the businessman once
more, the salesman displaying his wares. The first thing that
Abse would see upon awakening would be the dramatically
situated object. His own voice, from behind, would then
break the spell with some trifling comment; and the magic—
broken—would partly retreat into the depths and so be
sealed in the viewer's mind. Hopefully, the object's attrac-
tiveness would be enhanced by this.

The stirring of a hand. A slight cough. A gesture suddenly frozen, never to be completed . . .

He drew it out for perhaps six seconds, then said, "Like it?"

The boy did not reply immediately, but when he did, it was with the words of a younger child, rather than those with which he had entered the studio. Gone was the faintly hidden contempt, the feigned weariness, the ostentatious sense of duty to a parent who had decided upon that as the ideal birthday present for a son who had little else to desire.

"That's it . . ." he said. "That's it!"

"I take it, then, that you are pleased?"

"Lords!" The boy rose and moved toward it. He put his hand out slowly, but did not touch the crystal. "Pleased . . . ? It's great." Then he shuddered and stood silent for a time. When he turned, he was smiling. Morwin smiled back, with the left corner of his mouth. The boy was gone again.

"It is quite pleasant," and he made a casual gesture toward it with his left hand, not looking back. "Have it delivered and bill my father."

"Very good."

Morwin rose as Abse moved toward the door that led to the front office and out. He opened it and held it for the boy. Abse halted before passing through and looked into his eyes for a moment. Only then, after a moment, did he return his glance to the globe.

"I—would like to have seen how you did it. It's too bad that we did not think to record the act."

"It's not all that interesting," said Morwin.

"I suppose not.—Well, good morning to you." He did not offer to shake hands.

"Good morning," said Morwin, and watched him depart.

Yes, being spoiled would have been pleasant. Another

year or two and the boy would have learned . . . everything that he would ever know.

Alyshia Curt, his secretary-receptionist, cleared her throat within her alcove around the corner behind the door. Holding to the frame with both hands, he leaned to his right and peered down at her.

"Hi," he said. "Have Jansen pack it and deliver it; and send the bill."

"Yes, sir," and she gestured with her eyes. He followed them.

"Surprise," said the man seated by the window, without any inflection in his voice.

"Michael! What are you doing here?"

"I wanted a cup of real coffee."

"Come on back. I've got some simmering."

The man rose and moved slowly, his bulk, his pale uniform, his albino hair reminding Morwin for the dozenth time of ice ages and the progress of glaciers.

They passed back into the studio and Morwin sought two clean cups. Locating them, he turned to discover that Michael had crossed, silently, the entire length of the studio, to regard the latest creation.

"Like it?" he asked.

"Yes. It's one of your best.—For that Arnithe kid?"

"Yeah."

"What did he think of it?"

"He said he liked it."

"Hm." Michael turned away and moved to the small table where Morwin sometimes took his meals.

Morwin poured the coffee and they sipped it.

"The *lamaq* season opens this week."

"Oh," said Morwin. "I hadn't realized it was getting around to that time of year. You going out?"

"I was thinking of the weekend after this. We could skim up to the Blue Forest, camp out a couple nights, maybe bag ourselves a few."

"That sounds like a good idea. I'm with you. Anybody else coming along?"

"I was thinking maybe Jorgen."

Morwin nodded and drew on his pipe, his thumb covering the insignia on its side. Jorgen the giant Rigellian and Michael of Honsi had been crewmates during the war. Fifteen years earlier he would have shot either one of them on sight. Now he trusted them at his back with guns. Now he ate, drank, joked with them, sold his works to their fellows. The DYNAB insignia, Fourth Stellar Fleet, seemed to throb beneath his thumb. He was squeezing it tightly, feeling ashamed that he sought to conceal it from the Honsian but unable to uncover it. If we had won it would have been the other way around, he told himself, and nobody would have blamed Michael if he wore that damned big battle ring of his backward or on a chain around his neck, out of sight. A man has to make his life where he finds things best. If I had stayed in the DYNAB, I would still be juggling electrons—in some damned laboratory—on starvation wages.

"How much longer've you got till retirement?" he asked.

"Around three years. Still a lot of looking forward left."

Michael leaned back then, and with his right hand withdrew a news printout from his tunic.

"Looks as if a certain friend of yours plans never to retire."

Morwin took the paper, ran his eyes along the columns.

"What are you referring to?" he asked, for the sake of form.

"Second column. About halfway down."

" 'Explosion on Blanchen'? That one?"

"Yes."

He read the report slowly. Then, "I'm afraid I don't understand," he said, while a certain thing like pride occurred within him. He kept it there, inside.

"Your old fleet commander, Malacar Miles. Who else?"

" 'Six men dead, nine injured . . . Eight units destroyed, twenty-six damaged,' " he read. " 'No clues have been found the Service is working on . . .'—If no clues have been found, what makes you suspect the Commander?"

"The contents of the warehouses."

"What was in them?"

"High-speed voice-translation units."

"I fail to see—"

"—Previously only produced in the DYNAB. These were first ones manufactured on CL worlds."

"So they're cutting into *that* DYNAB industry too."

Michael shrugged.

"I guess they have a right to make what they want. The DYNAB simply was not turning them out fast enough. So, some Leagues industrialists went into that line. That was the first batch. As you know, they are precision instruments—one of the few machines that requires considerable manual adjustment. Lots of skilled hand labor makes for high over-head."

"And you think the Commander was involved?"

"Everybody *knows* he was responsible. He's been doing things like this for years. He forgets the war is over, the armistice signed . . ."

"You can't very well go into the DYNAB after him."

"No. But some powerful civilian may someday—some-body who gets tired having his property destroyed, or his friends or workers murdered."

"It's been tried, and you know what happened. Anybody

who tries it now will be snapping at an even more indi-
gestible mouthful."

"I know! It could lead to big trouble—to a thing we don't
want."

"Supposing the Service caught him, red-handed, putting
a knife into somebody's back here in the CL—is it still what
they used to say?"

"You ought to know the answer."

Morwin looked away.

"We never talk about such things when we talk," he
said, finally.

Michael ground his teeth and wiped his mouth with the
back of his hand.

"Yes," he said, then. "It still has full force and effect.
We would have to return him to the DYNAB. We would
then file a complaint with DYNAB Central, which of course
would do nothing to their only surviving retired fleet commander. Legally, we would have to return him—so if there
are too many witnesses, that's what gets done. If only they
hadn't made him their representative at the First SEL Conference. It does seem as though they planned it then and
are encouraging him now. I wish there were some way to
get him to admit that it is a lost cause, or for us to get his
diplomatic immunity revoked. The situation is very embar-
rassing."

"Yes."

"You served under him. You used to be a pretty good
friend of his."

"I guess so."

"Well. You still are, aren't you?"

"As you know, I go to visit him occasionally—for old
times' sake."

"Any chance you could talk some sense into him?"

"As I said, we don't talk about things like that. He wouldn't listen to me if I did."

Morwin poured more coffee.

"No matter what he once was, he is a murderer and an arsonist—among other things—now. You realize that, don't you?"

"I guess so."

"If he were ever to go too far—if he were ever to pull off something resulting in a really large-scale disaster—it *could* possibly lead to war. There are a lot of political and military types who would love an excuse to take on the DYNAB again, to dispose of it for once and ever."

"Why are you telling me about it, Mike?"

"I'm off duty and I'm not under orders. Hopefully, my superiors will never find out that I mentioned it to you. It's just that you are the only man I know of—living right here in town and a friend of mine—who actually knows the man and even sees him sometimes. Hell! I don't want another war! Even if this time it would be an overnight affair. I'm getting old. I just want to retire and hunt and fish.—You were his EO. He'd listen to you. He even gave you that fancy pipe when it was all over. Isn't it a Bayner-Sandow briar? They cost something. He must have liked you."

Morwin's face reddened and he nodded into the smoke, got it in his eyes, shook his head.

And I sold him out, the same as all the others, he thought, when I moved to the CL and started taking their money.

"I haven't seen him in a long time. I'm sure he wouldn't listen."

"I'm sorry," said Michael, staring down into his coffee. "I was way out of order, suggesting something like that. Forget it, huh?"

"You working on the Blanchen thing?"

"Only peripherally."

"I see. I'm sorry."

There was a long silence, and then Michael gulped his coffee and stood.

"Well, I've got to be getting back to work," he said. "I'll see you in eleven days, my place. Sunrise. Right?"

"Right."

"Thanks for the coffee."

Morwin nodded and raised his hand in a half-salute. Michael closed the door behind him.

For a long while, Morwin stared at the boy's frozen dream. Then his gaze fell upon his coffee cup. He watched it until it rose into the air and dashed itself against the wall.

Heidel von Hymack stared down at the girl and returned her faint smile. About nine years old, he guessed.

". . . And this is a Claanite," he explained, adding a stone to the row beside her on the counterpane. "I picked it up a little while back on the world called Claana. I've polished it a lot since then, but I didn't do any grinding. That's its natural shape."

"What is Claana like?" she asked him.

"Mostly water," he said. "It's got a big blue sun in a sort of pinkish sky and eleven small moons that are always doing something interesting. There are no continents, just thousands of islands all over the place. Its people are batrachians, and they spend most of their lives in the water. They do not have any real cities that anybody knows of. They are migrants and traders of sorts. They trade things they find in the oceans for knives and duralines and things like that. This stone comes from their seas. I found it on a beach. It gets its shape from all that grinding against sand and other stones while it is being washed ashore. The trees there spread out for great distances—and they push extra roots out over the ground to reach the water. They have many very large leaves. Some have fruit. The temperature is almost always pleasant, because there are always winds coming in off the water.—And any time you want, you can climb up on something high and start looking off in all directions. You will always find a dark place where it is raining, somewhere. Anything seen through the rainwall is misty and distorted, sort of like the far shores of fairyland. Also, there are mirages. You see islands in the sky, with trees growing upside down. One of the natives told me that that's where they go when they die. They think that their ancestors are up there looking down at them—staring into the seas, watching.—If you like that stone, you can have it."

"Oh yes, Mr. H! Thank you!"

She clutched the stone and rubbed it with her hand. She polished it on the front of her hospital gown.

"How are you feeling today?" he asked.

"Better," she said. "A lot better."

He studied the small face, dark eyes beneath dark bangs, freckles sprinkled everywhere. There was more color to it than there had been a day and a half earlier when she had received the treatment. Her breathing was no longer labored. She was now able to sit up, propped with pillows, and could speak for fairly lengthy periods of time. Her fever was down and her blood pressure was almost normal. She was displaying curiosity and recovering the animation one would expect in a child her age. He considered the treatment a success. He no longer thought of the nine graves in the forest, or the others that lay farther behind him.

". . . I'd like to see Claana someday," she was saying, "with its blue sun and all those moons . . ."

"Perhaps you will," he told her, guessing far ahead, however, and seeing her with some local boy, a housewife in Italbar for all the days of her now recovered life, with perhaps only an orange stone to remind her of the dreams of childhood. Well, it could be worse, he decided, remembering that evening in the hills above the city. A town like Italbar might be a pleasant place to end one's wanderings . . .

Dr. Helman entered the room, nodded to them both, took her left wrist in his hand and watched his chrono.

"You are a bit excited, Luci," he announced, lowering the wrist. "Perhaps Mr. H has been telling you of too many adventures."

"Oh no!" she said. "I want to hear them. He's been everywhere.—See the stone he gave me? I'll bet it's a lucky one. It's from Claana—a world with a blue sun and eleven moons. The people live in the sea . . ."

The doctor glanced at the stone.

"It is quite pretty. Now I want you to get some rest."

Why doesn't he ever smile? Heidel asked himself. He should be happy.

Heidel scooped up the rest of his stones and deposited them in the monogrammed *kuhl*-skin bag he carried.

"I guess I'd better be going now, Luci," he said. "I am glad that you are feeling better. If I don't see you again, it has been pleasant talking to you.—Be good."

He stood and moved toward the door, along with Dr. Helman.

"You'll be coming back, won't you?" she said, sitting up away from the pillows, her eyes widening. "You'll come back—won't you?"

"I can't say for certain," Heidel told her. "We'll see."

"Come back . . ." he heard her say, as he passed through the door and into the hallway beyond.

"She has responded amazingly," Helman said. "I still find it difficult to believe."

"What of the others?"

"All the ones you visited have either had their conditions arrested or are undergoing small rallies. I wish I understood how it worked.—Your blood, by the way, is even more of a mess than those reports indicated—according to our laboratory. They would like more samples, to send to Landsend for further analysis."

"No," said Heidel. "I know my blood is a mess, and they won't discover much new about it by sending it to Landsend. If they are especially interested, they can request very detailed reports concerning it from Panopath in SEL. It has been tested in every possible way, and the reports are still inconclusive. Besides, it will be getting dangerous again soon. I have to be going."

The two men moved toward the lift shafts.

"This 'balance' you speak of," said Helman. "There is no such thing. You speak as if the pathogens formed ranks, warring against one another, and then sign a truce for a time where none of them misbehaves. This is nonsense. The body does not work that way."

"I know," said Heidel, as they entered the lift. "It's just an analogy. As I said, I'm not a doctor of medicine. I've coined my own simple, pragmatic terms for referring to what occurs to me. Translate them as you would. I'm still the expert on the effects."

The lift dropped them to the ground floor.

"Shall we stop in the office?" said Helman, as they emerged. "You say you have to be going soon, and I know when your air car is coming in. This means you want to go up into the hills and undergo another coma. I'd like to arrange to observe it and—"

"No!" said Heidel. "That's out. Definitely. I don't allow anybody near me when I do that. It's too dangerous."

"But I could put you in isolation."

"No, I won't allow it. I've been responsible for too many deaths already. Things like what I did here are my way of trying to partly make up for them. I won't chance causing more by having people around me during the coma—even trained people. Sorry. No matter what the precautions, I'd still be afraid that something would go wrong."

Helman shrugged slightly.

"If you should ever reconsider, I'd like to be the physician in charge," he said.

"Well . . . Thanks. I'd better go away now."

Helman shook his hand.

"Thanks for everything," he said. "The gods have been kind."

To your patients, maybe, Heidel thought. Then, "Good afternoon, Doctor," he said; and he walked through the door that led to the lobby.

". . . Bless you," she was saying. "May the gods bless you!"

She had seized his arm and drawn him near as he passed her chair.

He looked down into the tired face with its red-rimmed eyes. It was Luci's mother.

"She'll be all right now, I think," he said. "She's a nice little girl."

While she clung to his left arm, his right hand was taken and pumped by a thin man wearing light slacks and sweater. His weather-beaten face was split by a smile that showed a row of irregular teeth.

"Thank you so much, Mr. H," he said, his palm moist against Heidel's. "We must have prayed in every house of worship in town—and all our friends were doing it too. I guess our prayers were answered. May all of the gods bless you!—Would you care to come home with us for dinner tonight?"

"Thank you, but I really have to be going," said Heidel. "I have an appointment—something I have to take care of before my transportation arrives."

When he was finally able to draw away from them, he turned to find the lobby filling with people. Among the sounds of many voices, he heard the words "Mr. H" being spoken over and over again.

". . . How did you do it, Mr. H?" came from five different directions. "—May I have your autograph?—My brother has an allergy. Will you . . . ?—I would like to invite you to attend services this evening, sir. My parish . . .—Can you heal at a distance?—Mr. H, would you care to make a statement for the local . . . ?"

"Please," he said, turning his head from face to camera to face. "I *must* be going. I appreciate your attention, but I have nothing to tell you. Please let me through."

But the lobby was filled and the front door was held open by the pressure of bodies pushing forward. People were raising children into the air to see him. He looked to the coat rack and saw that his staff was missing. Looking through the glass wall beyond that place, he saw that a crowd was forming in front of the building.

". . . Mr. H, I have a present for you. I baked them myself . . .—May I drive you to wherever you're going? —Which gods do you pray to, sir . . . ?—My brother has this allergy . . ."

He backed to the desk and leaned toward the woman who had received him there.

"I wasn't warned of this," he said.

"We didn't expect it either," she told him. "They assembled in a matter of minutes. There was no way of knowing. Get back in the corridor, and I'll tell them no one is allowed beyond here. I'll call for someone to show you out the back way."

"Thanks."

He passed through the door once more, waving and smiling to the people.

A cry went up as he departed. It was a combination of "H!" and a cheer.

He stood in the corridor until an orderly appeared and conducted him to the rear of the building.

"May I drive you a distance from here?" the man inquired. "If the crowd sees you walking nearby and recognizes you—well, they might follow and be a bother."

"All right," said Heidel. "Why not take me half a dozen blocks or so in the direction of those hills."

He gestured toward the ones he had crossed in coming to Italbar.

"I can take you right up to the foot of them, sir. Save you some walking."

"Thanks, but I want to stop somewhere and pick up some supplies—maybe even get a warm meal—before I head on up. Do you know any place in that direction where I could?"

"There are several. I'll take you to a small one on a quiet street. I don't think you'll be troubled there.—That's my car," he indicated.

They encountered no difficulty in reaching the place the orderly had recommended—an old-smelling, narrow store with wooden floors, walls lined with uncovered shelves—selling food retail in the front and serving it in a tiny dining room in the rear. Only one thing disturbed Heidel. When the vehicle had halted before the establishment, the orderly had reached down inside his collar and fetched forth a green amulet—a lizard with an inlaid line of silver down its back.

"I know this sounds sort of silly, Mr. H," he said, "but would you touch this for me?"

Heidel complied, then asked him, "What did I do?"

The young man laughed and looked away, depositing the carving within his shirt once more.

"Oh, I guess I'm a little superstitious, like everyone else," he said. "That's my good luck piece. With everyone talking the way they are about you, I figured it couldn't do any harm."

"Talking? What are they saying? Don't tell me that 'holy man' thing has followed me here too?"

"I'm afraid that it has, sir. Who knows? There may be something to it."

"You work in the hospital. You spend a big piece of your time among scientists."

"Oh, they're the same way, most of them. Maybe it has to do with living this far away from things. Some of the preachers say it's sort of a reaction because we're close to nature again, after our ancestors had spent centuries living in big cities. Whatever the reason, thanks for humoring me."

"Thanks for the ride."

"Best of luck."

Heidel stepped out and entered the store.

He replenished his supplies, then seated himself at a table in the windowless back room. The room was lighted by eight ancient, insect-specked glow-globes set in the walls, and was almost adequately air-conditioned. Despite the fact that he was the only customer, it was a long while before he was served. He ordered a local steak and brew and refrained from inquiring as to the nature of the beast from which the steak had been cut, a policy he had long before determined to be prudent when on brief visits to strange worlds. As he sipped the brew and waited for the meat, he reflected upon his condition.

He was still a geologist. It was the only thing he could do well and do safely. True, none of the larger companies would take him on as an employee. While none of them knew for certain that he was H, they all knew there was something strange about him. Perhaps they had him listed as an accident-prone. For that matter, though, he would not in good conscience hire on, anyway, and run the risk of being assigned to a place he did not wish to work—that is, any place near groups of people. Most of the companies, though, were happy to take him on as an independent con-tractor. Strangely, this had resulted in his making more money than ever before in his life. Now that he had it, though, he had little use for it. He stayed away from cities, from people, from all the places where money is spent in large quantities. Over the years, he had come so to accept a solitary existence that now the presence of people—even in far smaller groups than that crowd at the hospital—tended to cause him distress. He anticipated a solitary existence—a cabin on some far outback, a shanty near a quiet beach—in his old age. His cigars, his mineral collection, a few books and a receiving set that could pull in News Central—these were all that he really desired.

He ate slowly, and the owner of the store came back and wanted to talk. Where was he going with that pack and those rations?

Camping, up in the hills, he explained. Why? He was about to tell the old man it was none of his affair, when it occurred to him that perhaps he was lonely. Neither the store nor the dining room looked as if they drew much business. Possibly the man did not see many people. And he was old.

So Heidel made up a story. The man listened to it, nodding. Soon Heidel was listening and the storekeeper was doing all the talking. Heidel nodded occasionally.

He finished his meal and lit a cigar.

Gradually, as the time wore on, Heidel realized that he was enjoying the man's company. He ordered another brew. Finishing his cigar, he lit a second one.

Because there were no windows, he did not see the long shadows begin. He spoke of other worlds; he showed the man his stones. The man told him of the farm he once had owned.

As the first stars of evening gave their light to the world, Heidel glanced at his chrono.

"It can't be *that* late!" he said.

The old man looked at Heidel's, looked at his own.

"I'm afraid that it is. I didn't mean to keep you if you were in a hurry . . ."

"No. That's all right," said Heidel. "I just didn't realize what time it was getting to be. I've enjoyed talking with you. But I'd better be going now."

He paid his bill and departed quickly. He was not eager to push his safety margin.

He turned right when he left the store, walking through the twilight, heading in the direction from which he had originally come. After fifteen minutes, he was out of the business district and passing through a pleasant residential section of the city. The globes glowed more brightly atop their poles as the sky darkened and stars were splashed across it.

Passing a stone church, a faint light coming from behind its stained glassite windows, he felt that old jittery sensation that churches always gave him. It had been—

what?—ten or twelve years ago? Whatever the interval, he recalled the event clearly. It still troubled him on occasion.

It had been a stifling summer day on Murtania and he had been caught out in the noonday heat, walking. He had sought refuge in one of those underground Strantrian shrines, where it is always cool and dark. Seating himself in an especially shadowy corner, he had rested. He closed his eyes when two worshipers appeared, hoping to appear appropriately contemplative. The newcomers, instead of praying quietly as he had expected, did not seat themselves, but commenced an exchange of excited whispers. One of them departed, and the other moved forward and took a seat near to the central altar. Heidel studied him. He was a Murtanian, and his branchial membranes were swollen and flared, which indicated excitement. His head was not bowed; instead, he was staring upward. Heidel followed the direction of his gaze, and saw that he was looking at that row of glassite illustrations which formed a continuous band of deities, passing along all the walls of the chapel. The man was staring at the one among all those illustrations which was now glowing with a blue fire. When his own eyes fell upon it, Heidel felt something akin to an electric shock. Then his extremities tingled and there came a feeling of dizziness. Not one of the old diseases acting up, he hoped. But no, it did not behave that way. Instead, there was a strange exhilaration, like the first stages of drunkenness, though he had had nothing alcoholic to drink that day. Then the place began to fill with worshipers. Almost before he realized it, there was a service being conducted. The feeling of exhilaration and power began to heighten, and then specific emotions appeared—oddly contradictory emotions. One moment, he wanted to reach out and touch the people about him, call them "brother," love them, heal them of their ills;

the next moment, he hated them and wished that he had not just undergone catharsis, so that he might infect the entire congregation with some fatal disease that would spread like flames in a pool of gasoline and kill them all in a day. His mind cycled back and forth between these desires and he wondered if he were going mad. He had never exhibited schizophrenic tendencies before, and his feelings toward humanity had never been characterized by either extreme. He had always been an easygoing individual who neither gave trouble nor sought it. He had neither loved nor hated his fellows, but took them as they were and moved among them as best he could. Consequently, he was at a total loss to understand the mad desires that suddenly possessed him. He waited for the latest wave of hatred to pass, and when the lull came before the next upswing of amity, he rose quickly and pushed his way to the door. By the time he reached it, he was well into the other phase and he apologized to everyone he jostled. "Peace, brother. I crave your pardon.—Forgive me, for I love you.—I apologize with all my heart.—Excuse my unworthy passage, please." Once he made it through the door, up the steps and onto the street, he ran. Within a few minutes, all unusual feelings had departed. He had considered consulting a psychiatrist, but refrained because he later explained it to himself as a reaction to the heat, followed by the sudden coolness, in combination with all the little side effects that come of visiting a new planet. Then, too, there was never a recurrence of the phenomenon. From that day on, however, he had never set foot in a church of any sort; nor could he pass one without a certain feeling of apprehension which he traced back to that day on Murtania.

He paused at a corner to let three vehicles pass. While waiting, he heard a sound at his back.

"Mr. H!"

A boy of about twelve emerged from the shadows beneath a tree and advanced toward him. In his left hand he held a black leash, the other end of which was clipped to the collar of a green meter-long lizard with short, bowed legs. Its claws clicked on the pavement as it waddled after the boy, and when it opened its mouth to dart its red tongue in his direction, it seemed as if it were grinning. It was a very fat lizard, and it rubbed against the boy's leg several times as he approached.

"Mr. H, I went to the hospital to see you earlier, but you had to go back inside, so I only got a glimpse. I heard about how you healed Luci Dorn. It sure is lucky meeting you, just walking along."

"Don't touch me!" said Heidel; but the boy had clasped his hand too quickly and was looking up at him with eyes in which the stars danced.

Heidel dropped his hand and backed off several paces.

"Don't get too close," he said. "I think I'm catching a cold."

"Then you shouldn't be out in this night air. I'll bet my folks would put you up."

"Thanks, but I have an appointment."

"This is my *larick*." He tugged on the leash. "His name is Chan. Sit up, Chan."

The lizard opened its mouth, squatted, curled into a ball.

"He doesn't always do it. Not when he doesn't feel like it, anyway," the boy explained. "When he wants to, though, he's real good at it. He stabilizes himself with his tail.—Come on, Chan! Sit up for Mr. H."

He yanked on the leash.

"That's all right, son," said Heidel. "Maybe he's tired.

—Look, I have to be going. Maybe I'll meet you again before I leave town. Okay?"

"Okay. Sure glad I got to meet you. G'night."

"Good night."

Heidel crossed the street and hurried on.

A vehicle drew up beside him.

"Hey! You're Dr. H, aren't you?" a man called.

He turned.

"That's right."

"I thought I saw you at the corner back that way. Went round the block so I could get a good look."

Heidel drew back, away from the vehicle.

"Can I give you a lift to wherever you're going?"

"No thanks. I'm almost there."

"You're sure now?"

"Positive. I appreciate the offer."

"Well, okay.—My name's Wiley."

The man extended his hand out through the window.

"I have grease on my hand. I'll get you dirty," said Heidel; and the man leaned forward, seized his left hand, squeezed it briefly, then drew back into the car.

"Okay. Take it easy, then," he said, and he drove off.

Heidel felt like screaming at the world, telling it to go away and stop touching him.

He ran for the next two blocks. Minutes later, another vehicle slowed when its lights fell upon him, but he averted his face and it passed him by. A man sitting on a porch smoking a pipe waved at him and rose to his feet. He said something, but Heidel ran again and did not hear the words.

Finally, there were greater open spaces between dwellings. Soon the aisle of glow-globes ceased and the stars took on a greater prominence. When the road ended, he continued along the trail, the bulk of the hills now blocking half his prospect.

He did not look back at Italbar as he mounted above it.

Leaning far forward, her knees pressed hard against the plated sides of the eight-legged *kooryab* she rode, black hair streaming in the wind, Jackara raced through the hills above Capeville. Far below and to her left, the city crouched beneath its morning umbrella of fog. From over her right shoulder, the risen sun cast shafts down into the mist and made it sparkle.

There, the tall buildings of the city, all of silver, their countless windows taking white fire like gems, the sea beyond them something between purple and blue, clouds like one giant, frothing tidal wave, massed at the city's unguarded back, touched with pink and orange at its crest, there, halfway up the sky, ready to topple through the blue air and shave the entire peninsula from the continent, sinking it full fathom five, to lie forever dead at the ocean's bottom, becoming over the ages the lost Atlantis of Deiba, she dreamed.

Riding, clad in slacks and a short white tunic belted with red, a matching red headband keeping that fluttering hair from her bright blue eyes, Jackara cursed with the foulest oaths of all the races she had known.

Turning her mount and drawing it to a halt, so that it reared and hissed before it settled panting, she glared down at the city.

"Burn, damn you! Burn!"

But no flames leaped to do her bidding.

She drew her unregistered laser pistol from a holster beneath her garment and triggered it to cut through the trunk of a small tree. The tree stood for a moment, swayed, then fell with a crash that dislodged pebbles and sent them rolling down the hill. The *kooryab* started at this, but she controlled it with her knees and a soft word.

Reholstering her pistol, she continued to stare at the city, and unspoken curses were there in her eyes.

It was not just Capeville and the brothel in which she worked. No. It was the whole of the CL that she hated, hated with a passion only exceeded perhaps by that of one other being. Let the other girls visit the churches of their choice on this, a holiday. Let them eat candy and grow fat. Let them entertain their true loves. Jackara rode the hills and practiced with her gun.

One day—and she hoped that that day came during her lifetime—there *would* be fire, and blood and death within the blazing hearts of bombs and rockets. She kept herself as prepared as a bride for that day. When it came, she desired only the opportunity to die in its name, killing something for it.

She had been very young—four or five, she'd guessed—when her parents had emigrated to Deiba. When the conflict had begun, they had been confined to a Relocation Center because of the planet of their origin. If she ever had the money, she would go back. But she knew that she would never have it. Her parents did not live out the duration of the conflict between the Combined Leagues and the DYNAB. Afterward, she had become a ward of the state. She learned that the old stigma remained, also, when she came of age and sought employment. Only the state-operated pleasure house in Capeville was open to her. She had never had a suitor, or even a boy friend; she had never held a different job. "Possible DYNAB Sympathizer" was stamped on a file, in red, somewhere, she felt, and in it, probably, her life history, neatly typed, double-spaced, filling half a sheet of official stationery.

Very well, she had decided, years before, when she had sorted through the facts and achieved this conclusion. Very well. You picked me up, you looked at me, you threw me away. You gave me a name, unwanted. I will take it, removing only the "Possible." When the time comes, I will indeed be a canker at this flower's heart.

The other girls seldom entered her room, for it made them uneasy. On the few occasions when they did, they would giggle nervously, depart quickly. No lace and ruffles, no tridee photos of handsome actors, such as adorned their rooms—none of these occupied the austere cell that was Jackara's. Above her bed was only the lean, scowling countenance of Malacar the avenger, the last man on Earth. On the opposite wall hung a pair of matched whips with silver handles. Let the other girls deal with ordinary customers. She wanted only those she could abuse. And these were given to her, and she abused them, and they kept returning for more. And every night she would speak to him, in the closest thing in her life to prayer: "I have beaten them, Malacar, as you have struck down their cities, their worlds, as you still strike, as you shall strike again. Help me to be strong, Malacar. Give me the power to hurt, to destroy. Help me, Malacar. Please help me. Kill them!" And sometimes, late at night or in the early hours of morning, she would wake up crying and not know why.

She turned her mount and headed toward the trail that led through the hills toward the other shore of the peninsula. The day was young and her heart was light, filled as it was with the recent news of Blanchen.

Heidel drank one full canteen of water and half of another. The damp, past-midnight darkness lay upon his camp. He turned onto his back and clasped his hands behind his head, staring up into the heavens. Everything recent seemed so far past. Each time that he awakened from the thing it was as if he were beginning a new life, the events of previous days seeming for a time as cold and flat as a year-old letter discovered behind the waste container it had missed. This feeling would pass in an hour or so, he knew.

A shooting star crossed the bright heavens and he smiled. Harbinger of my final day on Cleech, he told himself.

He consulted his gleaming chrono once again, confirming the time. Yes, his sleep-filled eyes had not misread it. Hours still remained before the dawn.

He rubbed his eyes and thought back upon her beauty. She had seemed so very quiet this time. Though he seldom remembered the words, it seemed that there had been fewer of them. Was it sadness that had marked the tenderness? He recalled a hand upon his brow and something moist that fell onto his cheek.

He shook his head and chuckled. Was he indeed mad, as he had expected lives ago, back in that Strantrian shrine? To consider her as a real person was an act of madness.

On the one hand . . .

On the other . . . How do you explain a recurring dream, anyway? One that persists over a decade? Not the dream, exactly, though. Only the principals and the setting. The dialogue changed, the moods shifted. But each time he was taken with a sense of love and strength into a place of peace. Perhaps he should have seen a psychiatrist. If he had wanted to straighten himself out, that is. But he did not, he decided. Not really. Alone most of the time, who was there for him to harm? Awake when he dealt with others, he was not influenced by them. They gave him comfort and distraction. Why destroy one of the harmless pleasures of life? There seemed no progressive derangement involved.

So he lay there for several hours. He thought about the future. He watched the sky grow light, and one by one he saw the stars put away. He was curious as to the happenings on other worlds. It had been a long while that he had been away from News Central.

When dawn broke the world in two, he rose, sponged himself, trimmed his hair and beard, dressed. He breakfasted, packed his belongings, stowed his pack on his back and started downhill.

Half an hour later, he was passing through the outskirts of town.

As he crossed a street, he heard a bell tolling the same note over and over.

Death, he said; a funeral. And he passed on.

Then he heard sirens. But he continued on, not seeking their source.

He came to the store where he had taken a meal several days earlier. It was closed, and there was a dark remembrance set upon the door.

He walked on, suddenly fearing the worst, knowing it.

He waited for a procession to pass the corner where he stood. A hearse rumbled by, lights on.

They still bury the dead here, he reflected; and, Not what I think, he told himself. Just a death, an ordinary death . . . Who am I trying to fool?

He walked on, and a man crossed his path and spat upon it.

Again? What have I become?

He walked the streets, wending his slow way to the airfield.

If I am responsible, how can they know so soon? he asked himself.

They cannot, not for sure . . .

But then he thought of himself as they knew him. What? A god-touched being dropped into their midst. Mutual apprehension would prevail, along with the awe. He had stayed too long, that day, centuries ago. Now every moment's pleasure was refined, drained, siphoned, lessened by each bell-note. Every new moment here was closed to pleasure.

He moved along the street, cutting toward his right.

A young boy drew attention to him: "There he is!" he cried. "That's H!"

He could not deny it—but the tone made him wish he were catching his air car elsewhere.

He walked on, and the boy—along with several adults—followed him.

But she lived, he told himself. I made her live . . .

Big victory.

He passed a vehicle repair shop, and the men in blue uniforms who worked there sat in the front of the building, their chairs tilted back against the brick wall. They did not move. They sat there and smoked and stared at him as he passed by, silent.

The bells continued to ring. People moved out of doors and side passages to stare at him as he passed along the streets.

I stayed too long, he decided. It's not as if I wanted to shake anybody's hand. I never have this problem in a large city any more. They move me about in robot-controlled units, which they sterilize afterward; they give me a whole ward to myself, which they sterilize afterward; I only see a few people—immediately after catharsis; and I depart the way I arrived. It's been years since I visited a town this small for a job like this. I got careless. It's all my fault. It would have been all right if I hadn't talked too long after dinner. It *would* have been all right. I got careless.

He saw a casket being loaded onto a hearse. Around the corner, another hearse waited.

Then it's not a plague . . . yet? he decided. At that stage, people start burning bodies. They stay off the streets.

He glanced back, already knowing from the sounds they made what it was that he would see.

The individuals following him had become about a dozen. He did not look back again. Among the small noises that they made, he heard "H" spoken, several times.

Vehicles passed him, moving slowly. He did not look at them, consciously, though it seemed that there were many eyes fixed upon him.

He reached the center of town, passing along a small square situated there, a statue of some local hero/patriot/ benefactor turning green at its center.

He heard someone call out something in a language that he did not understand. He began to hurry; and now the sound of footfalls became more distinct at his back, as if the crowd had grown.

What were the words that had been spoken? he wondered.

He passed a church, and the sound of its bell was very loud as he moved before it. From behind him, he heard a woman utter an oath.

The touch of fear grew stronger. The sun had dropped a beautiful day about him, but he no longer took pleasure in its presence.

He turned to his right and headed toward the field, about three quarters of a mile distant. Now their voices rose, still not addressed to him, but talking about him. He heard the word "murderer" spoken.

He hurried, and as he moved he saw faces at windows. He heard curses at his back. No, it would not do to run. He crossed a street, and a vehicle swung toward him, then rushed away. He heard the strident cry of a bird, crouched beneath the eave of a house that he passed.

He had done it, they knew. People had died, and it had been traced back to him. The other day he had been a hero. Now he was a villain. And that damned primitive, superstitious aura that covered the town! All those references to gods, the talismans, the good luck charms—they added up to something, something that made him hurry his pace. Now, in their minds, he felt himself to be associated with demons rather than gods.

...If only he had not dwelled so long over his dinner, if he had fled from passers-by ...

I was lonely, he told himself. If I had been as wary as I was in the old days, it could have been avoided, there would have been no infection. I was lonely.

He heard someone call out, "H!" but he did not turn.

A child, standing beside a garbage can in an alleyway, shot him with a squirt gun as he passed.

He wiped his face. The bells continued their mournful clanging.

When he paused at a thoroughfare, someone flicked a cigarette butt in his direction. He stepped on it and waited. His followers massed behind him. Someone pushed him. It felt like an elbow in his kidney, though it could have been the heel of a hand. They jostled him, and he heard the word "killer" repeated several times.

He had encountered things of this nature previously. His past experience did not hearten him, however.

"What're you going to do now, mister?" someone called.

He did not answer.

"Infect more people?"

He did not answer.

Then he heard a woman coughing, suddenly, spasmodically, at his back.

He turned, now that he was clean and could help.

A woman had collapsed upon her knees and she was spitting blood.

"Let me through," he said, but they did not.

Held back by a wall of shoulders, he watched her die or go into a coma. She looked dead to him.

He tried to walk away, hoping that they would not notice, now that their attention was focused elsewhere. He moved to the next corner, crossed, began to run.

They were again at his back.

Running had been a mistake, for now he felt the first blow that was not administered by a hand. Someone had thrown something.

The stone clattered upon the pavement. It had glanced off his shoulder, inflicting no real damage. Still, a bad sign.

Now that he had begun the thing, however, he could not halt. The speed dictated more speed. He shed his pack and raced ahead.

The stones came clattering around him.

One touched his scalp, mussed his hair.

"Murderer! Killer!"

What will they take? he wondered.

He reviewed his assets and thought of possible bribes. He had been able to buy his way out of some tight situations in the past. This one, though, did not seem of a negotiable nature.

A small stone missed him and struck against the side of

a building. The next one did not; it hit him on the arm, causing considerable pain.

He carried no weapons. There was nothing he could do to avert their madness; and mad was what he judged them.

Another stone passed by his ear. He shook his head.

"Bastard!" someone called.

"You don't know what you're doing!" he cried out. "It was an accident!"

He felt moisture on his neck. He touched it, and his fingertips came away bloody. Another stone struck him.

Could he dash into a store? Might he seek sanctuary in some place of business? He looked about, but could discover none that seemed to be open. Where were the police?

Several rocks fell against his back. He swayed, for they were thrown with some force and he felt sharp pains.

"I came here to be of help . . ." he began.

"Murderer!"

Then they rained against him, knocking him to his knees. He rose and ran. More of them hit him, but he stumbled on.

He continued to look for some place of refuge—any place—saw none, lengthened his strides.

There were more things thrown, and he fell. This time he did not rise so quickly. He felt several kicks, and someone spat into his face.

"Killer!"

"Please . . . Listen to me! I can explain."

"Go to hell!"

He crawled, huddling finally against a wall, and now they came in close. There were kicks, spit, stones.

"Please! I'm clean again!"

"Bastard!"

Then came the fury. It was not right that they use him

so, he felt. He had come to their town for a humanitarian purpose. He had undergone hardship to reach Italbar. Now he was bleeding on its streets and being cursed. Who were they to judge him as they had done, to call him names and abuse him? This thing rose up within him, and he knew that, had he the power, he would have reached out and crushed them all.

Hatred, that thing nearly unknown to him, suddenly filled his body with cold fire. He wished that he had not undergone catharsis. He would be the plague-bearer, infecting them all.

The kicks and missiles continued.

He drew his arms across his abdomen, hands before his face, and suffered them.

You'd better kill me, he said to himself. Because if you don't, I'll be back.

Where had he felt this way before? He did not seek the memory, but it returned.

The church. The Strantrian shrine. That was where he had experienced something akin to this hatred. Now he saw that it was right. Strange not to have realized it back then . . .

His ribs felt broken, his right kneecap dislodged. He was missing several teeth, and the blood and sweat kept filling his eyes. The crowd continued to abuse him, and he was never certain when it was that it let up.

Perhaps they thought that they had killed him, for he lay there very still. Or perhaps it was that they grew tired or ashamed. He never knew.

He lay there, huddled on the pavement, his back against the wall that had not opened to give him refuge. He was alone.

Something, like a dream of mumbling and cursing and receding footsteps, flickered through his consciousness.

He coughed and spat blood.

All right, he said. You tried to kill me. Probably think you did. You made a mistake. You let me live. Whatever your intentions were, don't ever ask me for forgiveness, or for mercy. You made a mistake.

Then he passed out again.

The rain fell gently upon his face. This was what had awakened him. It was into the afternoon of the day, and somehow he had been transported into an alley. He had no memory of having crawled to the place, but then he was certain that no one would have assisted him in achieving it.

Again there was a lapse of consciousness, and when it returned the sky was dark.

He was drenched now, and the rain still fell—or perhaps it had just begun again; he had no way of telling. He licked his lips.

How much time had passed? He drew his chrono near. It was broken, of course. His body insisted, though, that he had endured the ages.

All right.

They had harmed him. They had cursed him.

All right.

He spat and tried to see whether it was blood that mixed with the rainslick.

Do you know who I am?

I came here to help. I *did* help. If I inadvertently caused some deaths while trying to be of assistance, do you seriously think that this was intentional?

No?

Then why this?

I know.

We do things because we *feel* that we must. Sometimes

we get hooked by our emotions, our humanity—as I did the other day. I probably did infect one or all of the people I was with.

But to die . . . Would I cause another human being to do it, intentionally?

Not then. Not a while ago.

Now, though, you've showed me another side of life.

I have emotions, too, and they have turned. You beat the hell out of me while I was simply trying to make it to the airfield. Okay.

You have me for an enemy now. Let us see whether you can take it the way that you give it.

Do you know everything that I am?

I am walking death.

You think that now you have done with me?

If you do, you are mistaken.

I came to help.

I will stay to slay.

He lay there for long hours before he could rise and move on.

Dr. Pels regarded the world.

They had had something for him. They had given him a lead.

Deiban fever. That had been the beginning. It had served to put him onto the trail of H. Now as the night without end containing days without number wore on about him, certain other thoughts came and went, remained longer and longer, stayed.

H.

H was more than the key to *mwalakharan khurr* . . .

The very presence of H had served to remedy many unusual conditions.

Is this the real reason, he asked himself, that I abandoned twenty years' labor in favor of this line of attack? H cannot live forever, whereas I may—like this. Am I being completely scientific about this one?

He prepared the *B Coli* for distance-hopping. Then he reread the notice he had received.

The sounds of *Death and Transfiguration* moved about him.

Heidel woke once again. He was lying in a ditch. There was no one near. It was still night. The ground was damp, muddy in places. But the rain had stopped.

He crawled, got to his feet, staggered.

He continued on, toward the field where he had been headed. He remembered something of its layout. He had seen it while strolling, later on on that day when he had given the blood—when?

When he arrived, near to its perimeter, he sought the shed he had seen.

There . . .

It was unlocked and there was a warm corner. Covers for some sort of equipment had been thrown there. They were heavy with dust, but it did not matter. By then he was coughing again, anyhow.

A couple days, he told himself. Let the scar tissue start. That's all.

Malacar kept abreast of the news. He pulled it in, listened, turned it off. He thought about it, digested it, turned it back on again.

The Perseus slid beneath the suns . . .

He drowsed through weather reports for one hundred twelve planets. He grew bored while listening to News Central. He meditated sleepily upon sex while hearing a program out of Pruria.

He rushed on. His ship was in hd, and it would not stop till he was home again.

We did it, said Shind.

We did it, he answered.

And the dead?

I would say we will have a tally before we strike home port.

Shind did not reply.

CHAPTER 2

Within the highest tower of the greatest port, he sat, one man opposing an empire.

Idiotic? he asked himself. No. Because they cannot hurt me.

Glaring down at the ocean, now momentarily visible, he inspected the wet miles of distance that lay beyond the Manhattan Citadel, his home.

It could be worse.

How?

When there's nobody else in port, you sometimes get fidgety . . .

Looking at the waters, he watched the great plume cover them again, like an opening fan.

Someday, maybe . . .

Dr. Malacar Miles was the only man on Earth. He was lord, he was monarch here. And he did not care. The Earth was his. Nobody else wanted it.

He stared through the bubble-window. It afforded him a prospect of half of what remained of Manhattan.

The smoke was a great cloud, and a mirror that hovered showed him the orange burning when he maneuvered it at the proper angle.

It blazed.

His shields absorbed this.

It burned; it was radioactive.

His shields absorbed this too.

There had been a time when he had actually paid attention to it.

He stared upward, and the Earth's dead moon in quarter-phase was there before his eyes.

For three, ten seconds, he waited.

Then came the ship, and he sighed.

My brother is hurting, said Shind. *Will you give him more medicine now?*

Yes.

I saw this thing long ago. Beware.

Before moving to the laboratory, Malacar stared down at the thing which had once been New York City's heart. Long gray vines had whipped their ways around the bases of killed buildings, climbed high. Their leaves were coarse, long, rustling. The smoke blackened them, withered them. Still they grew. He could actually see the movement. No human being could live in those canyons of masonry they wound. For no special reason, he pressed a button and a low-yield atomic missile destroyed a building miles away.

I will have to use karanin on your brother. It will impair his respiratory functions a bit.

It will do more good, will it not? Over-all?

Yes.

Then we must.

Go get him. Take him to the laboratory.

Yes.

He looked out one more time, out across his kingdom and the patches of its ocean that showed through smoke. Then he departed the high deck.

The winds that swirled about the world had deposited their rubbish as he had watched. As always. The only human inhabitant of the place, he was neither especially paternal nor antagonistic about the view.

The drop-tube took him to the lower level of his citadel. To test them, he broke three alarm circuits as he moved along a corridor. Entering the laboratory, he saw Shind's brother Tuv waiting.

He extracted the medication from its wall-slot and blasted it into the small creature.

He waited. Perhaps ten minutes.

How is he?

He complains concerning the sting of the injection, but he states that he begins to feel improvement in his condition.

Good. Can you unwind your mind now and tell me a little more about Morwin's visit?

He is your friend. Mine too. From long ago.

So why the "Beware" business?

It is not he himself, but something that he brings which may lead you to danger.

What?

Information, I feel.

News that may kill me? Those CL radicals with their rockets did not exactly accomplish the job. What has Morwin got?

I do not know. I speak only as a member of my race who occasionally glimpses a fragment of future truth. Sometimes I know. I dream it. I do not understand the process.

Okay. Monitor your brother's condition and tell me about him now.

His breathing is a trifle labored, but his hearts beat more easily. We thank you.

It has worked again. Good.

It is not good. I see his life as coming to an end in two-point-eight Earth years.

What do you want me to do?

He will require stronger drugs as time goes on. You have been kind, but you must be kinder. Possibly, a specialist . . .

All right. We can afford it. We will get him the best. Tell me more about what is wrong.

The blood vessels will begin to deteriorate at a more rapid rate soon. It will take approximately sixteen Earth months before the harm is widespread, however. Then he will go quickly. I do not know what I will do.

He will depend upon my care, and it will not be prominent by its absence. Talk to him and make him comfortable.

I am doing that now.

Pipe me in.

Bide a moment.

. . . Then into the mind of a Mongoloid child, but more. Snatched up by the currents, drawn in, he knew and he saw.

. . . Everything that had fallen before those eyes was there, and Malacar had seen to it that they had looked upon many things.

You do not toss away a tool such as this because of a doctor's bill.

Malacar gazed into that dark place, the mind, moved through it. Shind maintained the bond and Malacar regarded the medium which held him. Skies, maps, millions of pages, faces, scenes, diagrams. It might be that there was no understanding in the idiot creature's mind, but it was a place where everything his yellow eyes had fallen upon had found a home. Malacar moved carefully.

No, that furry head was a storage house; and not to be surrendered readily.

Then, all about him, rang the feelings. Suddenly, he was near the spot of pain and death-fear—only partly understood, and more awful thereby—the seething nightmare place where half-formed images crawled, writhed, burned, bled, froze, were stretched and torn. Something within his own being echoed it and moved toward congruency. It was the basic terror of a thing confronting nothingness, attempting to people it in some fashion with all the worst gropings of the imagination, succeeding in this latter and, failing to comprehend, repeating it.

Shind! Pull me out!

... And he stood there again, beside the sink. He dumped a retort, rinsed it.

The experience was of value?

He decided so.

I will increase the dosage on a very slow basis. Do not permit him to exert himself unduly.

You like his memory?

You are damned right I do, and I will act to preserve it.

Good. The estimate I gave you concerning his life expectancy might be several months off.

I will be judicious in acting upon it.—Tell me more of Morwin.

He is troubled.

Aren't we all?

He will be landing soon and coming by. It seems that his mind is invaded by fears given there by people of the place that you hate.

Likely. He lives among them.

• • •

He only glanced at the vision of his world.

He had activated the screens which showed him much of the Earth, to while away a few minutes. He shut them down because the changed map bored him. Living beside a volcano, simply because the site had once meant something, had accustomed him to the worst that the screens could show. It still meant something to him, but there was little he could do to change the landscape. Now he followed the trail of the ship and watched Morwin emerge.

Fixing a tracer on the man, he primed several weapons systems.

This is ridiculous, he decided. There must be somebody a man can trust.

He observed Morwin's progress all the way to his gate, however; and followed him with a hover-globe that could pour fiery death in an instant.

The space-armored figure halted and looked upward. Fracture lines crossed the globe. Malacar struck the recall button on his massive Weapons Console.

A white light blinked, and he turned a dial, bringing in words and static:

"I'm just here to say 'Hi,' sir. If you want me to go away, I will."

He touched Broadcast.

"No. Come on in. It's just the old precaution business."

But he tracked Morwin every step of the way, feeding the movement patterns into his battle computer. He X-rayed him, weighed him, determined his heartbeat rate, blood pressure and electroencephalographic indices. He fed this data to another computer which analyzed it and routed it back to the battle computer.

Negative, was the reading, as he had expected it to be.

Shind? What do you read?

I would say that he is just stopping by to say "Hi," sir.

Okay.

He opened the front gate of his fortress and the artist entered.

Morwin moved into the massive front hall. He seated himself upon a drifting divan.

Stripping, Malacar stepped into a screen of hazes that bathed him and shaved him as he passed. Moving to a closet, he dressed quickly, concealing only the ordinary weapons on his person.

He tubed then to ground level and entered the main hall of his fortress.

"Hello," he said. "How are you?"

Morwin smiled.

"Hello. What were you shooting at when I came down, sir?"

"Ghosts."

"Oh. Hit any?"

"Never.—It's a pity that all Earth's vineyards are dead, but I still have a good supply of their squeezings. Would you care for some?"

"That would be fine."

Malacar crossed to a wine chest, poured two glasses, passed one to Morwin, who had followed him.

"A toast to your health. Then dinner."

"Thank you."

They touched glasses.

He stood. He stretched. Better. Much better.

He tested his legs, his arms. There were still painful spots, cramped muscles. These he massaged. He brushed at his clothing. He moved his head from side to side.

Then he crossed the shed and peered out through its grimy window.

The lengthening shadows. The end of day once again.

He laughed.

For an instant, a sad blue countenance seemed to swim before his sleep-spotted eyes.

"Sorry," he said; and then he moved to sit upon a box while he waited for the night.

He felt the power singing in his sores, and in a new, unhealed lesion which had occurred on the back of his right hand.

It was good.

Deiling of Digla meditated, as was his custom, while awaiting the ringing of the tidal bell. His eyes half-lidded, he nodded, there on his balcony, not really seeing the ocean he faced.

The event had been one for which his training in the priesthood had not really prepared him. He had never heard of a similar occurrence, but then it was an ancient and complicated religion wherein he held his ministry.

It was inconceivable that the matter had not been called to the attention of the Names. Traditionally, the lighting was a galaxy-wide phenomenon.

But the Names were strangely indifferent to the doings of their own shrines. Generally, the Name-bearers only communicated with one another on matters of worldscaping, in which nearly all of them engaged.

Would it be impertinent for him to submit an inquiry to one of the Thirty-one Who Lived?

Probably.

But if they were truly unaware, they should be advised. Should they not?

He pondered. For a long while, he pondered.

Then, with the ringing of the tidal bell, he rose and sought the communications unit.

It was unfair, he decided. It was what he had wanted, and it was appropriate, so far as he was now concerned. But the intention had been lacking at the time of the act, and this took away a taste which would have been far sweeter upon his lips.

He moved through the streets of Italbar. There were no lights. There was no movement beneath those blazing stars.

He tore down a quarantine sign, stared at it, ripped it across. He let the pieces fall to the ground and walked on.

He had wanted to come in the night, touching door handles with his wounds, running his hands along banisters, breaking into stores and spitting on food.

Where were they now? Dead, evacuated, dying. The town bore no resemblance to what he had seen that first evening, from the hilltop, when his intentions had been far different.

He regretted that he had been their agent of destruction by accident rather than by design.

But there would be other Italbars—worlds, and worlds filled with Italbars.

When he passed the corner where the boy had shaken his hand, he paused to cut himself a staff.

When he passed the place where the man had offered him a lift, he spat.

Having led a solitary life for so many years, he felt that he could see man's basic nature far, far better than those who had dwelled in cities all their lives. Seeing, he could judge.

Clutching his staff, he passed out of the town and into

the hills, the wind tumbling his hair and beard, the stars of Italbar in his eyes.

Smiling he went.

Malacar stretched his arsenal arms and legs and stifled a yawn.

"More coffee, Mr. Morwin?"

"Thank you, Commander."

". . . So, the CL is thinking of further hostilities and they want to use me as an excuse? Very good."

"That's not exactly the way it was put to me, sir."

"It amounts to the same thing."

Too bad I cannot trust you, Malacar decided, even though you consider yourself trustworthy. You were a good Exec, and I always liked you. You artistic types are too unstable, though. You go where they buy your art. With that mind trick of yours aimed at a fusion reactor we could do some good work together again. Too bad. Why don't you smoke that pipe I gave you?

He is thinking of it now, said Shind.

What else is he thinking?

Whatever the information I feared, it is not foremost in his mind. Or if it is, I do not recognize it as such.

"Mr. Morwin, there is a favor I would like to ask of you."

"What is it, sir?"

"It concerns those dream-globe things that you make . . ."

"Yes?"

"I'd like you to make me one."

"I'd be only too happy. But I don't have my equipment with me. If I had known you were interested, I could have brought the gear along. But—"

"I understand, in principle, what it is that you do. I

believe that my laboratory facilities would be sufficient for us to work something out."

"There are the drugs, the telepathic linkage, the globe—"

"—And I'm a doctor of medicine with a telepathic friend who can both receive and transmit thought-images. As for the globe, we should be able to manufacture one."

"Well, I'll be glad to try."

"Good. Why do we not begin this evening? Now, say?"

"I have no objections. Had I known of your interest earlier, I would have offered to do it long ago."

"I only thought of it recently, and the present seems a particularly appropriate time.

So very, he reflected. And late.

He moved through the great rain forest of Cleech. He passed beside the River Bart. By boat, he traveled hundreds of miles along that watercourse, stopping at villages and small towns.

By now, his appearance was indeed that of a holy outcast—somehow stronger and taller, with voice and eyes that could catch and draw the attention of crowds, his garments in tatters, hair and beard grown long and unkempt, body covered with countless sores, blotches, excrescences. He preached as he passed, and men listened.

He cursed them. He told them of the violence that lay in their souls and of the capacity for evil which informed their beings. He spoke of their guilt, which cried out for judgment, announced that this judgment had been rendered. He stated that there is no such act as repentance, told them that the only thing remaining for them was to spend these final hours in the ordering of their affairs. None laughed as he said these words, though later many did. A few, however, moved to obey him.

Thus tolling the Day of Annihilation, he moved from town to city, from city to metropolis; and his promise was always kept.

The few who survived considered themselves, for some obscure reason, as the Chosen. Of What, they had no idea.

"I am ready," said Malacar, "to begin."

"All right," Morwin agreed. "Let's."

What the hell does he want with it? he asked himself. He was never especially introspective or aesthetically inclined in the old days. Now he wants a highly personalized work of art created for him. Could he have changed? No, I shouldn't think so. His taste in decorating this place was as abominable as ever, and nothing has changed since last I was here. He talks the same as he always did. His intentions, plans, desires seem unaltered. No. This has nothing to do with his sensibilities. What then?

He watched Malacar inject a colorless fluid into his arm.

"What is the drug you took?" he asked.

"A mild sedative, somewhat hallucinogenic. It will be a few minutes before it takes effect."

"But you haven't told me yet what thing I am to look for—to attempt to induce, if necessary—for the work."

"I'm making it easier for you," Malacar told him, as they reclined upon their couches before the globe they had erected. "I will tell you—via Shind—when it is ready. Then all you will have to do is hit your controls and capture it, exactly the way that it is."

"That would seem to imply a moderately strong element of consciousness on your part. This invariably interferes with the strength and clarity of the vision. That is why I prefer to use my own drugs, sir."

"Don't worry. This will be strong and clear."

"How long do you feel it will be before it occurs just as you would have it?"

"Perhaps five minutes. It will come in a flash, but it will remain long enough for you to activate your controls and impose it."

"I will try, sir."

"You will succeed, Mr. Morwin. That is an order. It will be the most difficult one you have ever attempted, I am certain. But I want it—there, before me—when I awaken."

"Yes, sir."

"Why don't you relax for a while? Make whatever mental preparations you do?"

"Yes, sir."

Shind?

Yes, Commander. I am watching. He is still puzzled. He is wondering now why you want it and what it will be. Failing to arrive at any conclusions, he attempts to dismiss these questions for the moment. Soon he will know, he tells himself. He tries to relax, to follow your order, now. He is very tense. His palms perspire and he wipes them on his trousers. He regulates his breathing and his heartbeat. His mind becomes a more peaceful place. His surface thoughts diminish. Now! Now . . . He does a thing with his mind that I cannot follow, understand. I know that he is readying himself for the exercise of his special talent. Now he does indeed relax. He knows that he is ready. There is no tension in him. He allows himself the joy of reverie. Thoughts arise unbidden, vanish in like fashion. Wisps, rag-tails, highly personal, nothing strong . . .

Continue to follow him.

I do. Wait. Something, something . . .

What is it?

I do not know. The globe—something about the globe . . .

This globe? The one we made?

No, the globe seems only to have served as the stimulus, now that he is relaxing and there are free associations . . . This globe . . . No. It is another. Different . . .

What is it like?

Big, and with a backdrop of stars. Inside . . .

What?

A man. A dead man, but he moves. There is also much equipment. Medical equipment. The globe is a ship—his ship. B Coli . . .

Pels. The dead doctor. Pathologist. I've read some of his papers. What of him?

Nothing to Morwin, for the thing is gone now from his mind, and the wispy thoughts have come again. But there was something there for me.—My dream-thing. The thing of which I warned you, the thing that I said he would bear— this is it, somehow. Or connected with it.

I will find out.

Not from Morwin, for he does not know. It is simply the fact that there is knowledge you will gain in connection with Pels, and that he has brought into your presence a thought of the dead doctor, which menaces you. I—Commander, for- give me! I am the agent! Had I not told you of my dream of weeks ago, discerned its key just now and told you of this, also, there would be no danger. The way to trouble is through Pels, not Morwin. Better I had remained completely silent.—Simply avoid anything connected with the dead doc- tor.

Strange. A very strange twisting. But we have uncovered the information we desired. We can deal with it later. Let us get on with the "dream."

Wait. Let there be no later. Dismiss Pels from your thinking and never recall him.

Not now, Shind. Now you must help me seek through your brother's memories.

Very well. I will assist you. But—

Now, Shind.

Then he was there again, moving along aisles of that library, the brother-thing's mind. In it, everything the creature had experienced, from vague pre-birth feelings through present awareness, lay before him. He sought the sad, sore spot he had come upon earlier. Locating it, he drew nearer. Shaken, at the pain-death-fear nightmare-place, he forced himself to bore deep within it. It was a dream Tuv had had earlier, but the preservative quality of the memory made it hang there, like all the others, in the gallery of his agony. It was a corkscrew-twisted blot, with two streamers like writhing legs, the whole penetrated by spark-lines, as from the tail of a green comet; there was a faint lightening near its bottom, featuring a vague, facelike area—suggesting no creature Malacar had ever known—the horrid face-place, lying at that instant between life and death, red tears emerging in all directions therefrom, falling into the blot and beyond, into a faintly silver landscape of crystal or of thin-flamed silver fire. Into the center of this thing, from out his own memory on such matters, Malacar cast the main stat-map of the CL, each sun so faint—like cells in a dying body! The whole took but an instant, and Malacar said, *Now, Shind!* and heard Morwin scream. But he also heard the jets come alive.

He realized then that he was screaming too; and he continued to, until Shind pulled him out. Then blackness, like lightning, struck him.

The world called Cleech fell away at his back. Within a matter of hours, he would be outside that small system and able to enter subspace. He turned from the console and fetched a long, slim cigar from a supply he had taken from the dead man's counter, there in the dead men's space port.

It had been much faster this time, had gone through a larger area almost immediately. What had it been? He had not even recognized the condition. Could it be that he had somehow become a breeding place for new diseases?

He lit the cigar and smiled.

His tongue was black and the sclerae of his eyes had grown yellowish. Very little healthy tissue was now visible upon him. He had become a discolored mass of sores and swellings.

He chuckled and puffed smoke until his eyes fell upon his reflection in the dampened screen to his left.

Then he stopped chuckling and the smile went away. He put the cigar aside and leaned forward, studying his face. It was the first time he had seen it since—How long ago? Where? Italbar, of course. Where it had all started.

He regarded the lines, the places that looked like burns, the dark ridges that crossed the cheeks.

Something inside him chose, at that moment, to close its fingers about his stomach and squeeze.

He turned away from the screen, his breath quickening. Suddenly, he found that he was panting. His hands began to tremble.

My appearance need not be so extreme to achieve the desired effect, he decided. Three weeks in sub before I reach Summit. Might as well go into remission and clean up a bit.

He located the cigar and continued to puff on it. He placed his left hand where it was out of sight. He did not look back at the screen.

After he had entered hd, he turned on the forward screen and regarded stars. Centered about a point directly before him, they moved in long, burning spirals, some clock-wise, some counterclockwise. He hung there, absolutely still, and for a time he regarded the universe as it moved about him.

Then he reclined the seat, closed his eyes, folded his arms and followed the long trail he had not taken since before Italbar.

... *Walking, quickly, through the mists. Blue, blue, blue. Blue flowers, like the heads of serpents. A more exotic perfume in the air. Blue moon above, blue vines across the shallow stairs.*

Up into the garden . . .

Blue insects swarmed about him, and as he gestured to brush them away he saw his hand.

Something is wrong, he decided. Whenever I come to this place I am whole again.

He advanced into the garden and felt a subtle change, though there was no specific thing to which he could attribute it.

He cast his eyes upward, but there was only the motion-less moon.

He listened, but there were no birdsongs.

The mists snaked about his ankles. The first glittering stone, when he came upon it, still cast its prisms. The but-terflies, though, were missing. Instead, it was partly covered by a webwork within which dozens of fat blue caterpillars hung suspended, turning, contracting into U's and straight-ening again, slowly. Beneath knobbed horns, their faceted eyes blazed like sapphire chips. As he watched, they all con-trived to turn in his direction and raise their heads.

He did not look upon the other stones as he passed them, but pressed forward with increasing distress, seeking a certain high stand of shrubbery.

When he located it, he hurried in that direction; and as always, the light faded at his approach. He saw then the summerhouse.

It stood as he had never seen it before. Shaded, peaceful, cool, it had always been. Now, however, each stone was clearly delineated, burning with a cold blue light. Inside, there was absolute blackness.

He halted. He succumbed to a chill that gave way to a shudder.

What is it that is wrong? he asked himself. *It has never been this way before. Could she be angry with me? Why? Perhaps I should not enter. Perhaps I should wait here until it is time to go back. Or perhaps I should return immediately. There is an electrical quality to the air. Like just before a storm . . .*

He stood there, watching, waiting. Nothing occurred within the stillness.

The tingling sensation increased. The back of his neck began to throb, then his hands and feet.

He decided to depart, discovered that he could not move.

The throbbing spread throughout his entire body.

He felt an urge to move forward. It was not a desire, but a compulsion. Throbbing, he moved ahead once more.

When he entered, his feelings were not as they had been on prior occasions in the place. This time he hoped that he would not even glimpse a smile, a fluttering eyelid, an earlobe, a strand of hair, the sheen of blue moonbeams upon a restless forearm or shoulder. This time he was afraid to see anything of her. This time, he hoped she was not present.

He moved to the stone bench that ran along the wall, seated himself upon it.

"Dra Heidel von Hymack," came the words, and they

made him want to rise and flee, but he could not move. They were more sibilant than usual, and their breath came cold upon his cheek. He kept his face averted.

"Why do you not turn and look at me, Dra von Hymack? You have always desired this in the past."

He said nothing. She was the same—yet different. Everything had been altered.

"Dra von Hymack, you do not turn and you do not answer me. What is the matter?"

"Lady—"

"Then be unchivalrous. It is enough that you have come home, at last."

"I do not understand."

"You have finally done the correct thing. Now the stars have turned in their courses and the seas have come unchained."

It is a lovely voice, he decided. More so than before. It was the sudden alteration that startled me. The garden is prettier too.

"You have noticed the changes and you approve. That is good. Tell me what you think of your new strength."

"I like it. Men are worthless and they deserve to die. If my power were greater, more of them would."

"Oh, it shall be! Believe me. Soon you will be able to emanate spores that will slay across hundreds of kilometers. And there will come a day when you will need but set foot upon a world to kill everything which dwells there."

"It is only the people that I care about. It was they who hurt me. It is man who is unthinking and brutal. The other races, the other life forms—they do not disturb me."

"Ah, but if you would serve me fully—as you have chosen to do—then all of life is become your enemy."

"I would not go that far, Lady. For it was not all of life that attacked me."

"But to reach the guilty, you must strike among the innocent as well. It is the only way."

"I can avoid the non-human worlds."

"Very well. For a time, perhaps. Are you still happiest of all when you are here, with me?"

"Yes, Myra-o—"

"Do not barbarize my name. Speak it as it should be spoken—Arym-o-myra—when it must be spoken at all."

"Lady, I apologize. I had thought it otherwise."

"Cease thinking. Simply do as I tell you."

"Of course."

"With your new power, which grows in you by the day, you have the best of both worlds. It is only while you are here that your sleeping body does not bear all the marks of your power. It snores quietly in that little shell you use to cross between the worlds. When you awaken there, you will bear greater strengths and deeper marks than any you have thus far known."

"Why is this? I can recall when it was the other way about."

"It is because you have chosen to act as a man no more, but as a god, that godlike strengths have been granted you."

"I had thought that you might cleanse me for a time, for I discover that I grow increasingly ugly."

She laughed.

"You? Ugly? By all the Names, you are the most beautiful creature that lives. Turn now and fall upon your knees. Adore me. I shall require sexual worship of you, and then I shall confirm you as my servant forever."

He turned and finally beheld her face. Then he fell upon his knees and lowered his head.

♦ ♦ ♦

When he awakened, Malacar gave himself a genuine injection he had had ready, a tranquilizer. The first one he had taken had been distilled water. He did not allow himself to look at the globe during this time.

Then he rose to administer similar medication to the still unconscious Morwin. He hesitated, however.

Why is he still out, Shind?

The full strength of the death-dream came upon him in conjunction with his using his shaping power. It seems to have given it more force.

In that case, I am going to give him a sedative and put him to bed.

It was only after this was done that he returned to the laboratory and considered the globe.

He felt prickly sensations in unlikely places.

God! That's it! he decided. That is exactly what I saw! I never realized he was that good! He actually succeeded in stuffing a nightmare inside that globe. It is perfect. Too perfect, in fact. I did not want a work of art. That is what it is, though, when you see it like this—fully conscious. I think he does make small alterations . . . I will never know, for certain.—All I had wanted was a nasty, striking item to ship to the High Command in SEL—from Malacar, with love—to let them know I am on to their latest—to warn them. I wanted to tell them, by this, what I am going to try to do to their whole bloody CL. I will fail, of course, but I grow older and there is no successor in sight. When I do try that big one, it will be all over. They will be frightened of the DYNAB again, for a time. Perhaps during that time another Malacar will come along. That is what I will be praying when I carry the bomb into their E-Room. I almost hate to give them the globe, though. Too bad Morwin went over.

He isn't a bad sort. Those globes of his . . . Globes . . . What the hell!

He searched the laboratory. Not locating what he sought, he tried the monitor, checking all the rooms in the citadel.

All right, Shind. Where are you hiding?

No response.

I know you have some sort of mind-lock on me. I want you to release it.

Nothing.

Look, you know I can break it, now that I know it exists. It may take me several days, weeks even. But I will get through it. Save me the trouble.

There came to him the mental equivalent of a sigh.

I only did it for your own good.

Whenever people start talking to me about my own good, I reach for my gun.

I would like to discuss the advisability of not removing it before—

Take it off! That's an order! No discussion! Take it off the easy way now, or I will have to sweat it the hard way later. Either way, it is coming off.

You are a very stubborn man, Commander.

You're damned right I am! Now!

As you say, sir. It will be easier if you calm down a bit.

I am calm.

There came the sensation of a dark bird passing through his head.

The globe, Dr. Pels . . . Of course!

Now that you recall it, you can see that it is slim indeed. The stuff of dreams; an impossible, bootstrap-type paradox—

But you felt strongly enough about it to attempt to sup-

*press my memories of the matter. No, Shind. There is some
thing here that bears further inquiry.*

What are you going to do?

*I am going to read Pels' latest papers, and I am going to
ascertain where his current interests lie. I am also going to
determine his present physical whereabouts.*

Once more, there came to him the mental equivalent of
a sigh.

That night he sent a request for a special messenger ship
to come to Earth and pick up a parcel for delivery to the
High Command on Elizabeth. The expense would be astro-
nomical, but his credit was good. He personally crated the
globe and included a "Gentlemen: Best wishes.–Malacar
Miles, Flt. Cdr., Ret., 4th Stlr., DYNAB" note. Then he began
reading–and in some cases rereading–the writings of
pathologist Larmon Pels.

When morning lightened the mists over Manhattan, he
was still reading. He glanced at his notes. Aside from jottings
with respect to medical items in which he was personally
interested, he had written only two things he felt to be important: "Deiban fever" and "Special interest in the H case."

At that point, he debated retiring, decided against it, hit
himself with a stimulator.

Morwin might have something else I want, he decided.

Later that day, as they sat to lunch, Morwin was saying,
". . . Pretty rough one you sprang on me, sir. I've done things
verging on nightmare before, but nothing that emotionally
charged. It kind of drained me. I didn't mean to pass out on
you like that, though."

"I'm sorry I did it to you. I hadn't guessed it would
affect you the way it did."

"Well . . ." Morwin smiled and took a sip of coffee. "I'm glad you liked it."

"You're sure you won't take my money?"

"No thanks.—May I go to the upper deck again after lunch, to see the volcano?"

"Certainly. I'll go with you. Finish up, and we'll take a walk."

They rose to the upper levels, where they looked out and down and around. The sun had changed portions of the prospect to golden confetti. The collapsed skyline leaned like an ancient fence. Fires bubbled orange within a dark caldron. Molten stones were fired upward, filling portions of the air like flak. Occasionally, a faint tremor was felt. When the winds rose or shifted there was sometimes a parting of the agitated curtain; then sections of the dark Atlantic, especially that neck which curved inward, lapping about the base of the cone, would become visible through the distorting lens of the gases. The leaves of the man-thick vines grew green at their bases; the upper ones were black as crows.

". . . Hard to believe that the whole world is like this," Morwin was saying, "and that it happened during our lifetimes."

"Ask the CL about it. They did it."

". . . And that nobody will ever live here again, on the home planet."

"I live here—to remind them of their guilt, to stand as a warning of their own fate."

". . . There are many worlds such as this once was. There are millions of innocent persons on them."

"In reaching all the guilty one sometimes strikes the innocent as well. Generally, I'd say. It is the way of revenge."

"And if revenge is abandoned, a few generations will level both the guilty and the innocent, anyhow. The new generation, at least, will be totally blameless for this—and worlds will endure."

"That's too philosophical an outlook to accept—for a man who has lived through some of the things I have."

"I lived through them too, sir."

"Yes, but—"

He bit off his words.

They stared outward for a time, then, "Has that disease specialist, Larmon Pels, stopped by Honsi recently?" Malacar asked.

"Yes, as a matter of fact. Was he here too?"

"Some time ago. What was he looking for on your world?"

"Some general medical information, vital statistics and a man who wasn't there."

"The man . . . ?"

"Hyneck, or something like that, I believe. There was no record of him with us either, though.—Look at that flare-up, will you?"

H? Malacar asked himself. Could this Hyneck or whatever be the disease pool? I never heard of him either, but if he is—

Deiban fever has, for the first time, been detected on worlds other than Deiba, he remembered reading. *It is invariably fatal, save for one known exception. I refer, of course, to the case of H. The agent of transmission is not yet known.*

If this man were H, could he possibly also be the unwitting transmitter of the condition? It would be simple enough to obtain the exact name cited in Pels' request. I will, of course.

The outbreaks of Deiban fever on worlds other than Deiba were always accompanied by the occurrence of half a dozen other exotic diseases. Their presence, simultaneously, had never been adequately explained. But H had had countless diseases and survived them all, been pronounced cured. Could it be that some unknown cue within H caused them to recrudesce simultaneously—all mutually contagious?

The possible military applications flashed through Malacar's mind like the orange flare-up below him.

Everybody is prepared for bacteriological warfare, on one level or another—even combined approaches, he decided. But here would be a random assault, shotgun-style, attributable to knowable yet still unclassified natural causes. If this is possible and H is the key to controlling the process—or somehow *is* the process—then I hear the tolling of the death bell. I could hurt the CL more than I'd thought. It but remains to determine whether this Hyneck is indeed H; and if so, to locate him.

For hours they stood and watched the flames and the seething lava, the shifting patterns of sky and sea. Then Morwin cleared his throat.

"I'd like to rest for a time now. I still feel somewhat weak," he said.

"Of course, of course," said Malacar, suddenly withdrawing his attention from something distant. "I believe I will remain here myself. It looks as if another flare-up is due."

"I hope you didn't mind the unexpected company."

"Far from it. You've raised my spirits more than I can tell you."

He watched him go, then chuckled.

Perhaps that dream-globe you created was true, he decided. An accurate prediction of things to come. I never

actually had hoped to succeed, unless . . . How does it go?
Those lines I learned at the university . . . ?

> Unless the giddy Heaven fall,
> And Earth some new Convulsion tear;
> And, us to joyn, the World should all
> Be cramp'd into a *Planisphere.*

If I'm correct on this thing, I am going to cram it all there—
all of the CL, just as you did that vision—into a planisphere.

Shind! he called out. *Do you know what has happened?*

Yes. I have been listening.

*I will ask Morwin to stay and mind the shop. We our-
selves will soon be leaving on another journey.*

As you say. Where to?

Deiba.

I feared as much.

Malacar laughed at this retort, and the mist ran away
with the noon.

He watched the spiraling stars, like the distant fireworks
of childhood. His hand fell upon the monogrammed bag
fastened at his belt. He had forgotten it was there. He
glanced downward when he heard the clicking sound, and
for a moment he forgot the stars.

His stones. How lovely they were. How could he have
pushed them from his memory with such ease? He fingered
them and smiled. Yes, these were true. A piece of mineral
never betrays you. Each is unique, a world unto itself and
harmless. His eyes filled with tears.

"I love you," he whispered, and one by one he counted
them out and replaced them in the bag.

As he tied them again at his belt, he watched the movements of his hands. His fingers left moist smudges upon the material. But his hands were beautiful, she had told him. And she was correct, of course. He raised them near to his face and a surge of power swept through his body and settled within them. He knew that he was stronger now than any man or nation. Soon he would be stronger than any world.

He turned his attention once more to the bright whirlpool that sucked him toward its center: Summit.

He would be there in no time at all.

When the message arrived, his first reaction was a very loud "Damn! Why ask *me?*" But since he already knew the answer he restricted his subsequent reactions to the expletive.

Pacing, he paused to flip a toggle and postpone his lunch until further notice. After a time, he noted that he was in his rooftop garden and smoking a cigar, staring into the west.

"Racial discrimination, that's what it is," he muttered, then moved to a hidden plate, thumbed it open and flipped another toggle.

"Send me a light lunch in the manuscript library in about an hour," he ordered, not waiting for a reply.

He continued to pace, breathing in the smells of life and growth that surrounded him and ignoring them completely.

The day grew gray and he turned to the east where a cloud had covered his sun. He glared at it and after a few moments it began to dissipate.

The day brightened once more, but he growled, sighed and walked away from it.

"Always the fall guy," he said, as he entered the library, removed his jacket, hung it on a hook beside the door.

He moved his eyes along the rows of cases which contained the most complete collection of religious manuscripts in the galaxy. On shelves beneath each case were bound facsimiles of the originals. He passed into the next room and continued his search.

"Way up there by the ceiling," he sighed. "I might have known."

Setting the foot of the ladder within three feet of the Qumran scrolls, he adjusted its balance and climbed.

He lit a cigarette after he had seated himself in an easy chair with a fac-copy of *The Book of Life's Manifold Perils and Pleas for Continued Breathing*, in ancient Pei'an script, across his knees.

It seemed but moments later that he heard a click and a programmed cough at his right elbow. The robot had entered, rolled silently across the thick carpeting, come to rest beside him and lowered the covered tray to a comfortable eating level. It proceeded to uncover it.

He ate mechanically and continued reading. After a time, he noted that the robot had departed. He had no memory whatever of what it was that he had eaten for lunch.

He continued to read.

Dinner passed in the same fashion. Night occurred and the lights came on about him, brightening as the darkness deepened.

Sometime in the middle of the night he turned the final page and closed the book. He stretched, yawned, rose and staggered. He had not realized that his right foot had grown numb. He reseated himself and waited for the tingling to pass. When it did, he climbed the ladder and replaced the volume. He restored the ladder to its corner. He could have had robot-extensors and grav-lifts, but he preferred libraries of the old-fashioned sort.

He passed through sliding windows and walked to his bar on the west terrace. He seated himself before it and the light to its rear came on.

"Bourbon and water," he said. "Make it a double."

There was a ten-second pause, during which he could feel the faintest of vibrations through his fingertips resting on the bar. Then a six-by-six square opened before him and the drink slowly rose into sight, coming flush with the counter top. He raised it and sipped.

". . . And a pack of cigarettes," he added, remembering that he had finished his some hours before.

These were delivered. He opened the pack and lit one with what was probably the last Zippo lighter outside of museums. Certainly the last functioning one. Every piece of it had been replaced, countless times, by custom-made duplicates turned out solely to repair *this* lighter—so it was not, properly speaking, an antique; it was more in the nature of a direct descendant. His brother had given it to him—When? He took another sip. He still had the original around somewhere, all the broken pieces reassembled within its scratched case. Probably in the bottom drawer of that old dresser . . .

He dragged on the cigarette and felt the drink grow hot in his stomach, then move its momentary warmth into regions beyond. An orange moon hung low on the horizon and a rapidly moving white one was pacing midheaven. He smiled faintly, listened to the toadingales in their wallows. They were doing something of Vivaldi's. Was it from *Summer?* Yes. There it was. He took another swallow and swirled the remainder in his glass.

Yes, this was his job, he decided. He was really the only one of them with experience in the area. And of course the priest would rather send the inquiry to an alien than to one of his own people. Less of a chance for reprimand, for racial reasons; and if there was something dangerous involved . . .

Cynical, he decided, and you don't want to be cynical. Just practical. Whatever prompted the thing, it's yours now; and you know what happened the last time something like this occurred. It must be dealt with. The fact that there will be no element of control means that, ultimately, it will be aimed at everybody.

He finished his drink, ground out his cigarette. The glass dropped from sight. The panel slid closed.

"Give me another of the same," he said; and quickly, "Not the cigarettes," as he remembered the new servomech's program.

The drink was replaced and he took it with him into his study. There, he dropped into and semi-reclined his favorite chair. He dimmed the lights, caused the room temperature to drop to 62 degrees Fahrenheit, moved a control which brought about the ignition of real logs in the fireplace across the room from him, dropped a tri-dee night winter scene upon the room's one window (it would have taken him several hours to arrange for the real thing), extinguished all the lights now he saw that the fire was taking and settled back into his favorite thinking environment.

In the morning, he switched on his automatic Secretary and Files unit.

"First order of business," he dictated. "I want to talk with Dr. Matthews and my three best programmers immediately after breakfast—here in my study. I want breakfast, by the way, in twenty minutes. You estimate the eating time."

"Do you wish to speak with them singly or as a group?" came the voice from the hidden speaker.

"As a group. Now—"

"What would you like for breakfast?" S & F interrupted.

"Anything at all. Now—"

"Please be more specific. The last time you said 'Any-thing'—"

"All right. Hamandeggsandtoastandmarmaladeandcof-fee. Now, the second thing I want is for someone high up on my staff to contact the Surgeon General or the Director of Health or whatever the hell his title is, in the SEL complex. I want full access to that Panopath computer of theirs no later than tomorrow afternoon, local time, via remote input from here on Homefree. Third, have the port hands start checking over the *T* for distance-jumping. Fourth, find out who it belongs to and get me the dossier. That's it."

Approximately an hour and a quarter later when they had assembled in his study, he waved them toward chairs and smiled.

"Gentlemen," he said, "I require your assistance in obtaining some information. I am not certain as to the specific nature of the information or the questions I must ask in order to come by it, though I do have some vague notions. It will concern people, places, events, probabilities and diseases. Some of the things I wish to know concern happenings fifteen or twenty years past, and some quite recent. It could take a long while to come up with sufficient information for me to act upon, but I do not have a long while. I want it in two or three days. Your job, therefore, will first be to assist me in formulating the appropriate questions, and then to place those questions on my behalf before a data source which I believe capable of providing what I need. That is the general situation. Now we shall discuss specifics."

Late that afternoon, after they had departed, he realized

that there was nothing more he could do for the time being, and so turned his attention to other matters.

That evening, however, as he wandered through his arsenal, it was for purposes of making a routine safety check, he told himself. But as time passed, he found that he was checking only the smaller, more lethal pieces, such as might be borne easily by one man, perhaps carried concealed and capable of striking from a distance. When he realized what he was doing he did not stop, however. As, among other things, the only living deicide in the galaxy, he felt it his bounden duty always to be prepared, just in case.

Thus did Francis Sandow spend the days before his departure for Deiba.

Anxious to test his new powers on a smaller scale before moving on to the large urban centers of Summit—a far more heavily populated world than Cleech—Heidel von Hymack orbited the world at a great altitude while he studied its maps and read statistics concerning that synthetic planet.

Then, careful to avoid the traffic control centers of the great space ports, he dropped into a thinly populated, backwoods area of its second major continent, Soris. There, in a canyon, he concealed the vessel he had used, beneath an overhang of rock. He locked its controls and its ports, and with a tiny beamer he had found in a rack, he cut brush for camouflage and arranged it about the jump-buggy.

Moving away, staff in his mottled hand, walking, he broke into song. At an earlier date, this would have surprised him, for he did not understand the words that he sang and the tune was a thing out of dream.

After a time, he saw a small farmhouse built against the side of a hill . . .

The music throbbed about him as he set his laboratory in order. He cleaned, adjusted, locked down, put away everything which would not be needed for a time. His giant, ghostlike figure drifted about the ship, straightening, ordering.

I'm becoming a bit old-maidish, he chided himself, smiling inwardly. A place for everything and all of it there. What will it be like if I have the opportunity to go back, be around people again, readapt? Of course, I adapted to deep space . . . Still, it would be quite a change. There is nobody who could tackle my condition yet, if H cannot do anything for me. So it would be years off. Several centuries, most likely. Discounting some unexpected breakthrough. What will it be like if it takes several centuries? What will *I* be like by then? A ghost of a ghost? The only human alien to his own species? What will my descendants say?

Had there been functioning lungs within him, he would have chuckled. Instead, he moved forward and seated himself within the observation section of the *B Coli*. There, he watched the stars spin, as in a cosmic centrifuge, about him. A Gregorian chant provided the sound track as he hung and they wheeled, on his way to Cleech, Heidel von Hymack's last reported destination.

CHAPTER 3

It was late on a rainy night when she first saw him in the flesh.

Having no customers that evening, she had descended and visited the small newsstand off the lobby. She knew that the front door of the establishment had been opened because of the sudden draft and the amplification of noises from the street and the storm. Selecting her reading materials and depositing her coins, she took her papers and turned to cross the lobby.

That was when she saw him, and the papers fell from her hand. She took a step backward, confused. It was impossible that they should ever be this near to one another. She felt dizzy, and her face began to burn.

He was big, bigger even than she had imagined. His hair was mainly black—just a few light touches of gray at the temples—she noted; but then, of course, he would have had the S-S treatments and aged more slowly than other men. This pleased her, for she would have hated to see him in his decline. And those hawklike features and those blazing eyes! He was more impressive in person than on record or in tridee. He wore a black rain garment and bore two huge pieces of luggage—one a clothing case of sorts and the other a perforated box with a handle. The rain sparkled in his hair and eyebrows, glistened on his forehead and cheeks. She felt like running forward and offering her blouse as a facecloth.

She stooped and gathered the papers. Rising, she lowered her head and raised them before her, so that her face was partly hidden. Then she moved into the lobby, as though reading, and found a chair near to the main desk.

"Room and girl, sir?" she heard Horace saying.

"That will be fine," he said, lowering his luggage to the floor.

"There are many vacancies," said Horace, "because of the weather," as he pushed the album across the counter. "Let me know what strikes your fancy."

She heard him turning the pages of the big book and she counted, because she knew them by heart: . . . *Four, five.* A pause. . . . *Six.*

He had stopped.

Oh no! she thought. That would be Jeanne or Synthe. Not either one of them, not for him! Meg, perhaps, or Kyla. But not that cow-eyed Jeanne, or Synthe, who was twenty pounds heavier than her photo indicated.

She ventured a glance and saw that Horace had moved away and was reading a paper.

Deciding quickly, she rose to her feet and approached him.

"Commander Malacar . . ."

She tried to say it boldly, but her voice dropped to a whisper because of the dryness of her throat.

He turned and stared down at her. Glancing at Horace

from the corner of his eye, he raised his right forefinger and crossed his lips with it.

"Hello. What is your name?"

"Jackara."

Her voice was better this time.

"You work here?"

She nodded.

"Occupied this evening?"

She shook her head.

"Clerk!" He turned.

Horace lowered the paper.

"Yes, sir?"

He jerked a thumb at Jackara.

"Her," he said.

Horace swallowed and looked uncomfortable.

"Sir, there is something I had better tell you—" he began.

"Her," Malacar repeated. "Sign me in."

"Just as you say, sir," said Horace, producing a blank card and a writing stylus. "But—"

"The name is Rory Jimson, and I am from Miadod, on Camphor. Pay now, or pay later?"

"Pay now, sir. Eighteen units."

"How much is that in DYNAB dollars?"

"Fourteen and a half."

Malacar produced a roll of bills and paid him.

Horace opened his mouth, closed it, then said, "If everything is not satisfactory, please let me know immediately."

Malacar nodded and stooped for his bags.

"If you'll wait here, I'll ring you a rob."

"That won't be necessary."

"Very well. In that case, Jackara can show you to the room."

The clerk picked up the stylus, fidgeted with it, replaced it. Finally, he returned to his paper.

Malacar followed her toward the lift shaft, studying her form, her hair, trying to recall her face.

Shind, prepare to transmit and relay, he said, as they entered the shaft.

Ready.

—*Do not look startled, Jackara, or give any outward sign of hearing me. Tell me how it is that you know me.*

—*You are a telepath!*

—*Just answer the question, bearing in mind that I can destroy half this building by waving my arm in the proper way.*

"This is where we get off," she said aloud, and they left the lift and she turned to the right, leading him along a tiger-striped corridor where lights glowed only in the base-boards. The effect was tantalizing as well as stark. It gave a somewhat animal-like aura to the girl moving before him. He sniffed and detected faint narcotic fumes in the air. They were stronger near the ventilators.

—*I have seen your picture many times. I have read much about you. That is how I knew you. As a matter of fact, I have all your biographies—even the two CL ones.*

He laughed aloud and gave Shind the shorthand signal for "End transmission. Continue to receive," then, *Is she telling the truth, Shind?* he inquired.

Yes. She admires you considerably. She is quite excited and extremely nervous.

No trap, then?

No.

She halted before a door, fumbled with her key for a time, unlocked it.

She pushed it open and instead of entering or stepping

aside, moved to bar it, facing him. Her face twisted and untwisted and she looked as if she were about to cry.

"Do not laugh when you go in," she said. "Please. No matter what you see."

"I won't," he said.

Then she stepped aside.

He entered the room and looked about. His eyes fell first upon the whips, then moved to the picture above the bed. He lowered his luggage to the floor and continued to stare. He heard the door close. The room was a study in asceticism. Gray walls and gleaming fixtures. The one window was shuttered tight.

He began to understand.

Yes, said Shind.

Prepare to transmit and receive.

Ready.

—*Is this room monitored in any way?* he inquired.

—*Not exactly. That would be illegal. There are ways that I can request assistance or activate monitors, though.*

—*Are any of them activated right now?*

—*No.*

—*Then no one will hear us if we speak.*

"No," she said aloud; and he turned to look at her where she stood with her back and palms pressed against the door, eyes wide, lips dry.

"Don't be afraid of me," he said. "You sleep with me every night, don't you?"

Feeling awkward when she did not reply, he removed his coat and looked around.

"Is there a place where I can hang this to dry out?"

She moved forward and seized the garment.

"I'll take it. I'll hang it in my shower."

She jerked it from his hands, passed quickly through a

narrow door and closed it behind her. He heard its lock click. After a time he heard sounds of retching.

He took a step in that direction, about to rap and ask if she were all right.

Do not, said Shind. *Let her be.*

All right.—Do you want to be let out?

No. I would only upset her further. I am quite comfortable.

After a time, he heard a flushing sound, and a little later the door opened and she emerged. He noted that her eyelashes were wet. He also noted the bright blue of her eyes within them.

"It will be dry before too long," she said, "Commander."

"Thank you. Please call me Malacar, Jackara. Or better yet, Rory."

He rounded the bed to study the picture more closely.

"That's a good likeness. Where's it from?"

She brightened, followed to stand beside him.

"It was a plate, from your biography by that man Gillian. I had it enlarged and tridized. It is the best picture I have of you."

"I never read the book," he said. "I am trying to remember where the picture was taken, but I can't."

"That was right before the Parameter Eight Maneuver," she said, "when you were preparing the Fourth Fleet to rendezvous with Conlil. It was taken about an hour prior to your departure, according to the book."

He turned and looked down at her, smiling.

"I believe you're correct," he said, and she smiled at this.

"Cigarette?" he offered.

"No, thank you."

He took one himself, lit it.

How the hell did I walk into this? he asked himself. A

real patho case of hero worship—with me as its object. If I say the wrong thing, she'll probably go to pieces. What is the best tack to take with her? Perhaps if I let her think *I* am nervous, then ask for her confidence on something unimportant . . .

"Listen," he said, "you startled me downstairs because nobody knew I was coming to Deiba, and I did not think too many people remembered my face. I came to this place rather than one of the hotels because nobody here cares about faces or names. You surprised me, though. I wanted to keep my presence a secret, and I thought I'd been uncovered."

"But you're immune to the laws, aren't you?"

"I'm not here to break them. Not this time, anyhow. I came to obtain some information—quietly, confidentially."

He stared directly into her eyes.

"Can I trust you to keep my presence a secret?"

"Of course," she said. "What else would I do? I was born in the DYNAB. May I assist you with whatever you are doing?"

"Perhaps," he said, seating himself on the edge of her bed. "If the DYNAB means something to you, what are you doing here?"

She laughed as she moved to seat herself in a chair across from him.

"Tell me how to get back. Look at the only job I can have in this town. How long do you think it will take me to save the price of a ticket?"

"Are you indentured, or under any sort of contract?"

"No. Why?"

"I don't know much about the local laws. I was just considering whether I would have to get you out of here the hard way."

"Get me out of here? Back to the DYNAB?"

"Of course. That's what you want, isn't it?"

She turned away from him then and began to cry, silently. He did not move to interfere.

"Excuse me," she said, "I never— I never expected anything like this to happen to me. Malacar to walk into my room and offer to take me away. It is something I have dreamed of..."

"Then I take it your answer is 'yes'?"

"Thank you," she said. "Yes, yes it is! But there is something else..."

He smiled.

"What? Perhaps a boy friend you want to take along? That can be arranged too."

She raised her head and her eyes flashed.

"No!" she said. "It is nothing like that! I would not have one of these men!"

"Sorry," he said.

She stared down at her sandals, her silvered toenails. He flicked his cigarette above a black metal ashtray on the table beside the bed.

When she spoke again, she spoke very slowly and did not look at him.

"I would like to do something for the DYNAB. I would like to help you with whatever you are about in Capeville."

He was silent for a time. Then, "How old are you, Jackara?" he asked.

"I am not certain. Around twenty-six, I think. At least, that is what I tell people. Perhaps twenty-eight. Maybe twenty-five. But just because I'm young—"

He raised a hand and silenced her.

"I am not trying to talk you *out* of anything. In fact, it is possible that you could be of some assistance to me. I asked your age for a reason. What do you know of *mwulukhurun khurr*, which is generally called Deiban fever?"

She shifted her gaze to the ceiling.

"I know that it is not too common," she said. "I know that when it does hit you, there is a high fever and a darkening of the complexion. It is supposed to attack the central nervous system. After that, the breathing and the heartbeat are affected. And there is something about the liquids. The body does not exactly lose them, but cellular fluids go extracellular. That's right. And the cells do not reabsorb. That is why you get so thirsty but liquids do not help. You're a doctor, though. You know all that."

"What else do you know about the condition?"

"Well, there is no cure and it always kills you, if that is what you mean."

"Are you certain?" he asked. "Have you never heard of anyone living through it?"

She looked at him, puzzled.

"Nobody?" he said. "Nobody has ever lived through it?"

"Well, they said there was one man. But I was very young then, and it was right after the conflict. I do not remember very much."

"Tell me what you do remember. There must have been some talk about it later on."

"He was just a man who lived through it. They never even gave his name."

"Why not?"

"After he had been pronounced cured, they were afraid that he would still panic people if they knew who he was. So they withheld his name."

"H," he said. "Later on, they referred to him as H."

"Maybe," she said. "I do not know. That's about it, I guess."

"Where did they treat him? What hospital?"

"Here in town. But the place is gone now."

"Where did he come from?"

"The Mound. Everybody called him 'the man from the Mound' for a while."

"Was he a local man?"

"I do not know."

"What is the Mound?"

"It is sort of a plateau. You leave the peninsula and go about thirty miles inland, to the northwest. There is a ruined city there—Pei'an. Deiba used to be a part of the old Pei'an Empire. The city is all fallen down, and about the only people interested in it are archaeologists, geologists and visiting Pei'ans. They found him up there while they were deactivating part of the early warning equipment from the war, I guess. Anyhow, there was some sort of military installation set up there then, and when they went up to do something to it, they found this man. They brought him back in an isolation boat and he recovered."

"Thank you. You've been helpful."

She smiled, and he returned it.

"I have a gun," she said, "and I practice with it. I am very accurate, and fast."

"That is excellent."

"If there is anything dangerous that you want done—"

"Perhaps," he said. "You speak of this Mound as if you are familiar with the area. Can you get me a map, or draw me one?"

"There are no good maps," she said. "But I have been up there many times. I ride a lot too—the *kooryab*—and sometimes I ride inland. The Mound is a very good place for target practice. Nobody bothers you there."

"It is completely deserted?"

"Yes."

"Good. Then you will be able to show it to me."

"Yes, if you wish. There is not much to see, though. I had thought . . ."

He mashed out his cigarette.

She is clean, Shind?

Yes.

"I am *really* interested," he said, "and I know what you thought. You thought that I had come here for purposes of sabotage or revolution. This is more important, however. While a small act of violence may annoy the CL, they can live with it. But if the Mound can furnish me with the information that I want, I will have a clue as to the nature of the greatest terror weapon in the galaxy."

"What is it?"

"The identity of H."

"How could that help you?"

"I am keeping that to myself for now. I had better start by looking up there, though. If my man had a camp up there on the Mound, some traces might still remain. Of what sort, I do not know. But I'm sure that whoever brought him back would have left his gear alone or destroyed it—if they found it at all, that is. If it is still there, I want it."

"I will help," she said. "I want to help. But I do not get time off until—" and he rose to his feet, towered above her, leaned down, touched her shoulder.

She shuddered at the contact.

"You don't understand," he said. "This is your last day in this place. You're your own person now. In the morning I would like you to make arrangements for the purchase or rental of a couple or three of those *kooryabs*, and all the gear we will need to ride to the Mound and spend some time there—maybe a week or so. I don't want to lift ship and have any curious young port controllers track me. When we do ride out of here tomorrow, though, that will be the end of the story so far as you and this place are concerned. You do not have to concern yourself over 'time off' or 'time on.' You are quitting with minimum notice. That's legal here, isn't it?"

"Yes," she said, sitting straight-backed and gripping the arms of the chair.

I did not want to, he thought. But she can help me in this respect. And she is a DYNAB girl the damned CL has driven half-nuts. She comes along.

"Then that is settled," he said, moving back to the bed and lighting another cigarette.

She seemed to relax.

"I believe that I will take a cigarette now—Malacar."

"Rory," he corrected.

"Rory," she agreed.

He rose again, gave her one, lit it for her, returned.

"I never heard anywhere about you being a telepath," she said, after a time.

"I'm not. It's sort of a trick. Tomorrow I might show you how I do it."

But not tonight, he thought. Gods! If it's taken this long to get you half-relaxed, I am not going to introduce you to a hairy Darvenian with eyes big as teacups. You would probably scream and they would bring on the bouncers.

"Mind if I open those shutters for a minute?" he asked.

"Let me do it."

"No, that's all right."

But she was already on her feet and halfway across the room.

She located a control beneath the sill and they slid back into the wall.

"Would you like the window opened too?"

"A little," he said, coming up and standing beside her.

The window responded to another control, and he inhaled the moist night air.

"Still raining," he observed, and he extended his hand and flicked an ash outside.

"Yes."

Looking out over a low rooftop, they watched the quiet city through the drops and rivulets on the half-raised pane. The lights below were fractured, shifted slightly. With the mild draft that entered, there came the faint salt odor of the sea. "Why do you keep it closed?" he asked her; and, "I hate the sight of that city," she replied, without emotion. "It is not too bad at night, though, when you can't see anything." A faint thunder-rumble rolled down from the hills. He rested his elbows on the sill and leaned forward. After a moment's hesitation, she did too. She was quite close to him then, but he knew that if he touched her the moment would be shattered.

"Does it rain often here?" he asked.

"Yes," she said. "Especially at this time of year."

"Do you do any sailing, or swimming?"

"I swim, to keep in practice, and I know how to handle small vessels. But I do not especially like the sea."

"Why not?"

"My father was drowned. This was after my mother died and they had put me in with the children. He tried to swim around Point Murphy one night. I guess that he was attempting to escape from the Relocation Center.—At least, they told me he had drowned.—It might be that one of those damned guards shot him."

"Sorry."

"I was just a child. I didn't know enough to hate them until later."

He flicked more ashes through the window.

"What will it be like after you win?" she asked.

He threw away the cigarette.

Staring, he saw it become an instant's comet.

"Win?" he said, turning his head and looking at her. "I am going to fight until I die, but I will never break the CL. I will never win, in that sense. My objective is the preservation of the DYNAB, not the destruction of the CL. I want to keep thirty-four little worlds from becoming subservient to the whims of fourteen leagues. I can't hope to beat them, but maybe I can teach them some respect for the DYNAB—enough so that the DYNAB might have a chance to grow and expand to the point where it can achieve League status itself one day, rather than being reapportioned and absorbed by the others. If we had a chance to colonize a few dozen more worlds, if we were unhampered by the Leagues instead of being boycotted and cut out every time we tried our hand at something new, then we'd have a chance. I want us to join the CL—not break it—but on our terms. Sure, I hate them, for what they did to us. But they're the best civilization we've got. I want to be in on it—but as an equal."

". . . And the thing on the Mound? The identity of H?"

He smiled crookedly.

"If I can get control of H's secret, I'll go down in history as one of the blackest villains who ever lived. But, by the gods! I'll scare the holy hell out of the CL! They'll leave the DYNAB alone for a long time afterward."

She tossed her cigarette after his and he lit them two more.

They listened to the voice of a faraway storm-buoy and saw into the distance whenever the lightning flickered. When it flashed far ahead, the skyline was silhouetted dark and gap-toothed before them; when it came from behind, the windows of Capeville each seemed to catch some of its burning and spill it in a different way. Mainly, though, there were only the fractured lights of the city.

I haven't talked like this in ages, he thought. I don't always have Shind sitting there to tell me who I can trust, though. She's a likable child. Certainly pretty. But those whips, and that funny way the desk clerk acted ... She hates everybody here. I didn't think they went in for the fancier stuff in government-run places. Maybe I'm old-fashioned ... Of course I am. Too bad about her. Perhaps one day she will find somebody, back in the DYNAB, who will be kind to her in just the right ways ... Hell! I *am* getting old! That air feels good. Nice view.

A low-flying aircraft passed slowly, circling like a luminous insect. He watched it move off in the direction of the field where he had landed.

Could be a jump-buggy, he decided. About the right size. Who would come down on a night like this when he could stay in a nice, warm, dry orbit until things blow over?—Not counting me, of course.

The vessel swung through a slow, circular pattern, then hovered as though awaiting landing clearance.

"Jackara, would you turn the light out?" he asked, and she stiffened beside him. ". . . And if you have binoculars, or a telescope of some kind," he continued quickly, "please get it for me. I'm curious about that vessel."

She moved away and he heard a closet opening. After perhaps ten heartbeats, the room grew dark.

"Here," she said, coming up beside him again.

He raised the glass to his eye, swung it, adjusted it.

"What is it?" she asked. "What's the matter?"

He did not reply immediately, but continued to sharpen the focus.

There was another flash, from behind them.

"That vessel is a jump-buggy," he stated. "How many come to Capeville?"

"Quite a few, of the commercial kind."

"This one's too small. How many private ones?"

"Tourists, mainly," she said. "A few every month."

He collapsed the tube and returned it to her.

"Maybe I'm overly suspicious," he said. "I'm always afraid they will find a way to keep track of me—"

"I'd better get the light again," and she retreated through the darkness, then made it go away.

After he heard the closet close, he continued to watch the city for a long while.

At his back, he heard a muffled sob and he turned slowly.

She was lying on her side on the bed, her legs scissored out behind her, hair hiding her face. She had unbuttoned her blouse and he saw that she had on black underwear.

He stared for a long moment, then went and sat beside her. He brushed her hair aside and pushed it back over her shoulder, letting his hand rest between her shoulder blades. She continued to cry.

"I'm sorry," she said, not looking at him. "You wanted a room and a girl, and I can't. I wanted to, but I can't. Not with you. Not so that you would enjoy it. There is a very nice girl named Lorraine and another named Kyla. They are quite popular. I will get one of them to come and be with you tonight."

She began to rise, and he reached out with his other hand and touched her cheek.

"Whichever one you bring, she'll get a good night's sleep," he said, "because that's about all I'm fit for right now."

She looked at him then.

"You wouldn't lie to me?"

"Not about that. I'm very sleepy. If you'll just turn back the covers, you can tell me in the morning if I snore."

She swallowed, nodded vigorously and moved to obey him.

Later, he heard her emerge from the bathroom and felt her enter the bed. She had forgotten to close the window. As he liked fresh air, he did not remind her. He lay there, breathing the ocean and listening to the rain.

"Malacar," he heard her whisper, "are you asleep?"

"No."

"What about my things?"

"What things?"

"I've got some nice dresses and some books and—well—just things."

"We can pack them in the morning and have them shipped to the port and held there until we're ready to leave Deiba. I'll help you."

"Thanks."

She turned and twisted some, then lay still. The storm-buoy sounded. He wondered about the jump-buggy that had passed. If the Service had somehow tracked him from the Sol-System, there was nothing they could do to him. On the other hand, he never wanted them to connect him with Deiba or H. If it was indeed a Service ship that had passed, how had they done it? Morwin? He had mentioned a friend in the Service. Could he have notified him or hung some sort of tracer on *The Perseus?* But Shind had said that he was clean . . .

I must be getting paranoid, he decided. Forget it.

But he opened his eyes and stared at the ceiling. The girl moved again, slightly. He moved his eyes about, and through the darkness he could make out the darker outline of her whips on the wall. He winced. Him staring down on all that from the wall. A fake holy picture in a brothel. It amused him and hurt him at the same time. Again the buoy, and the night air coming more chill. A flash, a bit of thunder, the rain. Again. The play of brass butterflies upon the ceiling, the walls . . .

He must have dozed, for he was aware of coming awake once more, with the touch of her hand upon his shoulder.

"Malacar?"

"Yes?"

"I'm cold. May I come closer?"

"Sure."

He moved his arm and she was beside him. She clung to him as though he were floating and she were not. He put his arm about her shoulders, drew her head onto his chest and returned to sleep.

In the morning, they breakfasted at a place several doors up the street from the brothel. Malacar noticed a group of women at a far table who kept darting glances in his direction.

"Why do those women keep looking at me?" he asked softly.

"They work where I do," she told him. "They are wondering about the fact that you spent the entire night with me."

"This doesn't happen very often?"

"No."

Returning, they obtained cartons and Malacar helped her fill them with her belongings. She was silent as they packed, as silent as she had been most of the morning.

"You are afraid," he said.

"Yes."

"This will pass."

"I know," she said. "I thought that I would feel many things if this day ever came, but not afraid."

"You are leaving something that you know for something unknown. It is understandable."

"I do not want to be weak."

"Fear is not a sign of weakness." He patted her shoulder. "You finish packing now. I'll call the port and arrange for them to pick up your stuff and hold it."

She drew away.

"Thanks," she said, returning to her packing.

I hope she leaves the picture and those damned whips, he thought.

After he had made arrangements for a messenger pickup, he had his call transferred to the flights controller's office. He kept the screen blanked.

"Can you tell me," he inquired, "whether the jump-buggy which landed last night during the storm was a Service ship?"

"It was not," came the reply. "It was a privately owned vessel."

Which means nothing, he told himself. If the Service asks for secrecy, they get cooperation. I might as well push this as far as I can, though.

"Would you identify the vessel for me?"

"Surely. It is the *Model T*, out of Liman, Bogotelles. Signor Enrico Caruso is logged here as master and owner."

"Thank you."

He broke the connection.

It still proves nothing, he decided. Except, there is the fact that the Service has always been quite open when it comes to following me about. A warning, actually, when they do it. I must be getting paranoid. No sense checking on this Caruso. If he is real, nothing. If he is not, it will take too long to pierce his disguise. Furthermore, I should not really care. Unless he is an assassin. But even then . . .

"I'm ready," she said.

"Good. Here is some money. Count it and tell me if there is enough. I'll wait here for the messenger while you get us mounts and equipment."

"There is more than enough," she said. "Malacar . . ."

"Yes?"

"When should I tell them that I am quitting?"

"Right now, if you want. Or write them a note if you don't want to talk with them."

She brightened.

"I'll write them a note."

That afternoon, they moved into the hills, pack animal trailing behind, tethered to Jackara's saddle. She drew rein and turned to regard the city below them. Malacar halted his mount also, but he watched her rather than Capeville. She said nothing. It was as if he were not present.

Her eyes were narrow and her lips pressed so tightly together as to be all but invisible. Her hair was bound with a ribbon and he watched the wind play with its ends. She sat so for perhaps half a minute. He felt as if a wave of pure hate were passing, flowing down the slopes, breaking upon the city. Then it was gone, and she turned and her mount moved forward once again.

I see the dream, Jackara, he said to himself. The one that Morwin would do you . . .

All that afternoon they rode, and he saw the opposite shore of the peninsula where the waters were lighter in color and there was no city. He made out a few shacks on the distant shore, but between their beach and the hills rose a tangle of green, where runners like grapevines crossed from tree to tree and dark birds fluttered and lit, fluttered and lit, among the leaves. The sky was half overcast, but the sun occupied the other half and the day was still bright. The trail remained damp, tacky from the previous night's rain, and they muddied clear puddles as they passed. He noted that his mount's hoofprints were triangular in shape, and it occurred to him that the beast he rode could be a vicious fighter. Far below, there were some whitecaps on the water, and he saw that the trees were moving.

The wind has not hit this high yet, he thought. But it will probably rain again tonight, judging from those clouds. Tarps might have been better than those flimsies she bought if the winds get bad up here . . .

They halted before dusk and took a meal. By then, Capeville was out of sight. Shind sprang down from the pack mount he had been riding and sat with them. Jackara smiled. She seemed to have taken a liking to the Darvenian. This pleased Malacar, who decided, She hates all the people she has known so much that it is probably easier for her to be friends with an alien.

He ate his food while the sky darkened. It was now completely overcast, and the night was near. Occasional gusts of wind struck them.

"Where should we camp, Jackara? And how soon?"

She raised a finger, swallowed, then said, "About six more miles and we will come to a place sheltered on two sides. We can pitch our flimsy there."

By the time they reached the site it was already raining.

Lying there, still wet, listening to the movements of the *kooryabs*, feeling the wind and sometimes the rain, hearing both, holding her, looking up the walls of gray stone at their bridge, night, he planned ahead, selecting worlds for death. He conceived a master plan then, turned it over in his mind, decided it would work, filed it for future implementation. He was ready. Two more days and they would reach the Mound. Beside him, Jackara made small noises in her chest.

Good night, Shind.

Good night, Commander.

Is she having a nightmare?

No. Her dream is pleasant.

Then I shan't awaken her. Sleep well.

And yourself.

He lay there for a long while listening to the night, and then he joined it.

They departed the peninsula late the following morning, turned to the northwest, headed inland. Their way continued as a gradual ascent until they reached a tableland which they crossed that afternoon. This brought them to the foot of another line of hills. Within these lay the Mound, Jackara told him. They would sight it before nightfall.

Nor was she incorrect. They topped a rise, she gestured, he nodded. A gigantic, flat-topped mass of rock lay a few miles away. Between themselves and the mesa was a wide canyon through which they must pass to achieve it. The *kooryabs* picked their way almost casually among the boulders.

By nightfall, they had crossed and were ascending an easy trail that began at the southern foot of the Mound and worked its way westward and up. By then, Malacar had grown at ease with his mount, and trusting its hoofs beneath stars was not difficult.

It was not until morning, when he could properly survey the ruin, that he began to realize the scope of the task which lay before him. True to Pei'an architectural precedent, none of the buildings had been especially close together. They were spread over an area approximately two miles in length and a quarter mile across. The remains were mainly foundations. Here and there, a wall still stood. There was much debris on the ground and grasses and vines grew among it, covering or partly covering some of the rubble. The place was virtually devoid of trees. Outside the general lines of what had once been the town stood a small, square structure, sunbleached, and weather-worn.

"Is that the war installation?" he asked, gesturing.

"Yes. I've been inside it. The roof is partly fallen in and it is full of insects and smells bad. They took everything with them when they abandoned it."

He nodded.

"Then to start, let's just walk a bit and you can give me a rough idea of what's what."

Shind accompanied them, a small shadow passing among stones.

For several hours they walked, and she told him what she knew of the place. After this, he selected the most prominent of the ruins for close scrutiny, hoping it would be one of these which would have attracted H. But when lunchtime arrived, he was no nearer satisfaction than he had been at sunrise.

After lunch, he climbed the highest accessible point (a wall) and from there sketched the best map he could of the entire area. Then, point by point, he marked it off in his mind and gridded the map to follow. That afternoon, he placed a marker at each spot where the lines crossed.

"We are going to explore it section by section?" she asked.

"That's right."

"Where will we begin?"

"Choose one," he said, proffering the map.

She gave him a quick glance, saw that he meant it.

"All right. Here—in the middle."

That day they searched two of the squares he had drawn, going through them foot by paced foot, crawling through cellars and subcellars, turning blocks, tramping down or separating long weeds or grasses. They worked until they could see no longer, then returned to the camp they had made and kindled a fire.

Later that night as they stared at stars, she broke a long silence by saying, "We're off to a good start."

He did not reply, but lay there smoking. After a while, she found his hand with both of hers and squeezed it so tightly that it almost hurt.

What's wrong with her now, Shind?

She is trying to comfort you. She feels that you are unhappy that you did not locate what you sought today.

Well, she is correct, of course. But then, I did not really expect to come across anything the first day.

Perhaps you ought to tell her that. Her mind is a strange place. She is unhappy because she thinks that you are.

Oh, hell!

Commander . . .

Yes?

I wish I had never told you about that dream.

I already know that.

It is still not too late.

Go to sleep, Shind.

Yes, sir.

"Hey, Jack?"

"Yes?"

He reached over with his free hand, placed it on the back of her head and turned her toward him. He leaned and kissed her forehead, then released her.

"You're a good guide and today was a good start," he said.

Then he turned away and went to sleep.

Star light, star bright, she thought over and again—because there were so many of them—give him his wish.

In the morning they began again, and by noon they had worked their way through three more of the squares. They located a hopeful sign—old cooking utensils of a local make and a dirt-covered flimsy—in the day's fourth square. But although they excavated for yards about the area, they uncovered nothing else.

"This might have been his camp," she said.

"Or anyone else's. There is nothing here of value."

"If this is the place, though, it could mean that he was working nearby."

"Perhaps. Let's finish this square and take the one below afterward."

They continued, completing eight squares. There were no more finds that day.

Shind?

Yes, Jackara?

Is he asleep?

Yes. But even if he were not, he would not hear us if I did not choose. What do you wish?

Is he distraught?

Not especially. He is always very quiet when he works. He is—occupied. You have done nothing to disturb him.

You have known him for a long while?

Over twenty Earth years. I was his personal translator during the war.

And you fight with him still, for the DYNAB. From among all his command, you stayed with him to continue the battle.

I am sometimes helpful to him.

It is good to hear of such loyalty to the cause.

One cannot long share thoughts as we have done without either going insane or coming to love. Mine is a personal feeling toward Malacar. The DYNAB is only incidental. I serve it because it still means something to him.

You love him? You are a female?

As a matter of fact, I am a female of my kind. But this, too, is only incidental. It would take months to teach a human the way a Darvenian thinks . . . and feels. And it would serve no useful purpose. Call it love.

I did not realize this, Shind.

The mental equivalent of a shrug followed.

You say that you are good with a gun.

Yes, she replied.

Then keep it ready whenever you are near him and be prepared to use it instantly, should he be threatened.

Threatened?

I have had many misgivings concerning this expedition. I feel that there is danger, though I do not know how or why it will arrive.

I will be ready.

Then I shall rest more easily. Good night, Jackara.

Good night, Shind.

She moved her pistol to a position from which it could be fired quickly, and she slept with her hand upon it.

• • •

As they worked their way through the third day, Malacar heard a faint sound from above and scanned the sky. A jump-buggy was moving from the south toward the northwest. Jackara stopped her work and stared at it also.

It seemed to grow as they watched it.

"It's coming this way. It may pass overhead."

"Yes."

Shind. Can you—?

No, the distance is too great for me to read anything.

If it goes overhead . . . ?

I will see what I can do.

Within a matter of minutes it had reached the mesa. It cruised slowly, several hundred feet above the ground, and began to pass over the ruins. When it reached a position where the pilot could not but have seen them—looking groundward as he must have been—it came to sudden life and sped on to the northwest, gaining altitude as it went. Soon it was gone from sight.

It contains one occupant, a man, Shind said to both of them. *He was curious about the ruins. This is all that I was able to read.*

"Sight-seeing, perhaps."

"Then why did he run when he saw us?"

"No way of telling."

Malacar returned to the camp and unpacked a laser sub-gun, which he strapped to his shoulder. Jackara checked her own weapon when she saw what he was doing.

They moved back to the square they had been working.

"I have an idea," she said.

"Tell me about it."

"The Pei'ans are Strantrians, and Strantrian shrines are nearly always underground. We have not come across one yet. If, as you guess, your H was an amateur archaeologist—"

He nodded vigorously and studied the map again.

"I'm going to climb that wall once more," he said, looking over his shoulder. "An underground chamber the size of a Strantrian shrine might be partly caved in after all these years. I'll look for sinkholes."

He mounted the wall and turned his head slowly, from left to right. Then he withdrew the map, marked it, checked it against his observations once more.

He climbed down and moved to Jackara's side.

"I saw six dark places," he said, exhibiting the map. "We will probably come across more holes, but those six were the only ones I could make out from up there. So we will start with them. Pick one."

She did, and they moved off in that direction.

The fourth cavity they investigated was a Strantrian shrine.

Lying spread-eagled, he flashed his light downward through the gloom. It had once been a five-sided chamber, he saw. Below, ahead and to his left lay the remains of what must have been the central altar. An enormous mound of rubble blocked his view to the front and the far left. Edging forward and turning to his right, he saw the low archway and a portion of the foyer that lay beyond it. From there, a flight of steps normally led upward to . . .

He estimated the approximate aboveground position, crept back from the hole and went to the shattered building. He pulled on his gloves, stooped and began throwing pieces of masonry aside.

"This is the way," he said. "It shouldn't be too difficult to clear. This stuff is fairly loose."

"What about lowering ourselves through the hole?"

"It collapsed there once. It's weak. We'll go the safe way."

She nodded, donned her own gloves and joined him.

By nightfall, they had cleared the surrounding area and, he estimated, about two thirds of the stairwell.

"Sit on the top step and hold the light for me," he ordered; and he worked for another two hours.

"You must be getting tired," she said.

"A bit. But I've only a few more feet to go."

He passed her with a melon-sized stone in his arms.

There is somebody else on this plateau with us, said Shind.

Where? asked Malacar, dropping the stone onto a heap.

I cannot say for certain. It seems to be to the northeast of here. It is a general sense of presence that I have. Nothing specific.

Could it be some animal? asked Jackara.

This is an intelligence of a higher sort.

Try to read it.

I am trying, but it is too distant.

Well, keep on with it and let us know when you succeed.

Malacar moved near to Jackara.

"Turn off the light," he said.

She did, and he unslung his weapon and held it in one hand.

"Let's wait here awhile," he said, seating himself beside her.

There is only one, said Shind.

Could it be the same one who passed us in the jump-buggy this afternoon? asked Jackara.

I cannot tell.

"The jump-buggy could have returned at a low altitude," she said, "and landed in one of the canyons near here."

Is it moving in this direction? he asked.

It seems to be stationary.

They waited.

After a quarter of an hour, Shind said, *It still has not moved. It may have made camp.*

"What are we going to do, Malacar?"

"I am deciding whether I should go have a look, or try to break through here tonight."

"He has no way of knowing where *we* are. If it is the jump-buggy man, we are nowhere near the place we were when it passed. Why go looking for trouble?"

"I'm curious."

"Shind can tell you if he moves. If I go farther down the stairway, the light will not be visible above the ground. We could probably be inside in an hour or so. If we locate what you are looking for, we can move out tonight and let him camp here as long as he wants."

"You are right, of course—tactically."

He rose.

"Careful on those steps."

Shind, tell us immediately if he moves. Have you any idea how far away he is?

I would judge about two miles. If I were to advance a few hundred yards, I might be able to obtain stronger impressions.

Go ahead.

Malacar stood ten feet beneath the ground and Jackara was to his left and above him. He reslung his subgun and renewed his assault on the rubble. Perhaps ten minutes passed before a gap appeared near the top of the archway.

Commander, I am still advancing. The impressions are stronger. It is a masculine mind. It seems to be about the business of bedding down for the night.

Good. Continue to monitor.

He enlarged the opening he had made. He cast the stones beside him on the stair. Jackara leaned her back against the wall, holding the light in her left hand. Her right hand rested upon the butt of her pistol.

"Pretty soon," said Malacar, drawing three large stones from the heap before him. Smaller ones rattled to the ground as he did so.

He twisted aside a metal strut which had bent downward. Taking a step back, he drove his heavy right boot forward into the top of the heap. Stones rattled to the floor inside, and dust rose about them. Jackara coughed and the light wavered.

"Sorry," he said. "I wanted to get the small stuff out of the way in a hurry. We should be able to get in in a few more minutes."

She nodded and the light nodded with her. Malacar tore into the heap.

Commander!

What?

I made contact with his mind, to probe it. He went away.

What do you mean, he went away?

I can no longer read anything, even the fact of his existence. He detected my presence when I made the attempt. Now he is shielding. He is a telepath himself—a skillful one. What should I do?

Come back. We are about to go in.—Of what race is this creature?

Your own, I think.

Humans aren't telepaths.

There are some, you know. It seemed *like the mind of a man.*

Malacar moved more masonry and twisted another strut out of the way.

"Our visitor is a telepath," he said. "He has blocked Shind. Shind is on her way back now.—There. I think we can get through that opening."

"Do you think we should? It might find us here."

" 'It' is apparently a human being," he said. "If he can read us anywhere, he can find us anywhere—back in camp, say. We might as well continue."

He leaned forward and crawled across the heap, passing beneath the archway and into the foyer. He regained his footing and stood.

"Come on in," he said.

He directed the beam ahead of her and she followed. She took his hand and came to her feet in the small room.

"This way."

They moved into the pentagonal chamber, and small things rushed away from his light and vanished into the shadows. He flicked the light beam about the room. There were overturned pews, dusty pews, pews which had sagged and broken. He turned to the altar—a green stone containing many fracture lines. Then he stared at the rows of glassite plates which surrounded them, depicting the Pei'an deities. There were hundreds of them upon the walls, some shattered, some hanging loosely. A few had fallen to the floor. Turning, he raked his light across them all.

"Pretty well preserved," he said. "How old is this place supposed to be?"

"Nobody knows for certain," she told him. "This city was here and in ruins when Deiba was discovered, about nine hundred Earth years ago."

I am here, said Shind, and a dark form entered through the passage they had cleared.

Good. What more of our visitor?

Nothing. I am going to attempt to shield us from him while you search this place.

Capital.

He began to scan the floors, moving among the remains of the pews. After an hour and a half, he had covered this area and located nothing. He moved to the altar and began sifting through the pieces of ceiling that lay about it.

"I think I've found something," he heard her say, from far ahead and to his left, where she was seeking along the walls with a small light of her own.

He went to her immediately.

"What is it?"

She pointed with her weak light toward a spot on the floor. He moved his own light to cover it.

A damp-looking notebook, covered with dust, lay at their feet.

Stooping, he touched it carefully. Then he lifted it and dusted its covers. It was a cheap, plasticovered tablet, bearing only its manufacturer's name. Removing his gloves and tucking them behind his belt, he opened it. The pages were damp, the lines blurred or blotted out entirely. One by one, he turned the leaves.

"Sketches," he said, "of this place. Nothing but sketches," as he closed the tablet.

"It means that *someone* was here," she said. "Why throw away a book you've spent so much time drawing in? Maybe this is where H was stricken."

She drew back suddenly.

"Could we catch anything from that book?"

"Not after all these years."

He shone his light about the area.

"If he left that, he may have—"

He held the beam steady. Within its spot lay something that was partly metal. Rotted cloth hung in strips and patches and there was a small container beneath it.

"Some sort of carrying case," he said, bending forward and touching it lightly.

Then he froze, seeing through the dust to the markings on the case.

Carefully, he raised it and blew upon it. Then the old visions of chaos and death swam through his mind once more, for it bore the initials *HvH*.

"This is it," he said softly. "I know who he is."

I feel him! said Shind. *Your find excited him and he gave himself away!*

Malacar whirled, dropping the case and extinguishing the light. He whipped the subgun from his shoulder.

"Peace!" cried a voice from above him. "I'm not pointing anything at you!"

Jackara's light went out at that moment, and he heard the safety catch *snick* on her pistol.

Through the hole in the ceiling, suddenly silhouetted against stars, he saw the form of a man.

"You make a good target," Malacar said.

"I exposed myself to show good faith, when I saw that you would hold your fire. I want to talk."

"Who are you?"

"What difference does it make? I know what you know now. Heidel von Hymack is the name I came here to verify."

While the man was speaking, a faint illumination appeared on the wall to the right. Malacar glanced at it. It was one of the glassite plates. It had begun glowing, giving off a faint green light. It bore the picture of a naked man, holding a thundercloud in one hand and a bow in the other. The face was partly hidden by the raised arm. At his hip hung a quiver of thunderbolts that matched the yellow sky above him.

"So you know his name," said Malacar. "What are you going to do with it?"

"Find the man it fits."

"Why?"

"He represents a very great danger to a large number of people."

"I know that. That is why I want him."

"And I know you, Malacar. You are a man I once admired very much—still admire. You are making a mistake in this matter, though. Heidel cannot be used the way you want to use him. If you try it, he will become uncontrollable. The DYNAB itself will be in danger, not just the CL."

"Who the hell are you?"

"Enrico Caruso," he replied.

He is lying, said Shind. *His name is Francis Sandow.*

"You are Francis Sandow," Malacar said aloud, "and I can see why you want to stop me. You are one of the wealthiest men in the galaxy. If I were to hurt the CL badly, I would be stepping on a lot of your interests, wouldn't I?"

"That is correct," said Sandow. "But that is not why I am here. I generally deal through representatives on all matters. This is an exception because of the nature of the case. You are a doctor of medicine. You are aware that there are many conditions which are not purely physical in origin."

"So?"

"You have been exploring down there for a long while. Did you find any indication that anyone else has been inside recently?"

"No, I didn't."

"All right, then. Without being able to see it, I will tell you something that I could not know by any ordinary means.—You are standing near to the place where you made your discovery, next to a wall. Have your woman keep me covered and turn your light onto that wall, up rather high. Above, or very near to the place where you located the thing, you will see a glassite plate. I will describe it: You will see the head and shoulders of a blue-skinned woman. She has two faces, one looking in either direction. The one to the left is attractive and there are flowers on that side of the picture—blue flowers. The gal on the right has pointed teeth and a sinister expression. Near to her there is a framework of blue snakes. Directly above, there will be a blue circle."

Malacar switched on the light.

"You're right," he said. "How did you know?"

"It is a representation of the goddess Mar'i-ram, the queen of healing and of disease. It was doubtless beneath her picture that von Hymack lay, somewhere between life and death. He bears, in a strange way, the blessing and the curse of that entity."

"You've lost me. Are you trying to say that the goddess is real?"

"In a sense, yes. There is a complex of energies which somehow possesses the attributes ascribed to that Strantrian deity. Call it what you would. It now inhabits the man we seek. I have been presented with satisfactory evidence that this is true. Now that I am aware of the identity of the individual involved, I must seek him."

"What will you do if you find him?"

"Cure him—or failing that, kill him."

"No!" said Malacar. "I need him alive."

"Don't be a fool," Sandow cried, as Malacar swung the light and it fell upon him.

Hand raised to shield his eyes, Sandow threw himself

backward as Malacar fired—not at him, but through the ceiling.

With a rattling and a crash, a section of roofing gave way. It seemed that a body fell.

"Hit it!" cried Malacar, falling flat and dragging Jackara with him.

He crawled forward and lay behind a low hedge of stone, subgun at ready.

He's alive! He's conscious! He's got a gun!

Malacar embraced the floor as a laser beam melted a stone near his left shoulder.

"Let a man finish talking, will you?"

"We've nothing to say to each other."

"Judge it after you hear it! I'll hold fire if you will!"

"Don't shoot," he said to Jackara. "We'll hear him out."

He drew a bead, then said, "All right, Sandow. What is it?"

"You know what I want. I want von Hymack. I will not argue the morality of what you are planning, since you have already made up your mind. I read it there. I would like to offer you a deal, however.—Damn it! Stop sighting in on me! No tricks involved here! You live on a dead, stinking, radioactive cinder—the Earth, the home planet of our species. How would you like to see it clean and green again? All those volcanoes dampened, the radioactives neutralized, dark soil, trees, fish in the oceans, the original continental configurations? I can do it, you know."

"That would cost a fortune."

"So? Is it a deal, then? The Earth the way that it was before the war, in return for you forgetting about von Hymack?"

"You're lying!"

He is not lying, said Shind.

"It would be another habitable world for the DYNAB," he was saying, "which you claim means so much to you."

All the while Sandow was speaking, Malacar attempted to control his thoughts—to operate automatically, as under battle conditions—and not to let any intention or desire pass through his consciousness. Carefully, soundlessly, he inched his way to the right, fixing on the voice. Now almost touching the wall, he could see the dim outline of the man's head and left shoulder. Gently, he squeezed the trigger.

His arm was numbed to the elbow with the force of the blow that struck him; and he saw his shot go wild, scoring the masonry high on the far wall.

With his left hand, he protected his eyes against the flying shards. Almost instantly he lowered it, however, to seize the gun and continue its upward arc.

The fires fell upon the ceiling and the ceiling upon the man.

Sandow was finally silent.

They lay there for a long while, listening to their breathing, their heartbeats.

Shind?

Nothing. You have killed him.

Malacar rose to his feet.

"Come on, Jackara. We had better be going," he said.

Later, before they broke camp, when she looked at him in the light, she said, "You are bleeding, Malacar," and she touched his cheek with her fingertips.

He jerked his head away.

"I know. I got cut when that damned picture of the green man fell on me."

He tightened his saddle cinch.

"Could he really have restored the Earth, Malacar?"

"Probably, but that would not have solved anything."

"You said you need more worlds for League status. Earth could have counted for one."

"To gain it, I would have had to surrender my weapon."

"How did he know about that picture of the goddess—Mar'i-ram?"

"All Strantrian shrines are laid out alike. He knew approximately where we were standing. Anyone who knows how their stations are set up could have said what was on the wall."

"Then he was making all that part up?"

"Of course. It was a ridiculous story. His interest in the matter was purely economic."

"Then why did he come in person?"

"I don't know.—There, I'm ready. Let's go."

"Aren't you going to put anything on it?"

"What?"

"The cut."

"Later."

Mounting, they hurried through the night toward Capeville and its rain.

CHAPTER 4

Dr. Pels studied the reports.

Too late, he decided; and, Something has gone very wrong. The *mwalakharan khurr* is there, all right, and a dozen other things. We cannot let him export them. Where is he? There is no record of his departure from Cleech. Yet there was a jump-buggy stolen from the space port, and the port was a point of infection. Was he trying to get away—to isolate himself—when he saw what was happening? Or was he simply going somewhere else?

Debussy's *La Mer* stirred about him and he regarded Cleech.

What to do? he thought. I have waited a long while and now the time for waiting has finished and the time for action is at hand. If I could have located him a month ago, this might not have occurred. I must find him as soon as possible now and speak with him, convince him to enter my care and remain until I solve this. I wonder whether he would be willing to undergo the process that keeps *me* going? Would he give up life as he knows it and become—a ghost—like me? Trade his present existence for the passionless, sleepless life of the void? If he is aware of what he is doing, I am certain that he would agree. This, or suicide— They would be about the only choices open to a sane, decent man . . . But what if he is no longer sane? Supposing he broke beneath the strain, or as a side effect of his condition? What then? This, too, could be an explanation for his disappearance.

And what if his condition proves as unassailable as my own? he wondered. Perhaps freezing would be the answer. It could be such a long wait, otherwise. But with no assurance of ever awakening, he may not consent. How shall I treat with him when I find him? The time for action is definitely at hand, and I do not know what to do. Wait, I suppose. There is nothing else.

After a time, he sent a message to the Public Health Coordinator for the planet, offering his services in dealing with the multiplicity of epidemics which so far had devastated two continents. Then he tuned his subspace receiving set to News Central. Since he could listen on a round-the-clock basis, he hoped that he would learn the next site of infection in time. He readied himself for departure on notice.

Then he listened to the news, and the impressions of a sea he had never seen accompanied it into his mind.

It went beautifully, Heidel told her. *A matter of minutes. Things seem to be somehow accelerated.*

It was because you were personally present. You are becoming a focal point. Soon you will be the still center of a cyclone. One day in the near future, there will be nothing able to stand against you. You will need but point your finger and will it and they will die.

Lady—I know now that you are real and not merely a dream born of fever. I know this because after I have awakened you keep the promises made in this place . . .

As do you. Which is why I reward you so.

You are not as you were before . . .

No. I am stronger.

That is not what I meant. Though this, too, is true, what I meant is that something has changed. What has happened? I find that I do not always think too clearly.

It is as I told you. You are becoming like unto a god.

Yet a part of me, somewhere, seems to be screaming.

This, too, will pass. It is but a phase.

. . . And you are not a dream. You are real. Who are you—really? And where am I, right now?

I am the goddess to whom you have sworn allegiance, and we dwell in my private heaven.

Where is that?

My kingdom is within you.

You do not truly answer me, Lady.

I give you the only true answers.

Where did we meet?

We have always known one another.

It was Deiba, wasn't it?

That was where we made formal contact, yes.

I cannot recall the introduction.

You were ill. We saved you.

"We"?

I. I saved you for this time, that we might benefit one another.

Why did you wait so long?

The time was not propitious—until recently.

He turned and regarded her. Quickly then, he bowed, as there was nothing but blue ice and blue flame before him.

What has happened? he muttered.

You have brought more here than is welcome, and less, Dra *von Hymack. The minor memories of a minor life have no part in our doings now. Bid them depart. You are no longer he whom you were on Deiba, or even on Cleech. Worship me now. I will sanctify you. I will grant you grace.*

I worship thee and adore thee.

When you awaken, you will walk until you come to a city. There, you will not speak a word. You will but point your finger at the first living thing you see . . .

. . . I will point my finger at the first living thing that I see.

You will feel the power open within you like a flower, rise like a serpent . . .

. . . I will feel the power.

Then you will go away from that place and seek another . . .

. . . I will seek another.

You are beautiful before me and I love you, Dra *von Hymack.*

He felt her cold lips touch his eyes, like coins for Charon. After a time, from somewhere, he heard her singing. The moon was blue. Blood dripped from her fingertips onto his palm. The song was a piece of forever.

He had given her a tranquilizer and sent her to her berth. It was either that or shut off the screens which were the apparent cause of her vertigo. He could have done without the screens, but she had been rubbing his nerve ends raw since their departure.

It is not just that she is a lovely girl who idolizes you and is afraid to let you touch her, he thought. It is not her incessant talk of The Cause either, or the fact that she wants you to reminisce aloud. What the hell is it then? Just being cooped up with another human being for two weeks in subspace? No, that is not it. Maybe it is the sudden weight of time. She brings to my attention a matter of years, the contrast between what I was and what I am now. Did I really hate with such fire in the old days that I would have burned the city to kill the rats? When did I start going soft, moving from pure revenge to these half-assed plans for League status? It was such a graduated thing, and with lapses, that I never caught myself until recently. I wanted whips, and now I am not so certain it is the right way. I wonder about Sandow. Could he really have helped the DYNAB? Would he have, if I had asked him? He had sounded reasonable. But all that crap about the Strantrian goddess . . . It had to be that, even if Sandow believed it himself.—This girl either brings out the worst in me or shuts me down completely. Not true. I did it myself. Still . . . I will try to sleep when she awakens. If Sandow's people ever tie me in with this, there is going to be trouble. They do not care about political boundaries. Well, another bridge, another day. It is going to be rough when I unleash von Hymack. Somebody is certain to try for me after that, once the connection is made. Stupid thing, sending that globe. I should have kept it, not shipped it. Am I diminished thereby? Debit me, one *memento mori?* Hard to tell. How many of those bastards in the CL High Command have I outlived? They did not pass out S-S the way we did.—Earth, of all places! Bifrost, I should have let it go at that. I should have dropped her on Bifrost. That's DYNAB.—So she gets to see the volcano, learn about tracing the routes of contagion . . . But why am I in such a hurry? Is it that I want done with this as quickly as possible? Probably.—God, don't give me a conscience now. I am not ready for one today. I have gone this long. I can go a little longer.—It is pretty, the way her hair falls, and those frightened eyes . . .

A blue star appeared at the whirlpool's center, and he watched it spiral outward, then fly like a stone from a sling, away.

"That ruined city of the Pei'ans is nothing but a quaint relic," he said, gesturing, "when you consider an entire planet in that shape."

Jackara stared at what remained of Manhattan.

"I've seen pictures," she said finally, "but . . ."

He nodded.

"I'll take you over the Mississippi this afternoon. I will show you where California once was."

He activated the screens, one by one, and the recon satellites flashed pictures of the other broken places.

"They were thorough," he said.

Why the hell is he doing it? thought Morwin, from where he stood, pretending to study a crater. Wherever he found that girl, he is turning her into something like himself. The way she spoke at dinner last night . . . Another year and she will be worse than he is. Maybe she is already. Is that what it takes to be a fleet commander? The power to bend other people's thinking until it is just like your own? None of my business, but she seems so young . . . Maybe it is me that needs bending, though. Maybe they *are* right. I have been getting fat since the war, while people like this have kept on fighting. What if it is not a lost cause? Supposing that somehow the Commander wins? There probably would not be much surface change.—The stuff of news items. Unreal . . . Still . . . Have I developed a sheep's mentality? Or played with dream-stuff too long? The girl must only barely remember the conflict, but she is with him. What does he intend for her?

"It is pretty awful," he found himself saying, shifting his eyes from the girl back to the screens. Then, after a time, "Commander, why your sudden interest in epidemics?"

Malacar studied him for half a minute; then, "It is a new hobby of mine," he said.

Morwin packed his pipe and lit it.

. . . Clearly out of order, he decided. What could they be planning, though? When I did that damned globe for him, it reminded me of things I had put aside years ago. What will become of the girl, I wonder? Will she get thrown to the wolves like all those others, to die praying for him and still believing he is correct? She ought to get out. She has too much life before her to waste it this way. Still, I envy that sort of dedication, whatever its object. How dangerous will his new tactic be, I wonder? Perhaps . . . Somebody should watch out for the girl.

He puffed smoke. He stroked his long red beard.

Finally, "I am interested in epidemics too," he said.

The first living thing that he saw that morning was a young man, walking along a narrow and deserted roadway. When he was near, Heidel stepped out of the bushes and stood before him. He heard him exclaim, "Good Lord!" and then he pointed his swollen finger.

The power was there. He felt it move within him, then leap like a spark crossing a gap.

The man staggered, almost fell, recovered. He touched his hand to his forehead.

"Who are you?" he asked.

He did not reply, but took several steps toward the man.

Bolting, the man ran by him and disappeared up the road.

Only then did he allow himself the faintest of smiles. No need to go farther. She had been correct.

Turning toward the misty hills to the south, at the first of which and beyond which lay much life, he continued his pilgrimage. A rainbow hung before him.

At the end of an Earth week, he was still not certain whether Malacar would allow him as company. A decision of some sort was now in order, however. It had become obvious from the preparations being made that Malacar was readying himself for departure within a day or so. He wondered what piece of news might have stimulated this. He was still not privy to his former commander's secrets.

Jackara, on the other hand, obviously was. He felt a twitch of jealousy at this.

He had made his own wishes obvious during the previous week. Now it was up to Malacar. He was willing to accompany him in the name of renascent anger and more than a little guilt. In analyzing these feelings, he knew that they went back to that night on the couch and the thing he had wrought out of dream. No matter. The source was unimportant. He wanted to be trusted now, trusted as Jackara was. Perhaps there should be blood as there had been in the old days. He began to feel the old infection, the old hates.

Where could he be going, though? And for what purpose? Morwin had listened to news summaries religiously, but he had detected nothing that offered opportunity for one of Malacar's hit-and-run sabotage operations. Of course, it could have been information from a non-public source—such as Malacar's underground in the CL. Whatever the source, he became irritated as the Commander grew more and more preoccupied.

He smiled somewhat maliciously as he recalled how, on the previous day, he had upset the old man.

Malacar had come onto the observation deck unannounced, as he had stood there with Jackara, explaining his means of earning a livelihood.

The great silver Service vessel stood before them like an exotic candleholder, in the midst of the steam and the smoke. It stood in a place where no sane pilot would have set it, near to the rim of the crater itself. When Malacar saw it, he crossed the deck in a series of blurred strides and his hands darted like flames across the console. Morwin did not see from where they emerged, but he felt the aftershocks of the missiles. As he turned his head from the Commander to the scene below and back again, the vessel slowly faded from sight. He snickered and Jackara laughed.

"There is nothing there!" said Malacar, regarding his instruments.

"Uh—No, sir," said Morwin. "I was just showing Jackara how I do dream-globes. I formed a picture out of the particles out there. That is—what you were shooting at."

Malacar snarled then, said, "Jackara, I want to talk with you," and the two of them departed. At dinner, Malacar had joked about the thing. By then Morwin was able to keep his laughter respectful.

Mr. Morwin . . .

Yes, Shind?

The Commander is going to ask you to accompany us on a journey we will be undertaking tomorrow evening.

Where to?

It was a choice between two worlds—Cleech and Sum-mit. He chose Summit, for various reasons.

What are we to do there?

It is in the nature of a recruitment operation. He will tell you as much of it as he feels you should know.

If I am to go along, I ought to know everything.

Please. This is not an invitation. I trust that he will never become aware of the fact that I have communicated with you.

What is it, then?

He requested my opinion as to whether you would be an asset to the expedition.

. . . And trustworthy, I daresay.

. . . And trustworthy, of course. My reply was in the affirmative. I am not unaware of your resurgent sympathies.

Thanks for the good word.

It was not to preserve your feelings that I made the rec-ommendation.

What, then?

I feel that this time the Commander will need all the assistance he can get. I wish to assure its presence.

What is wrong?

Call it a feeling and let it go at that.

All right. I will forget that we have spoken. Who else is coming?

Jackara. Myself.

I will go along, and be ready to help.

Good day, then.

Good day.

He looked about. Shind was nowhere in sight. From where had the creature reached him? It was always a strange feeling to speak with Shind in this fashion. It occurred to him that Shind might have been in another part of the citadel, at Malacar's side perhaps, the entire time.

He paced and reflected.

All right, he decided, it is not a typical Malacar operation. There has been no hint of planned mayhem. Yet Shind seems to feel that it is something more dangerous. If I can't be a fop or a good artist, perhaps I can be a decent assistant agitator. Wouldn't it be amusing if a real Service ship put down right now and Malacar thought it was another illusion? I don't think I could operate that console . . . —Would I, though? Would I actually fire and kill them, after all these years? In peacetime it is called murder. I wonder . . . ? The Commander certainly seemed upset, though. I understand that on other occasions he has actually allowed them to land here and even spoken with them. This thing must be big if he is jumpy.—I probably would fire, and regret it afterward.—What is Jackara's part in this? Is she sleeping with the Commander? Is she a professional member of the network with an assigned role in something that is to come? Possibly both—or perhaps a relative. She *could* be his daughter, I guess. Wouldn't that be something? Typical too. He seldom speaks of his personal life, and I have never heard him mention relatives. Strange girl—too hard and too soft by turns, and you never know which turn is coming next. Pretty, though. It would be good to know her real status, to decide what I would like mine to be. I will ask her, later . . .

After dinner that evening, Malacar carefully placed his utensils across his plate, looked at Morwin and said, "Do you want to accompany us to Summit?"

Morwin nodded.

"What's on Summit?" he asked, after a period of silence.

"A man I've been looking for," Malacar said. "A man

who might be able to help us. At least, I think he is there. I could be mistaken. It could be the wrong place. If so, I will simply have to keep looking. The indications are pretty good, though. What I want to do is locate him and persuade him to assist us."

"What has he got that makes him so special?"

"Diseases," said Malacar.

"Beg pardon?"

"Diseases, diseases! At certain times this man becomes a walking infection, a plague-bearer!"

"To what use would you put this condition?"

Malacar chuckled.

Morwin sat unmoving for several seconds, then resumed scooping at his lemon sherbet.

"I think I see," he said, finally.

"Yes, I think you do too. A living weapon. I intend for him to walk among our enemies. How does the idea strike you?"

"It—It is hard to say. I will have to think about it."

"But you *will* come?"

"Yes, I will."

"Jackara will be accompanying us, and Shind."

"Very good, sir."

"Have you no questions?"

"Not really. Not at the moment. Though I am sure I will think of some later. Well . . . What is the man's name?"

"Heidel von Hymack."

He shook his head.

"Never heard of him, sir."

"Yes you did. Only you called him Hyneck—the man Pels was looking for."

"Oh, him. Yes."

"Ever hear of a man called H?"

"It seems to me that I have, though I forget the circumstances. It was not as a disease-carrier, though. Doesn't he have a rare blood type or something?"

"Something. I will send some articles to your room later."

"Thank you."

He glanced at Jackara and returned to his sherbet.

God! It's like looking down into hell! she decided. It has been an entire week, and this is the first time I have seen it at night.

She stared into the smoldering place, nearer-seeming now that night had come.

I wonder how far down it has to go to find those fires? she thought. I will not ask. It would show my ignorance. No volcanoes on Deiba. Too old, perhaps. Dust and rain. I remember descriptions, pictures of volcanoes. Never realized they were like this . . .

The building trembled, slightly, and she smiled. It was good living so close to so much power, to dwell on the periphery of chaos.

Will he allow me to remain when this is all over? she wondered. Perhaps. If I prove useful on Summit. I could learn to help with things around here. I will make myself useful. He will come to rely on me.

She looked about.

He must know I am out here, she thought. He knows everything that happens in his home. I never walked alone up here before, but I don't suppose it would bother him. No. He told me to make myself at home. He would have said something if he did not want—

"Hello. What are you doing up this late?"

"John!—Oh, I couldn't sleep."

"Neither could I. So I decided to get up and take a walk.—Pretty spectacular, isn't it?"

"Yes. It is the first time I have seen it at night."

He moved near to her and pretended to study the flames.

"All set for the trip?"

"Yes," she said. "Malacar told me it would only take about eight days, sub-time."

"That sounds right. Are you related?"

"What do you mean?"

"Are you and Malacar relatives?"

"No. We're just—friends."

"I see. I'd like to be your friend too."

She seemed not to have heard him.

He turned then and stared down, and the smoke arced to the right and the left, came together, formed a great spark-shot heart in the midst of which her name appeared, then his. An arrow of flame pierced its center.

"Be my valentine," he said.

She laughed. Turning, he took her shoulders quickly and kissed her on the mouth. For a moment she relaxed, then struggled with surprising strength and pushed him away.

"Don't do that!"

Her voice was shrill, her face twisted.

He stepped back.

"I'm sorry," he said. "I didn't mean—Look! Don't be angry. It's just that you looked so pretty standing there . . . I hope my beard didn't tickle too much. I—Oh hell! I'm sorry."

He turned and regarded the dissolving heart.

"You surprised me," she said. "That's all."

He glanced at her again, and she was nearer to him.

"Thanks for the valentine," she said, and she smiled.

He hesitated, then reached forward slowly and touched her cheek. He moved his hand down it, traced her chin, her throat, then around to the back of her neck, rested it there a moment, then drew her toward him. She stiffened then, and he relaxed but did not remove his hand.

"If you don't have a man just now," he said, "and you might be interested ... If you and Malacar are *just*—friends—I would like to be considered in the running. That is all I was trying to find out and to say."

"I can't," she said. "It's too late. Thanks, though."

"What do you mean 'too late'? All I know is now, and now is all I care about."

"You don't understand."

"... And I don't care either. If you and Malacar are not really together, well, perhaps, you and I ... You know. For a while, at least ... If you decide you don't like it—Well, no hard feelings. I was thinking along those lines. Say something."

"No, not yet. Not now."

He marked the "yet" and, "Of course," he said, "I expected as much. Think about it, though. Yes, do that. Think about it. Please."

"All right. I'll think."

"Then I'll shut up. Whatever—at least—I hope that you will consider me a—friend."

She smiled, nodded, drew away.

"I think I had better be going now," she said.

He nodded.

She left him then, and he watched the exploding night.

That's something, anyway, he said to himself.

The heart had long ago turned to vapor.

• • •

Heidel burst upon the city like a pod spreading seeds. He pointed his finger and people fell.

Enough, he said to the thing within him. They go now the way of all the others.

As he departed, before he entered the place of mists, he encountered a boy with a hammer in his hand.

Standing well back, he inquired, "What are you doing, boy?"

The youth turned and said, "Collecting stones, sir."

He laughed, then, "Chop into that yellow place on your left," he said. "There should be blue crystals there."

The boy turned and obeyed him.

"Sir!" he cried out, after perhaps ten minutes. "There are indeed blue crystals!"

He continued to dig and chip.

Heidel shook his head and contorted his face.

"I had better be away," he said. He hurried off toward the mists.

Hammering at the hillside, the boy did not notice him go.

CHAPTER 5

Matching his orbital velocity with Summit's rotation, he hung starlike above the area in question.

"... A single individual," he repeated. "I am sorry that I cannot be more explicit. I am convinced he is the focus of the infections. You have to do more than simply quarantine the area. You have to locate this man and immobilize him. He should be moving somewhat in advance of the contagion course, as we must allow for an incubation period. From what you have told me so far, he seems to be headed southwest. I recommend you assume continuing movement in that direction, most likely on foot, and begin searching immediately. And get me more data! If possible, I would like to be in direct communication with the searchers."

"I will of course have to get authorization for all this, Dr. Pels, but I am certain it will not take long. In the meantime, there should be more reports coming in shortly. I will get them up to you as soon as we have them."

"Very good. I will be waiting."

Pels broke the connection.

Indeed, he said to himself, I am used to waiting. But this time—The news came so quickly, and I made it in time to be right on top. I know he is down there. These people will let me direct things. I know it. Nothing like this has ever happened here before. He seems to be getting worse. But I will find him this time. Time . . .

. . . Three, four, five.

"Hold it!" he said, but she had already tossed the sixth coin.

It hung there a moment, turning, jerking, then moved to join the other five in a slow figure-of-eight procession in the middle of the air.

"Just wait until I stabilize the thing . . . There! All right, add another—carefully."

Jackara flipped another coin upward. It overshot the group by several feet, froze as if suddenly transformed to a photograph, then commenced a tadpole-like wiggling that took it in the direction of the pattern. Moments later, it had joined the flow.

"Another!"

Laughing, Jackara tossed another coin. This one did not stop or even seem to slow, but moved to take its place in the procession immediately.

"Another!"

It was caught instantly, fitted into the circuit.

"Another . . ."

"I think you are going to break your record," she said, throwing it.

Catching it, he unfolded the design so that the coins now moved in a circle. The circle expanded and the coins flowed faster.

"Now. Another."

It fell into the pattern, which continued to expand, to accelerate.

"You did it! That's the most yet!" she said.

The shining round of coins drifted toward her, where she sat on the edge of the bunk. It moved to a position above her, descended, spun about her head.

I still cannot tell what it is that occurs in your mind when you do it, said Shind, *though I can recognize the process when it is operating. Actually, it is a very pleasant thing to contem—*

Malacar laughed.

The ring came apart. The coins clattered against the bulkhead, shot across the cabin, fell about Jackara.

She uttered a brief cry and drew back. Morwin shuddered and shook his head.

Chuckling, Malacar emerged from behind the partition that separated the controls from the living area.

"The Summit port authorities are most cooperative," he announced. "Really helpful."

Morwin smiled to Jackara. "It *is* a record," he said. Then, to Malacar, "How are they being helpful?"

"I just checked with them for a picture of the landing situation, expressing concern over rumors I had heard of the outbreak of various diseases. Was it safe to land at all? I asked. Or should I take my tour elsewhere?"

"Tour?" Jackara said.

"Yes. I decided to be a tour guide, for purposes of the communication.—Might even be a good story to stick with if we get into trouble. At any rate, they responded by detailing the areas presently under quarantine. I got conversational then and managed to obtain some dates and places. I have a pretty good idea of our man's progress within the area now."

"Very good," said Morwin, stooping and beginning to retrieve coins. "What are we going to do now?"

"Drop back into subspace—I told him we were calling the trip off—and reenter at another point. Their satellite warning system looks pretty simple. I ought to be able to slip through all right."

"Then land in the quarantined area and pick him up?"

"Exactly."

"Well, I've been thinking. What if we find him and he says he doesn't want to come with us, that he doesn't want to be a weapon? What do we do then? Kidnap him?"

Malacar stared at him, eyes narrowing. Then he smiled.

"He'll come," he said.

Morwin looked away.

"Just wondering . . ."

Malacar turned back toward the front of the vessel.

"I am going to change course now," he said. "I will be taking us back into subspace as soon as I am able."

Morwin nodded, jingled the coins, stood.

"I think it is about time for your next round of immunizations," Malacar called back as he rounded the partition. "See to it, will you, Shind?"

Yes.

Morwin threw the coins into the air. They became a glittering tornado, twisting and spinning for several moments, then descended with a clatter into his outstretched palm.

"Here's another," said Jackara, extending her hand.

The coin shot from her fingertips and joined its mates with a sharp *clink.*

She stared at him.

"Is something the matter?" she asked.

He dumped the coins into his pocket.

"I don't know," he said.

You do, though, said Shind. *His answer has caused you to think once more of your own position in this enterprise. And of all the things that follow.*

Of course.

You see now that he has changed, that he seems willing to use people in ways he might not have before.

It seems that way.

Jackara, for instance. Why is she here?

I've been wondering.

He has rationalized his way around it, but there is only one reason: She worships him, she thinks that everything he does is right. He will not admit it, but he needs that support now.

He is that uncertain of himself?

He grows older. Time moves more quickly for him, but his objectives seem no nearer to realization.

And of my own presence?

A version of the same thing. It is not just that you can cause a gun to misfire or sabotage a starship with your mind. Your respect reassures him. While he cannot fully trust you, he requires the old feeling of command your presence provides.

He is taking a chance, though, if he cannot trust me . . .

Not really, for he knows that he can control you.

How?

By his control of Jackara. He is aware of your fondness for her.

I did not think that it showed—and I had never thought him to be so perceptive.

He is not, normally. I told him of your feelings for her.

For God's sake! Why? My feelings are none of—

It was necessary. I would not have violated your emo-

*tional privacy if it were not. I did it only to assure his bring-
ing you along.*

Just because you are worried about him?

It is no longer so simple—

"Should I prepare the inoculations, Shind?"

Yes. Go ahead, Jackara.

Morwin watched her as she rose and moved to the rear
of the compartment. Then he looked away and seated himself on the bunk.

What do you mean, Shind?

*As we have observed, Malacar has changed. But then, of
course, so have we. He was always somewhat rash—and this
was once a virtue—so that I found it difficult to decide until
recently whether he had become more so, or whether I had
simply grown more conservative. Something happened
recently, however, which settled this question for me and
gave me cause for alarm. It was on Deiba, where we sought
clues as to the identity of H and found him to be this Heidel
von Hymack. We encountered another individual searching
for the same information. He was also successful, and he
tried to dissuade Malacar from using it as he intends. He
even offered him a tremendous price for his cooperation—the
restoration of the entire planet Earth to its pre-war condition.*

Preposterous.

*No. The man was Francis Sandow, and I was in his
mind as he spoke. He meant what he said. And he was very
concerned.*

Sandow? The planoformer?

*The same. He has long enjoyed an intimacy with the
Pei'ans, the oldest race of which we have knowledge. In his
mind there was a certainty that the man we seek has*

obtained an abnormal and highly dangerous relationship with one of the Pei'an deities, a goddess concerned with both healing and disease—

And you believe this?

What is important is not whether I believe it or whether the thing is truly a deity. I do believe there is something highly unusual involved, though. Sandow was convinced that there is a dangerous concentration of power here, and his conviction was based on considerable personal knowledge of the phenomenon. I have known several Pei'ans, and they are a very strange, gifted people. I have encountered Sandow, and I know that he is anything but a fool. I know too that he was afraid. That is sufficient. I believe there is reason for his fears. Malacar would not even discuss the matter with him, though. Instead, he tried to kill him. I told him that he had succeeded, in order to save Sandow's life. The man was actually only stunned.

What happened then?

We returned home. Malacar began his search for von Hymack.

Was Jackara with you when you met Sandow?

Yes.

Does she believe Malacar killed him?

Yes.

I see . . . And now Sandow's organization may be after us?

I think not. He sent no agents. He went to Deiba alone. It is therefore a thing he wishes to handle himself. I believe he will keep it that way.—No, it is not the wrath of Sandow that concerns me at the moment. I wanted you along for a different reason.

What, then?

I did not exaggerate my fear for Malacar's safety, nor

the peril that I feel lies ahead. I wanted you with us for the purpose of killing Heidel von Hymack, should we succeed in locating him.

That is quite a request.

But necessary. You must do it.

And if I refuse?

Thousands of people may die besides the Commander— needlessly, horribly. Possibly millions.

I do not know this for a fact.

But you know me—have known me for years. You know I am stable and not given to acting without considerable thought. You know my loyalty to the Commander, and you know that I would not defy him lightly. Would I have set things up as I have if I did not believe what I was doing to be correct? You know the answer. I see it in your thoughts.

Morwin bit his lip. Jackara approached with the pressure pens. He drew up his sleeve and extended his arm.

I will have to think about it.

Think all you want. I already know your answer.

With blankets and water, the searchers made the man as comfortable as they could, there beside the trail. While they waited for the transportation they had summoned, they listened to his words, sometimes scattered by the fever, tugged back to responsiveness by chills.

"... Correct," he said, looking past them at the sky. "Mad and correct. I don't know. Yes I do. He was thin ... Thin and dirty and covered with sores. I was at the supply depot when he came around. Never saw him before ... No. Hair like a dirty halo. There's your stranger for you. Came walking, someone said. Dunno from where ... Give me another drink, will you?—Thanks.—I don't know ... Where he was going ... ? He didn't say. He talked. He did that. I don't remember what he said—exactly. But it was strange . . . There's your stranger for you. Never said his name. Didn't seem to need one. Got up on a packing case and started talking. Funny . . . Nobody tried to stop him, tell him to go away . . . He—Don't remember what he said. Mad and correct . . . But we listened. Not that much happens around here—and he was different. Preaching, sort of—but not quite. Cursing, maybe. I don't know . . . Anyway—Wait . . . More water?—Thanks.—Funny, funny . . . Mad talker. Death and life . . . That's right! Right! Right . . . How everything is going to die. Couldn't stop listening. Don't know why. We knew he was mad. Everybody said so—when we talked about him—after he left. Nobody said a word while he was preaching, though. It was like—He made it sound right while he was saying it. And he was—right. Look at me! He was. Wasn't he? Mad and correct . . . —No. I didn't see which direction he headed afterward.—You want to hear him, though? Sam—who runs the place—recorded part of what he said. Played it back later. Different with him not being there, saying it. We laughed a lot when we listened, then. Just mad, that's all. You can ask Sam, if he hasn't erased it. You can hear him for yourself . . . That was when I started feeling shaky—God! He was right! He was, I think . . . Seems that way—anyhow . . ."

They reported this back to their section leader, and after the pickup they continued on, slowly, combing the countryside, halting to assist and record, to provide for the dead, the dying, the survivors, maintaining radio contact with the other groups, passing through open country, searching dwellings, climbing hills, the searchers.

From the far corners of the sky, the clouds began to advance, and they cursed the threat of the storm which would foul both their boots and the body-heat detection equipment. One, who knew his history, even cursed Francis Sandow, who had designed and built the world.

Clouds, unrolling like carpets, spreading, trailing wisps and rag-ends, rushed toward a point near midheaven, dampening the dayblue sky to a pearl-gray from which the translucence slowly ebbed, as additional layers were heaped above, banking, mounting higher, pressing lower, darkening, dimming, hazing the outlines of trees and rocky heights, transforming the lower figures of men and animals into shifting things a quarter of shadow and going for half, while the rains were yet withheld, the mists rolled and rose, dew came afresh to the grasses, windows were filmed and beaded, moisture collected, ran upon, dripped from leaves, sounds came distorted, as though the entire world had been bedded in cotton, birds flew near to the ground in their courses toward the hills, the winds died down and ceased, small animals paused, raised their muzzles, turned them slowly, shook themselves, cocked their heads, then moved as if seeking some hidden Ark, beyond the foothills, in the mist, above the places the searchers combed, and the thunder held its breath, the lightning stayed its stroke, the rain remained unshed, the temperature slipped downward, cloud fell upon cloud and, stopper drawn from the spectrum, the colors drained out of the world, leaving behind a newsreel frame or the impression of a cave, shadows sliding on its farther walls, changing, irregular, wet.

Dr. Pels listened again to the rasping, recorded voice, hooking his thumbs beneath his jaw, bracing his knuckles against his cheeks:

"I—Did someone say he has a right to live? I—There is no cosmic guarantee for this. Far from it! The only promise the universe makes and keeps is death . . . I—Who says that life must triumph? All evidence indicates the contrary! Everything that has risen from the primal slime has been beset and ultimately destroyed! Every link in the great chain of being attracts the nemesis which breaks it! Life feeds upon itself, is crushed by the inanimate! Why? Why not? I—

". . . You are to blame. For existing. Look within yourselves and you will see the truth . . . Regard the rocks of the desert! They breed not, nor do they harbor thoughts, desires. No living thing can compare to the crystal in its still perfection. I—

". . . Talk not to me of the sacredness of life, nor its adaptability. For every adaptation there is a new, dark answer, and the echo shatters the utterer. Only the stillness is sacred. The absence of hearing evokes the mystic sound. I—

". . . The gods erred in dumping their wastes. But you are to blame. For existing. This corner of the universe is polluted! From the stuff of divine garbage the disease of life was bred . . . There is your sacredness! Quarantined between darkness and darkness, allowed to run its course. And everything that lives is disease to something other! We feed upon ourselves, are gone! Soon now, soon . . . I—

"I—Brothers! Envy the stone! It suffers not! Rejoice in untainted water and air and rock! Envy the crystal. Soon we shall be like them, perfect, still . . .

"Do not ask forgiveness, but slowness in the disposition that is to come—that you may savor the return to delicious peace! I—I—I—

"Pray, weep, burn . . . That is all. I—Go . . . Go!"

Then he set it to replay and resumed his attitude. It was a troublesome emotion that he felt, not unlike the effects of Wagner, whom he kept to a minimum. But one more time . . .

"How does this help us . . . ?" he began, and then he smiled.

It did not really help. But it made him feel better.

A moment's respite, then.

Heidel von Hymack moved along the trail that wound its way up and over the shoulder of a rocky prominence. Pausing near its highest point, he looked back and down, across the fog-shrouded distance he had come. He blinked his eyes and rubbed his beard. His vague feelings of uneasiness had intensified. Something was wrong. He leaned back against the glass-slick rock and rested his hands on his staff. Yes, it was difficult to identify, but something had been altered in the world about him. It was more than a pre-storm tension. It was almost as if he were being sought, by someone he was not yet ready to meet.

Is she trying to tell me something? he wondered. Maybe I should hole up and find out. But that would take time, and I feel this need to keep moving. Ought to get out of here before the storm hits. Why do I keep looking back? I—

He ran his fingers through his hair and raked his teeth across his lower lip. A bit of sunlight leaked through a rift in the clouds and caused the mist about him to sparkle with momentary, dancing prisms. Eyes darting, forehead furrowed, he watched them for perhaps ten seconds, then turned away.

"Damn you!" he said. "Whoever you are . . ."

He banged his staff against a rock, crossed over the ridge, sought a downward track.

He sat upon a stone and hunted. After a time, he rose and moved on, tramping among the hills and over the trackless, rock-strewn plains, there in the region of mists. As he walked, birds dipped and darted about him, appearing out of and vanishing back into the shifting curtain of fog.

Hunting, he climbed partway up the face of a steep stone hill, seated himself on a narrow ledge, withdrew a cigar, bit off its end, lit it. As he stared across the plain, a wind washed over it, and for a while it lay bare and bleak beneath his gaze. A spined lizard whose skin reproduced the shifting color display of a soap bubble's surface descended from a rock and came to share the ledge with him, fork-tongue darting heart-red, yellow eyes fixed unblinking upon his face. It brushed against his hand and he stroked it.

"What do you think?" he said, after several minutes. "I can't spot a warm-blooded body or mind in the area."

He continued to smoke, and the mists crept back to cover the plain. Finally, he sighed, thumped his heels against the rock and rose. Turning, he lowered himself and began the downward climb. The lizard moved to the edge and regarded his descent.

Pacing another half mile, he acquired the company of a pair of weasel-like predators who frolicked about his feet, tongues lolling, as though greatly amused by the progress of his boots, tiny hisses and barking noises occasionally escaping their throats. They ignored the circling birds and the big-throated wadloper who emerged from his mudhole to follow after, until his awkward, shambling gait left him far behind—at which time he croaked twice and crept back to his wallow.

When, beside a rust-streaked boulder, he paused to hunt with his mind, the animals grew still. An icy stream trickled nearby, dark, diamond-leafed plants swaying in clumps on its banks, the mists skating over its surface. He stared, unseeing, at the flow, chewing his cigar, searching.

Then, "No," he said, and, "Why don't you go home? to the animals.

They drew back and watched him, and when he departed they made no move to follow.

Crossing the stream, he continued on his way, without map or compass, bearing toward the west, after detecting a party of unsuccessful searchers in the direction he had intended taking, eastward.

And as he walked, he cursed. Between damns, he threw away his cigar. Turning then to the east, he stared for perhaps half a minute.

A roll of thunder sounded in the distance. Moments later, it was followed by another. More occurred then, merging into a steady growling note that vibrated within the ground as well as the air. A wind arose in the west and rushed to investigate the storm.

He moved on, turning farther southward now, paralleling the storm for a time, then leaving it behind him. Half an afternoon later, there came a glimmer of something that drew him farther to the west.

"Who, I wonder?" he said to the shadow that sighed along the ground beside his feet. "Somehow familiar, but still too far . . . I had better be very careful."

Probing gingerly, he advanced, and the fogs rushed to conceal him and to muffle the sounds of his passage.

Hunched within his poncho, Morwin splashed forward, the center of a fifty-foot circle of visibility. Protected from the moisture without, he was nevertheless damp with perspiration, and the palm of his hand felt clammy whenever he touched it against the butt of his pistol. He thought of Malacar and Jackara, moving along a drier course from the cave where *The Perseus* lay hidden. He thought of the land-slide they had brought down to cover the cave mouth, and he tried not to think of the difficulties they might encounter in blasting their way out again.

Anything, Shind? he inquired.

If I locate anyone, you will be the first to know.

What of Jackara—and Malacar?

They are just emerging from the storm into an area of greater visibility. They continue to monitor the radio com-munications among the native searchers, as well as their conversations with Dr. Pels. It appears that these searchers have found nothing but bad weather, so far. Worse than here, actually. At least, they keep complaining about it.

The search parties are near enough for you to read?

No. I am obtaining this information only from Malacar's mind. It seems that the searchers are about four miles north of us, and farther to the east.

This Pels you mentioned—He is the same one—the Dr. Pels?"

It seems so. I gather that he is in orbit directly overhead at this moment.

To what end?

He appears to be in charge of things.

I assume he wants H also.

Most likely.

I don't like this, Shind—their being aware one man is causing it, and hunting for him at the same time, in the same place. And Pels being in on it. If I decide to do as you suggested, there may be more trouble than we anticipated.

I have been thinking about this also. It has occurred to me that it might be safest to see whether there is a way to assure his being turned over to Pels' searchers. If they take him into custody, our problem is solved.

TO DIE IN ITALBAR

How do you propose achieving this?

Overpower him, bind him. Bring him to their attention. Failing that, kill him and claim self-defense. They seem to think he is unbalanced, so it would sound plausible.

Supposing Malacar finds him first?

Then we will have to think of something else. An accident, I suppose.

I don't like it.

I know that. Have you a better idea?

No.

They continued on for the better part of an hour, achieving higher ground and emerging from the storm into a warmer, somewhat clearer place, more level in character, though still rifted, still dotted with boulders. Dark shapes occasionally passed overhead, emitting high-pitched, trilling notes. The wind continued to blow steadily from out of the west.

Morwin removed his poncho, folded it, rolled it, hung it from his belt. He withdrew a handkerchief and began to wipe his face.

There is someone up ahead, Shind told him.

Our man?

Quite possibly.

He loosened his pistol in its holster.

"Possibly"? he said. *You're the telepath. Read his mind.*

It is not that simple. People do not generally walk about concentrating on their identities—and I have never met the man.

I was under the impression you could do better than just pick up surface thoughts.

You know that I can. You are also aware that many factors are involved. He is still a good distance away, and his mind is troubled.

What is bothering him?

He feels that he is being pursued.

If he is von Hymack, he is correct. I wonder how he knows it, though?

This not at all clear. He is in an abnormal state of mind. Extreme paranoia, I would say—and an obsession with death, disease.

Understandable, of course.

Not to me, not completely. He seems aware of what he is doing, and he seems to delight in it. There is a sense of divine mission about it. Finally, he seems somewhat dazed. Yes, this is our man.

With a string of defense mechanisms.

Possibly, possibly . . .

How far ahead is he?

About half a mile.

Morwin moved forward, hurrying now, eyes straining against the gloom.

I have just been in contact with the Commander. He thought his instruments had detected someone, but it was apparently only an animal. I lied to him about our own situation.

Good. What is H doing now?

He is singing. His mind is filled with it. A Pei'an thing.

Strange.

He is strange. I would have sworn that for a moment he was aware of my presence in his mind. Then this feeling vanished.

Morwin increased his pace.

I want to get this over with, he said.

Yes.

They pressed ahead, almost running now.

• • •

Francis Sandow sighed. The *martlind*—out of sight, though still within reach of his mind—continued on at the sluggish pace that had carried it directly past Malacar and Jackara. As this occurred, he had retreated to a point near a powerpull, moving out of range of the other's detection gear. A quick mental probe showed him that Malacar had sighed also, accepting the beast's presence in place of himself.

Should have been more careful, he reflected. No excuse for a blunder like that. I get too cocky on my own worlds. And this calls for some small subtlety, not just force. Got to baffle that gear of his . . . There!

Moving swiftly, he again regarded the thoughts of Malacar, and of Jackara . . .

Bitter, so bitter he has become, he reflected. The girl hates too, but with her it is such a childlike thing. Would either of them really go through with it, I wonder, if they realized fully what the results would be? He cannot have lost his sense of process to that extent, so that he envisages only the deaths and not the dying. If he had come a greater distance on foot, had seen the results of von Hymack's passing—I wonder? Would he still feel as he does? He has changed, though, even in that short while since I met him on Deiba—and he was not exactly soft and reasonable that day.

It was then that the prickling sensation began within Malacar's mind, and Sandow dropped his own toward inertia, realizing that he could not withdraw undetected. He did not even curse, for there must be no emotion, no telltale reverberation of feeling. It must be as if he did not exist. No reaction, no response, whatever transpired. Even then . . .

Peculiar sensation. Two telepaths regarding the same subject at the same time. One hiding from the other . . .

Sandow passively noted an exchange between Shind and Malacar, learning in an instant their aims, their progress, reacting not at all. When the exchange had terminated, his mind moved once more, withdrawing, assessing. He brushed lightly against Jackara's mind, then shied away, almost stung by Shind's presence there now.

He withdrew another cigar, lit it.

Complicated, damn it! he decided. Searchers to the left, still far off, but moving this way. Malacar to the right. Shind liable to pick me up at any time if I am not careful. And somewhere up ahead, probably, my man . . .

He began to move, slowly, then, paralleling Malacar and Jackara, out of reach of the man-sniffer, brushing lightly against the fringes of their minds, alternately, at half-minute intervals, beginning with Malacar, walking westward.

Let them find him and then take him away from them? he wondered. But they might not . . . Then . . . No—

And then his questions became unnecessary.

Moving at a rapid pace, Morwin stumbled when he attempted an abrupt halt. He had mounted a rocky ridge somewhat in advance of Shind, and through the half-lit, eddying haze he had seen the man, thin, dark, staff in hand, standing unmoving, looking back. There was no doubt in his mind as to his identity, and he felt himself taken by confusion at this sudden presence. Recovering, he found that Shind was once more in his mind.

That is our man! I am certain! But something is wrong. He is aware! He—

Then Morwin clutched at his head, dropped back to his knees.

He had never heard a mental scream before.

Shind! Shind! What is happening?

I—I—She's got me! Here—

His mind swirling like the mists, there came a sudden series of superimpositions of images and colors, rising and mixing with a clarity and vividness which destroyed his ability to distinguish between that which was externally objective and that which was not. A changing blueness came to overlay everything, and in its midst a myriad of blue women danced, wildly, kaleidoscopically; and as he realized—for no rational reason—that their plurality was but some symbolic illusion, they began to collapse, coalesce, merge, fall in upon themselves, growing more and more stately, compelling, potent. It was then that he felt himself the subject of scrutiny on the part of the swaying women. And they resolved themselves into two: one, tall and soft and lovely, a madonna-like tower of compassion; the other, like yet unlike her in appearance, possessed of an aspect he could only consider menacing. Then these two merged, the countenance and mien of the latter growing dominant. Amid blue lightnings she stared with unblinking, perhaps lidless, eyes that stripped him in an instant of his flesh, his mind, that terrified him with their primal, irrational intensity.

"Shind!" he cried, and he had the gun in his hand, firing.

A wave of something like laughter washed over him.

Then, *She is using me!* Shind seemed to be saying. *I— Help me!*

The empty weapon slipped from his fingers. He felt himself in the midst of a dream, a cosmic nightmare. Moving without motion, thinking without thought, his mind twisted reflexively then and, as in all his workings with the stuff of dream, he seized the image and exerted his will. Driven this time by a terror that flashed like fire through the rooms of his existence, he found himself wielding a force he had never before possessed, striking out with it against the mocking woman-thing.

Her expression altered, all traces of amusement vanishing. Her figure dwindled, grew distorted, faded and returned, faded and returned. With each dimming he glimpsed the man, lying now upon the ground.

A painful wailing filled his head. Then it was gone, she was gone, and finally so was he.

"Stop!"

Malacar turned.

"What is the matter?" he asked.

"Nothing, now," she said. "But we are finished here. It is time to return to the vessel. We are leaving."

"What are you talking about? What is wrong?"

Jackara smiled.

"Nothing," she repeated. "Nothing, now."

As he regarded her, however, he realized that something *had* changed. It took him several moments to sort his impressions. The first thing that struck him was her relaxed appearance. It occurred to him that he had never seen Jackara's features pleasantly animated, and that her posture, her entire bearing, had been stiff, tense, semi-military up until then. Her voice, too, was altered. In addition to having grown softer, throatier, it now possessed an unmistakable resonance of command, silken, seamless, resilient.

Still searching for the proper question, he said, simply, "I do not understand."

"Of course not," she said. "But you see, there is no reason to look further. That which you seek is here. The man von Hymack is useless to you now, for I have found me a

better place. I like Jackara—her body, her simple passion—
and I shall remain with her. Together now, we shall accomplish all that you desire. And more. So much more. You
shall have your plagues, your deaths. You shall see the ulti-
mate disease, life, healed by that which shall come to pass.
Let us return to the vessel now and be borne to a populous
place. By the time that we reach it, I will be ready. You will
witness a spectacle which will satisfy even a passion such as
yours. And this will only be the beginning—"

"Jackara! I have no time for jokes! I—"

"I am not joking," she said softly, moving nearer to him,
raising her hand to his face.

She ran her fingertips up his cheek, bringing them to
rest upon his temple. He was paralyzed then by the vision of
carnage that swept through his mind. The dead, the dying
were everywhere. The symptoms of disease after disease
flashed before him, displayed on bodies without number. He
saw entire planets rolling in the grip of epidemics, saw
worlds stark and barren, emptied of life, their streets, homes,
buildings, dead fields filled with corpses, bodies awash in
their harbors, choking gutters and streams, bloated, decom-
posing. All ages and sexes were so strewn, like the after-
math of a killer storm.

He grew ill.

"My God!" he finally gasped. "What are you?"

"You have seen what you have seen, and still you do
not know?"

He backed away.

"There is something unnatural here," he said finally.
"The blue goddess Sandow said . . ."

"How fortunate you are," she told him. "And I also. Your
means are vastly superior to those of my previous acolyte,
and we have common goals—"

"How did you come to invade the person of Jackara?"

"Your servant Shind was linked with her mind when I encountered her. She was preferable to the man I knew. I came over. It is good to have this sex again."

Shind! Shind! he called. *Where are you? What has happened?*

"Your servants are unwell," she said. "But there is no need for them any longer. In fact, they must be left behind. Especially the man Morwin. Come! We will return to the ship."

But faintly, very faintly, like a dog scratching at a door, Shind touched his mind.

. . . Right . . . Sandow—was right . . . I have seen a mind—beyond comprehension . . . Destroy—her . . .

Still shaken, Malacar fumbled at his holster . . .

"Pity," she said. "It could have been pleasant. But I *can* go it alone now—and I fear that I must."

. . . And knew that he would be too late, for Jackara's gun was already in the hand of the stranger.

Rags of consciousness raised by a black tide, dropped, raised again. Streamers now, farther aloft. Then down. Up . . .

Morwin's eyes fell upon the pistol.

Even before he realized who he was, his hand groped for the gun, seized it. The cold congruence of palm and curved metal butt was security, comfort.

Blinking, he saw his way back into existence, followed it, lifted his head.

Shind? Where are you?

But Shind did not reply, was not to be seen.

Turning, he regarded the prostrate form of the man, perhaps twenty paces distant. There was blood upon him.

He got to his feet and moved in that direction.

The man was breathing. His head was turned away from Morwin, his right arm flung grotesquely to the side, the hand twitching.

Morwin stood over him a moment, then circled, knelt and stared into his face. The eyes were open but unfocused.

"Can you hear me?" he asked.

The man exhaled sharply, winced. A light came into his eyes and they moved, met with Morwin's own. His face was pocked, creased, sallow, dotted with raw sores.

"I hear you," he said softly.

Morwin shifted his grip on the pistol.

"Are you Heidel von Hymack?" he asked him. "Are you the man called H?"

"I am Heidel von Hymack."

"But are you H?"

The man did not answer immediately. He sighed, then coughed. Morwin glanced at his wounds. He appeared to have been hit in the right shoulder and arm.

"I—I have been sick," he finally said. Then he chuckled, a series of dry croaks. ". . . Now I feel fine."

"You want some water?"

"Yes!"

Morwin reholstered his gun, unstoppered his canteen, carefully raised the man's head and trickled water into his mouth. The man drank half the canteen before he gagged and drew away.

"Why didn't you say you were thirsty?"

The other glanced at the gun, smiled faintly, shrugged his good shoulder.

"Thought you might not want to waste it."

Morwin put away the canteen.

"Well? Are you H?" he said.

"What difference does an initial make? I was the plague-bearer."

"You have been aware of this fact all along?"

"Yes."

"Do you hate people that much? Or is it that you just don't give a damn?"

"Neither one," he said. "Go ahead and shoot me if you want."

"Why did you let it happen?"

"It does not matter now. She is gone. It is over. Go ahead."

He sat up, still smiling.

"You act as if you want me to kill you."

"What are you waiting for?"

Morwin chewed his lip.

"You know I'm the man who shot you—" he began.

Heidel von Hymack knit his brows and turned his head slowly, regarding his body.

"I—I did not realize I had been shot," he said. "Yes . . . Yes, I can see now. And I feel it . . ."

"What did you think happened to you?"

"I lost—something. Something in my mind. It is gone now, and I feel as I have not felt in many years. The shock of separation, the feeling of relief—I was—distracted."

"How? What was it that occurred?"

"I am not certain. One moment this thing was with me, and then I felt the presence of another as well . . . Then— everything departed . . . When I awakened you were here."

"What thing?"

"You would not understand. I don't myself, really."

"Does it involve a blue woman—like, a goddess?"

Heidel von Hymack looked away.

"Yes," he said. Then he clutched at his shoulder.

"I'd better do something about your wounds."

Heidel allowed him to bind his arm and shoulder. He accepted more water.

"Why did you shoot me?" he finally said.

"It was more reflex than anything else. The—thing you lost—scared the hell out of me."

"You actually saw her?"

"Yes. With the help of a telepath."

"Where is he?"

"I don't know. I am afraid she was hurt."

"Hadn't you better find out? You can leave me. I can't go far. Not that it matters now."

"I suppose I should," he said. *Shind! Damn it! Where are you? Do you need help?*

Stay, came a weak reply. *Stay there. I will be all right. I need only to rest . . . awhile . . .*

Shind! What happened?

Silence.

Shind! Damn it! Answer me!

Malacar, came the reply, *is dead. Wait now . . . Wait.*

Morwin stared at his hands.

"Aren't you going to?" Heidel asked him.

He did not reply.

Jackara! Shind! Is Jackara all right?

Nothing.

Shind! How is Jackara?

She lives. Wait now.

"What is wrong?" Heidel asked.

"I don't know."

"Your friend . . . ?"

". . . is alive. We have just been in contact. That is not the problem now."

"What, then?"

"I don't know. Not yet. I am waiting."

I am trying to find out, John. I have to be careful. That goddess-thing is there.

Where?

With Jackara.

How? How did it happen?

I believe that I was responsible, that she traveled by means of my link with Jackara. I am not certain how.

How did the Commander die?

She shot him.

Then what of Jackara?

That is what I am trying to find out. Leave me alone, and I will let you know when I do.

What can I do?

Nothing. Wait.

Silence.

After a time, "Do you know now?" Heidel asked.

"I know nothing. Except that I have lost something too."

"What is happening?"

"My friend is trying to find out. At least we know where your goddess went.—How do you feel?"

"I do not understand my feelings. She was with me a long while. Years. For a time, she healed through me those who had been stricken with peculiar ills. It was as if we carried both these things and their remedies within us. For I was always protected myself. Then in Italbar I was attacked for a slip of fortune, stoned. It was as if I had gone to die in Italbar. Everything was changed. Her nature, I learned then, was dual. In both aspects she functions to remove disease. In the form in which I first knew her, she sought to purify life in this fashion. In her other aspect, it is life itself that she deems the disease, and she seeks to purify matter by curing it of this ailment. Ironically—or perhaps not so—it

was by means of that which she had earlier viewed as disease that she sought to do this. She is a remedy as well as a
condition. I have served her as apostle in both extremes.
—What did she seem like when you saw her?"

"Blue and evil and powerful. Beautiful, too. She seemed
to mock me, threaten me . . ."

"Where is she now?"

"She has taken possession of a girl—not far from here.
She just killed a man."

"Oh."

"You have been the subject of quite a search."

"Yes, I guess I did know that—some way."

There came a roll of thunder near at hand. When its
echoes subsided, Morwin said, "She may have been right."

"About what?"

"Life being a disease."

"I don't know. It does not matter. Does it? I mean, that is
only one way of looking at things, no matter what her
power."

"Do you look at things that way?"

"I suppose so. I—worshiped—her. I believed her. I still
probably do."

"How's the shoulder?"

"Hurts like hell."

"She must have done some good too."

"I suppose so."

Bright flashes occurred to the south, followed by more
thunder. A few spatters of rain fell upon them, about them.

"Let's get over to those rocks," said Morwin. "They slant
some. Might keep us dry."

He helped von Hymack to his feet, drew his arm across
his shoulders, supported him in slow progress to the place
beside the stone.

There are two of them, came Shind, *and they are moving toward one another now.*

Two of what? What are you talking about?

But Shind seemed not to have heard.

They have awareness of one another, he went on. *I must be very careful. She hurt me so . . . Strange that I did not recognize his peculiarity when first we met . . . But then, it is nearer the surface now. Sandow, too, is accompanied by a shadowy Other.*

Sandow? He is here? With Jackara?

They are talking. She still holds the gun, but he stands too far away. I cannot tell, here at the edges of things, whether she is aware that he is unalone. He called her by name, which has gained her attention. She replies. He advances. It does not seem that she will shoot, for her curiosity is aroused. They speak in another language, but I catch at the rag-tails of their thoughts. He seems to know her, from somewhere—else . . . She awaits as he draws near. He salutes her in some fashion which she acknowledges. He tells her now that she has violated a rule which I do not understand. She is amused by this.

Morwin brought von Hymack into the shelter of the rocks. He lowered him to the ground, where he assumed a sitting position, back braced against the stone. He seated himself beside him and stared into the grayness. By then, the rainfall had become steady.

He tells her that she must go—I do not understand where, or how . . . She laughs. That painful laughter . . . He waits until she has finished laughing and begins to speak. It is some formal thing that he says—memorized, not spontaneous. It is intricate and rhythmical, containing many paradoxes. I do not understand it. She listens.

"Heidel, she is now with a man who is presumably trying to stop her. I do not know what will come of it. But it is for this that we are waiting. Whatever the outcome, I have no idea what will become of you. My commander, my best friend, is dead. He had plans for you which will never come to pass. They were not especially admirable plans. But he was a great man nevertheless, and I might have helped him with them. Then again, I might have killed you, because of a danger you represented to him. Either way . . ."

"I probably deserve anything unpleasant that happens to me."

"It strikes me that you were manipulated, both by circumstances and a parasitic autonomous complex with paranormal capabilities."

"You toss that off pretty glibly."

"I've been pestered by paranorm specialists most of my life. I'm an empathesiac telekineticist, whatever the hell that means—well, I move things around with my mind, and I can cause objects to induce specific feelings in people. I've absorbed the terminology. I sympathize with you. You have been used, and I would have been party to your continued exploitation. Tell me what it is that you want now."

"What? I don't know . . . To die? No. To go away, I'd say. Someplace far, isolated. That is all I ever really wanted. I haven't been myself for so long that I want to get to know me again. Yes, to go away . . ."

—has finished, and she is no longer amused. She has angry words for him . . . Threatening . . . But now the thing in his mind is much nearer to the surface—the thing so like herself, when first I felt her presence in von Hymack. He speaks of this thing, mentioning a name. Shimbo, it seems to be. She raises the gun—

There came a dazzling flash, followed by a crack of thunder. Morwin sprang to his feet.

Shind! What happened?

"What—?" said von Hymack, jerking his head about.

Morwin slowly sank back. The thunder came again, between small, steady flashes of light, a low, growling note that did not cease.

The bolt struck between them, Shind said. *She dropped the weapon and he took it, cast it away. But now he is no longer himself. Both their minds are mainly opaque. They are somehow akin, and there is an exchange of energies between them. I believe he bids her depart once more and she protests the unfairness of it. I feel that there is fear in her. He replies. She does something . . . Now he is angry. Again, he tells her to depart. She begins to argue and he interrupts her, asking whether she would carry the dispute to a contest.*

The thunder ceased. The winds grew still. Abruptly, the rain halted. The fog-hung air was instantly possessed of an unnatural stillness.

I detect nothing now, Shind said. *It is as though they have become a pair of statues.*

Shind, where are you right now, physically?

I am drawing quite near their position. I have been moving toward them since I recovered. I was hoping there might still be something I could do. Now, though, it is purely a matter of curiosity. We are only about a quarter of a mile from you.

Have you looked into von Hymack's mind recently?

Yes. He is still in a state of depression. Harmless . . .

What are we to do with him, now?

The searchers are drawing nearer. I suppose we might just let them find him.

Do you think they would hurt him?

Difficult to say. The group I can pick up seems pretty businesslike about the whole thing, but there are some angry, unstable types . . . Wait!—They are moving again! She raises her arm and begins to speak. He gestures also and joins her in whatever she is saying. Now—

The sky seemed to collapse in a blazing sheet, and the peal of thunder that followed was the loudest he had ever heard. When his senses finally cleared, he realized that it had resumed raining and that the taste in his mouth was blood, from where he had bitten into his lip.

Now what, Shind? he inquired.

Again, the silence.

Then, "Heidel, other searchers are fairly near here—the real thing," he said. "Of course, they want to find you in order to stop the epidemics."

"That should all be ended. I can feel myself changing. I know the safe feeling, and it is on its way. Almost here, actually."

"But inasmuch as you are the only one aware of this feeling, they will still doubtless want to take you into custody. I understand that Dr. Larmon Pels is associated with the search. He would probably have you quarantined, studied. So you may get your wish for isolation."

"May?"

"I am wondering about the searchers themselves. Some of them may have lost relatives, friends . . ."

"I suppose you are right. Any suggestions—beyond simple avoidance?"

"Not yet. If only we knew—"

I believe that the issue has been decided, Shind said.

Which way?

I cannot tell. They are both unconscious.

Were they injured?

It seems the result of some form of psychic shock, so I cannot be certain. Perhaps you should come now. Jackara will need you.

Yes. How do I find you?

Relax your mind and let me move further in. I will guide your steps to me.

Don't guide too quickly. Heidel is not so fast on his feet.

What do we need him for?

Nothing. He needs us.

Very well. Come.

"All right, Heidel," he said. "Now is the time."

They rose together and, under one poncho, leaning together, moved through the mist and the rain, moisture starring their faces, a fresh-risen wind at their backs.

When he finally came upon them, Morwin found Shind beside the man Sandow, who sat holding Jackara's hand and supporting her back with his arm.

"Is she all right?" he asked.

Sandow looked at Shind, then at Morwin. Then, "Physically, yes," he said.

He released von Hymack, who seated himself on a stone.

"Give this to that man," Sandow said.

"What?"

"A cigar. He'd like one."

"Yes.—How serious . . . ?"

We have both viewed her thoughts, Shind said. *She is a child again, in a slightly happier time.*

"But how severe is it?"

See whether she recognizes you.

"Jackara?" he said. "How are you feeling? It's John . . . Are you all right?"

She turned her head and stared at him. Then she smiled.

"How are you?" he asked.

There was a flicker, Shind said.

He extended his hand. She drew back, dropped her eyes.

"It's me. John. Wait!"

He fumbled in his pocket, withdrew a handful of coins, tossed them into the air. They swirled wildly, swarmed, fell into a pattern. Forming an ellipse, they danced before her, moving faster and faster. She raised her eyes and stared. She smiled again.

Perspiration broke out on his brow as they spun, sped, turned.

"Is it a record?" she said.

They showered, clattering, to the ground.

"I don't know. I wasn't counting. I think so. You *do* remember."

". . . Yes. Do it again—John."

The coins rose from the ground, hovered, began a Brownian movement before her.

"You do re—"

Do not force her to recall anything. She wants to be distracted. She does not want to remember. Make it easy. Just keep distracting her.

He juggled the coins, only glancing occasionally to see whether she was still smiling. He smelled the smoke from Heidel's cigar. He felt Sandow move within his mind.

—So that is what you hit her with, he said. *Now I understand—*

The thought terminated abruptly.

He dropped the coins again when the implication reached him.

"No!" he said. "Do not tell me that thing migrated to Jackara because I hit it with my mind! I—"

No, said Sandow, perhaps too quickly. *No. The girl was ideal, personality-wise, and there was a channel—*

—provided by me, Shind broke in.

All unknowing, Sandow said. *Leave it at that. There need be no external stimulus for such a transfer. I know of one other case. Life is sufficiently furnished that one need not go looking about for extra guilt. Let this one go.*

"Do it again," Jackara said.

"A little later," Sandow told her, rising and drawing her slowly to her feet. "Take his hand now," and he placed hers in Morwin's. "Shind tells me a searching party is drawing near, and I see that he is correct. I have no desire to get involved. You people are welcome to come away with me if you share these sentiments." He turned. "Since I see that you do, we had better get moving. I am parked back that way."

"Wait."

"What is it?"

"The Commander," said Morwin. "Malacar. Where is he?"

"Beyond those rocks. About fifty feet. The searchers will find him soon. There is nothing we can do."

But Morwin turned and started toward the rocks.

"I wouldn't take her there!"

He halted.

"I guess you are right. You take her again. Go ahead without me if you have to. I have to see him one more time."

"We will wait."

The searchers are very near!

I know.

The storm renewed its fury, but a slight distance to the southeast.

"Thanks for the cigar—sir."

"Frank. Call me Frank."

It is going to appear as if there has just been a murder, you know.

It will not be the first unsolved one in history.

When they identify him—

—there will be a stink. Yes. Think of the possible rumors. Of a political killing. He would be gratified to know that he may have done more for the DYNAB by dying here than by anything he has done since the war.

How so?

There will be a League status vote, suddenly, near the end of this session. The sentiments aroused by his death may be of benefit. He was a popular man once. A hero.

And he was tired, and more than a little bitter. It would be ironic . . .

Yes. The rumors will require careful handling. The restoration of the home planet, as part of the DYNAB, should also be of some benefit. I will not be able to get to the work for a couple of years, but I will time the announcement properly. Commercial agreements I have spent a long while negotiating are also about to be made public.

Then it is true what they say about you.

What?

Nothing.—What is to become of von Hymack?

That is up to him. But I will see that he talks to Pels first, whatever. If he wishes, he can come to the clinic on Home-free, and Pels can orbit there and confer with the staff. In fact, as one of the few people with any idea as to what really occurred here, it might be a very good place for him to be—at least until after the voting.—And yes, I was born on Earth, a long time ago.

". . . Soft," Jackara said, stooping to pet Shind.

And warm, Shind added. *It comes in handy in this weather. I think John is returning. Why don't you tell him where you want to go now?*

Jackara stared at the approaching figure, then, "John," she called out, "take me back to the castle with the fiery moat. To Earth."

Morwin took her hand and nodded.

"Let's go," he said.

CHAPTER 6

One day there came a spring, curled and dotted, soft, green and brown, moist, and birds wheeled in the blue, shedding tumultuous notes of inquiry; the breezes were salt and cool from the sea that rolled as it rolled five thousand years ago; and the fires of the world were contained in proper chambers far beneath their feet, as they passed, slowly, amid the trees, the fields, the fresh-scrubbed hills.

Walking on within the globe of his desire, he thought of Pels, for he thought of music, invisible, weightless, consistent in terms of its own logic. He did not think of Francis Sandow, Heidel von Hymack or even the Commander, for she had just said, "It's a nice day," and yes, he thought, cloud in the sky, squirrel on the branch, girl, give it that much, give it that.

A DARK
TRAVELLING

To Cathy Kavanagh
in particular
and all of the other teachers
at Rio Grande School
in Santa Fe
who taught my children
to enjoy reading.

Prologue

The candle's flame was a bright leaf. Beyond the window a full moon hung in the evening sky. The house was absolutely still.

She stared into the flame, where many pasts swam, along with a multitude of presents and a confusion of futures. With practice these could be sorted, however, and she had had a lot of practice.

She forgot the house. She did not see the moon. After a time she was not even aware of the flame. Only the images held her attention; pasts, presents, and futures were shuffled like cards. . . .

She smiled faintly. A past, then. A true past of this place, for anchorage. . . .

. . . The man had laid out the rods and rolled the brass wheels. Now he walked, the wheels still clicking in his hand, his dark cloak and the feather in his hat undisturbed by any wind. His path led him through a place of whiteness, as if snow were banked at either hand. But the whiteness churned

slowly, drifting. Mist, fog . . . He moved like a phantom through the pale places. Before him, finally, there came a lessening, a fading. Faint outlines were beginning to take form. He did not change his pace, however, but continued on his way. Abruptly the mists were gone and the outlines sprang into full relief. The man stopped in a grassy area next to a road, regarding the distant prospect of a great city, its towers gleaming in the light of early day. Overhead something was descending towards an unseen destination, something large and metallic, its wings unflapping. As he watched, a metal vehicle with no visible means of propulsion passed rapidly along the road to his left.

'Sapristi!' the man exclaimed.

After a time, he began walking again.

She nodded, and the image faded, to be replaced by another. Futures, now . . .

. . . A lithe, dark-haired man clad in black was rising to his feet, a silver earring glistening on the lobe of his left ear. His hair was long and black, secured behind his head. He was smiling as he raised his hands before him, and she felt that they held death. They were reaching directly towards her.

' . . . And his name is Crow.'

The words flowed unbidden into her mind. She shuddered. Better to shuffle this one away. It was too menacing, and she did not want it to come to be. Pass on.

Try Now . . .

. . . The walls of an arroyo slid past at a dizzying rate, small dark outlines she knew to be piñon and juniper trees passed at either hand. She sensed the runner's controlled breathing.

The big moon cast shadows within the pale glow it had spread across the land. There was something wild, almost frantic in the movements of the boy who ran and ran. Now he threw his head back, and his mouth was open. His pace did not slacken, however.

She sighed, for she knew that this meant she would be subjected to loud rock music before too long. Brothers can be so trying. . . .

. . . Then there was the power station, its vibrating towers haloed in blue, dark conduits like sea serpents coiled about their feet. A small army was camped before the installation, facing a range of hills, where another army held its position. An occasional flash of light occurred within one camp or another. Nothing here had changed. Time to move closer, to try for a contact—

Abruptly, the scene vanished. Puzzled, she tried summoning it again. It took form slowly, hovered an instant, then vanished once more. Again she tried. This time it did not come at all. She shook her head. It was not the first time she had encountered this phenomenon. Later.

More Now . . .

. . . A body garbed in a white gi passed through the air above the hip of another gi-clad figure, a dark belt about its waist. She sensed rather than heard the cry that accompanied this. The figure landed upon the mat, arm slapping simultaneously at a forty-five-degree angle out to the side. Barry was at it again . . .

Unbidden, a new image occurred. . . .

• • •

. . . Dead. A city of broken buildings. Dust blowing along its littered streets. Heaps of rubble at every hand. No window left unshattered. Nothing stirring but the wind and the dust. . . .

It began to fade just as an almost familiar figure rounded a corner. She let it go. She had not called for this one.

Then she realized that it had been a future rather than a present and she swore softly. She should probably have tried holding it for a better look.

She relaxed and continued to watch. . . .

. . . A wolf was running through a forest. . . .

She watched for a long while, but that was all there was to it. As monotonous as watching Jim running back in the arroyos. She dismissed the wolf. Nothing useful there. She tried again for the two armies, and the vision came and went and stayed away.

Suddenly she saw Tom, next door, down in the transcomp room, puttering with the machinery. She became aware that something was rushing towards him. From where, she did not know. What it was, she could not make out. But she knew that it was threatening and that it was on its way, right now, this minute, and she cried out, though she knew that he could not hear her. In that instant everything she had seen flowed together into a single general vision. She did not understand it, but for a moment she felt its connectedness.

She screamed, and the image went away and the candle went out. Only the pattern remained, signifying menace, overlaid with her sudden fear. But despite the fear she was on her feet and running, out the door, down a hallway, towards a stair. . . .

Smoking candle. Empty room.

CHAPTER 1

My father was the keeper of the Eddystone Light.... Know that song? If you don't, it doesn't matter. It's just that it always reminds me of home.

I'm a normal fourteen-year-old boy, my name is James Wiley, and I live in a large building in a southwestern state capital in the United States. My sister Becky is a witch, my older brother Dave lives in a castle, and our exchange student Barry is a trained assassin. I also have an uncle named George who is a werewolf. And my own palms do get itchy whenever there's a full moon, so I guess I have some of the same genes. It *must* be the genes. I try to be scientific about these matters, because I'm going to be a scientist one of these days.

Unfortunately, there was a full moon for a while earlier that evening. That's when the trouble began, and, of course, I wasn't home. I'd smeared on the cortisone cream Dr. Holmes had prescribed for what he called my 'monthly palmar dermatitis,' and it was working okay. But I also get restless on these occasions, and I take long walks in the arroyos out back. Well, I jog through them usually. But don't misunderstand. I don't change shape or anything like that. I don't even howl much.

I came in from my moonlight jog sweaty and very hungry—the same as always. The first thing I do at such times is raid the refrigerator. Then I take a shower. Then I put on more cream. Then I go to my room and play loud music and pace. This usually irritates Becky, whose room is two doors up the hall from mine, because whenever there's a full moon she turns out the lights in her room and stares at a candle flame for hours. She's weird.

I did not get as far as all that this time, though. I came in the back way, remembering the hamburger in the meat drawer, and Becky was waiting for me right by the door and she was holding a brown paper bag in her left hand and looking upset. Now, Becky is a tough little blonde thing and she is somewhere around my age, maybe even a little older—fifteen, say—and it had been a long time since I'd seen her upset about anything. So when she said, 'Come on!' and grabbed hold of my hand and turned away I followed her.

She led me through our part of the building and over to the heavy metal door that separates us from the foundation headquarters. Then she released me and stuck her right hand into the bag she was carrying. A moment later I heard a very suspicious *click* as she raised the bag and pointed it at the door.

'Becky!' I said. 'What have you got in that bag?'

'You already guessed,' she said, her voice steady. 'Just listen to me, Jim. I want you to go over to my left, reach across and unbolt the door, then give it a push and get back out of the way.'

'You've got to be kidding,' I said. 'You mean, you're going to start blazing away when that door opens?'

'Only if something tries to come through it,' she said.

'Uh, I don't know where you got it, but I think you'd better let me have the gun.'

'Nope,' she said. 'Because you might freeze up, and I know I won't.'

I looked at her narrowed green eyes, at her tight shoulders, and I thought of some things about her that I hadn't thought of for a long time. I knew then that she could do it if it needed doing, and I wasn't all that sure I could.

'Okay,' I said, and I moved into position, unfastened the door and gave it a push.

I stepped back fast, and a few moments later I sighed, for there was nothing there, nothing waiting to rush through and do us harm. I hadn't realized until then that I'd been holding my breath.

The light was on in the hallway and there was no one in sight in either direction. No unusual sounds came to us, either. There was a foreign human odour, though. Also blood.

'Now can you tell me what's going on?' I asked.

'If only Barry were here,' she answered.

Great! Nothing like it to make you feel important. *If only Barry were here.* He was not here, of course, because he was off at a dojo, kicking, blocking, and punching. Or was it the other dojo? In that case he'd be throwing, grappling, locking. Whatever, he was off practising those things Becky wanted him for now, things I gather he'd started doing at about the time he'd learned to walk. It irritated me that she talked about him as if he were an adult and still treated me like a kid. After all, he was only a year older than me.

Becky moved forward, throwing switches, lighting the way ahead. I followed her along the hallway to the right, which led to the reception area, peering into two vacant offices we passed.

I halted at the desk, behind which hung the sign reading TRANSIT FOUNDATION.

'Well, Barry *isn't* here,' I said. 'So I think you'd better tell me about it. I've already smelled blood.'

She turned suddenly then, beneath the big picture of Leonardo da Vinci standing with his back to a table on which a mess of brass gears and shafts is strewn. The corner of some construction juts from behind his left arm. He is smiling faintly. It is a self-portrait. It is not in any of the art books. No one has ever spotted it for what it was.

'Shh!' Becky said, raising one finger to her lips. Then she whispered, 'Just wait a bit!'

I nodded, and she turned away and I followed her. We inspected two more offices, a small conference room, and a coatroom. They were all, mercifully, empty. But I was already pretty sure of that, by sniffing.

We came to the foot of the stairs and she looked up into the darkness and shuddered. The smells were present here also.

'I can't!' she said softly. 'I can't—go upstairs.'

I put my hand on her shoulder.

'You don't have to,' I said. 'Do you?'

She continued to stare into the darkness.

'I guess not,' she said. 'There's probably nothing . . . really there. Now now.'

'I wish I knew what was going on.'

'Come on,' she said at last. 'I'll show you.' And, 'I'm sorry,' she added.

'What do you mean?'

'Just come,' she said, leading me away from the stair in

the direction of the small storeroom to the rear of the building.

I wanted to scream but I followed her instead. A nasty movie had begun playing in my mind and I couldn't switch it off. I'd been telling myself all along that she'd just heard a few noises and was nervous.

She led me into the storeroom, which was lit. We made our way past mops and buckets, a rack full of cleaning compounds, and a stack of folding chairs to the place where she began to fiddle with the hidden latch. A moment later a section of the wall swung away from us, revealing a short, narrow flight of stairs leading downward. This corridor was also illuminated, by an overhead fixture, and there was a metal door at its end. The hidden room behind the metal door was actually above ground level, despite the descent, because of the slope of the land. It was a windowless border place, designed so that anybody connected with the foundation who glanced out a window at that odd corner would think it a part of our living quarters next door, if they thought about it at all. And vice versa, if we had guests. We haven't had many, though, since my mother's death earlier in the year.

I followed Becky down the steps and up to the door. 'Are we going to do that SWAT team business again?' I whispered.

She just shook her head and pushed the door open.

I followed her into the transcomp room. The lights were on, and the place was a mess. Becky slumped into a metal folding chair, handed me the paper bag, and began to cry.

I looked around, and I saw a stain on the floor, over by the main console. I already knew what it was before I crossed the room and stopped to examine the smear. My sense of smell is abnormally acute, and it's even better on nights such as that one. I could tell that my father had been in here earlier, and I could tell that blood had been shed. I could have told these things with the lights out. There was also the stranger's odour, which I had detected upstairs.

When I rose I looked again at the transcomp, and I saw a place where it had been damaged. It was still switched on and humming faintly, but only one of the indicator lights was burning. Something had obviously shorted when it had been bashed. I reached over and flipped the power switch to off.

The logbook lay on the floor. I picked it up, smoothed some bent pages, and read the latest entry. Dad had signed in a little over an hour ago. That was all. No mention of what bands he'd be running or anything like that. I replaced the book on its shelf and looked in the drawer where he kept his revolver. The drawer was already partly open and, of course, there was no gun there, because it had to be in the bag I was holding.

I reached into the bag and removed the thing carefully. Yep. I held the weapon he normally kept in the drawer, easing the hammer back into position and popping the cylinder. I already knew that it had been fired, from the smell. I was curious, though.... Yes, one round had been discharged. Then I closed it again, not sure whether to put it back in the drawer or to keep holding it until I knew what had happened.

'Where'd you find the gun?' I asked Becky.

'On the floor,' she said, 'over there,' and she pointed to the far corner of the room.

'What were you doing down here anyway?'

'I was in my room meditating,' she said, 'and I kept getting these feelings that something terrible was going to happen. Then I heard the gunshot. So I ran downstairs and I listened by the door for a while. But I didn't hear anything else. Finally I opened the door and I came on down. The place was empty and looked just the way it does now—except for the gun,' she added, gesturing again.

'So what did you do?'

'I picked up the gun and put it in a paper bag I saw in the wastebasket—because I didn't want to touch it any more than I had to. But if something really bad was going on I thought I might need it. Then I went back upstairs and over to our place, and I locked the door. I went to the kitchen after that and waited for you.'

'You said you knew that the shot came from here,' I stated. 'How could you tell? It would be pretty muffled down here. It could easily have been from somewhere outside.'

She shook her head. 'Tom had just gone over,' she said. 'He told me he was going right before he went. Then about five minutes later I heard the shot. The timing was just right for him to have come down here, turned everything on, and logged in.'

I licked my lips, which felt very dry, and I nodded. Tom Wiley is my father. He is not Becky's father, though, so she calls him by his first name intead of Dad or something like that. It's the way they worked it out between them.

'Did he say anything about what he planned on doing here?' I asked.

'No.'

'Did he get any phone calls or visitors before he came over?'

'I didn't hear the phone ring,' she answered, 'or the doorbell either. Why?'

'I was trying to figure whether he was attacked from this side or some other.'

'Oh. I never thought of that.'

'In fact, a whole bunch of odd questions come to mind,' I said. 'First, whose blood is that on the floor? Dad's? Or the other guy's?'

'I'd guessed it was Tom's,' she said. 'If he'd hurt the other guy there would be no reason for him to run away. He'd have a wounded prisoner—or a corpse. Hey! Maybe he killed the guy and took the body away with him to get rid of the evidence somewhere.'

'I don't think so,' I said. 'If that had been the case he'd be back by now. It's been over an hour.'

'Could they have been fighting, got into the field and both been transitted out?' she asked.

I gestured at the console. 'Then how could the machine have been damaged after they were gone?'

'Okay. I'm not thinking clearly,' she said. 'But what are we going to do?'

I glanced back up the stairway.

'You're right. We'd better do something. I'll save my other questions for later. Come on.'

'Where?'

'We're going to close up here,' I said. 'Leave everything just the way it is for now. Then we're going back next door and I'm going to wake up the Golem.'

'Do I have to be there when you do it?' she asked. 'I don't like the thing at all.'

'I know,' I told her. 'But it has to scan you while I press the button, so it'll know you're okay and leave you alone.'

'But Tom did that one other time—'

'Yes, but it has to be reprogrammed each time it's turned on. It does work for *us*, though, you know. Besides I'm going to bring it over here to patrol the place. You won't even have to look at it then.'

'I know, but. . . . Okay, let's get it over with.'

We turned out the light, closed the door, and started up the stairway.

'Your face looks dirty,' she said.

'That shouldn't make any difference to a Golem,' I told her.

CHAPTER 2

We stopped on the way and hung the CLOSED sign in the window of the front entrance. I was afraid I'd forget to do it later, and I was sure that it would not be business as usual tomorrow. I realized as I did it that I should get on the phone and call Mrs. Dell, the secretary, and ask her to get in touch with everyone on the staff and tell them not to come in. As I decided this it also occurred to me that I should check the appointment book and see whether anyone was scheduled to stop by tomorrow. They should also be phoned and told to make it another time.

Damn! There was suddenly so much to do, and I was sure I hadn't thought of everything.

We returned to our side of the building and locked the door behind us. Then we climbed the stairs to the second floor and went into Dad's bedroom. Becky hung back at the doorway while I crossed to the area in front of the closet and rolled back the rug.

I caught hold of the recessed ringbolt and pulled

upward on it. The door in the floor creaked open, and I heard Becky say, 'Oh!'

I didn't blame her, actually, because Golly still scares me a little, even though I've done maintenance work on him and I know I'm safe so long as I do what I'm supposed to.

I start calling him Golly whenever I'm near him, possibly to make him seem less like something on a late night scare show. He's only a little over five feet tall, but he's much bulkier than any normal person you're likely to meet, unless you hang around in some awfully odd places. His skin, which is synthetic, is colourless; also, he has absolutely no hair, not even eyebrows. He hasn't got much in the way of a neck either, and his hands and feet are very large. He kind of reminds me of a short, mean-looking Mr. Clean. He's not really alive, he's awfully strong and fast, and he's not afraid of anything. All of the transit centres have one just like him around somewhere, in case of emergencies.

I knelt and removed the clear plastic wrapping covering him. He didn't stir, of course. He doesn't even breathe. I unzipped the top of his black jumpsuit and opened the panel on his chest.

When I pressed the button that says ACTIVATE he opened his very blue eyes, sat up, and then stood. He remained in that position and would continue to do so until he received further instructions.

I stood directly in front of him and pressed the PASS button. This was followed by a faint *click* from behind the panel.

'Okay, Becky,' I said. 'You've got to come here for a minute.'

She didn't answer, and when I turned and looked she was simply staring at Golly.

'I can't,' she said. 'You'll have to come and get me.'

'Okay,' I answered, and I went over and took her hand.

I led her back and she squeezed my hand very hard the whole way. As soon as I'd pushed the button and heard another *click* she let go and backed away fast.

'We're safe now,' I said, hitting FOLLOW. 'He knows we're okay.'

Then I took hold of Golly's hand, which feels something like a rubberized raincoat, and gave a slight tug. He responded by stepping up out of his storage cell and following me for a few paces. I left him to go back and close the hatch and to restore the rug to its former position. He stood stock still while I did this. When I returned to guide him again Becky was already waiting out in the hall.

He followed me along like a child, his grip strangely gentle, moving soundlessly on his large bare feet. Becky walked so that I was always positioned between Golly and her.

When we reached the downstairs hallway I heard a knocking sound coming from the metal door. It struck me that it might have been going on as a kind of background noise for some time, and that I'd been partly aware of it while I was occupied upstairs.

Somehow I didn't think that the one we were worried about would be knocking. Sneaking about, yes. Knocking, no.

So I called out, 'Who's there?'

'Bill Jeeter,' came the reply from beyond the door, 'with your cleaning service. I came in the back way and I just now saw your sign out front. I wanted to know if you'd be needing us tomorrow night.'

'No,' I said, thinking fast. 'I think they're planning some remodelling. In fact, it would be better if you don't clean tonight either. It'll just get messed up again.'

There followed a moment of silence, then, 'I'll still have to bill you for coming out,' he said.

'That's okay,' I answered. 'I'm sorry they didn't notify you.'

'Me, too,' he answered gruffly, and I heard something like the rattle of a bucket handle. 'Tell them to call when they want us back, will you?'

'I will,' I said, and again, 'sorry.'

I heard the rattle once more and the sound of footsteps going away.

I sighed.

'It's hard to think of everything,' I said.

Becky glanced at Golly.

'Now what?' she asked.

'We have to give them time to clear out,' I said, 'before I set him to patrolling in there.'

I opened the closet door, led Golly inside, and left him.

'Do you really think there could still be someone else here?' she asked.

'Maybe upstairs next door,' I said. 'Maybe not, too. But I don't want to go and look. As soon as it's clear, Golly can go and check the place out. If there's someone there, he'll capture whoever it is and we can question him.'

'Or it,' she said. 'You still haven't said why you think someone would still be there after this much time.'

'The transcomp was broken, and it had to be done from this side. That means someone had to be there to break it. And that means that person couldn't use it afterwards to get away himself.'

'Or itself,' she said. 'I see what you mean. So it's either still in there somewhere or it's taken off outside.'

'I think so,' I said, turning away and heading for the kitchen. I was still starved.

'So where's Tom?' she asked.

'I think he was hurt but got away through the machine,' I told her. 'Whoever was responsible couldn't follow for one reason or another. So he damaged the equipment so no one else could follow Dad either.'

'Stranding himself here?'

'Yes.'

'Why?'

'I don't know,' I answered as I opened the refrigerator. 'But I'm sure nothing good is involved.'

I opened the meat drawer and located the package of hamburgers.

'So why not the other way around?' she asked.

'What do you mean?'

'Say the attacker got away and Tom fell against the equipment and damaged it. Then he crawled off and. . . . ' Her voice faded.

I shook my head.

'Doesn't make sense,' I answered. 'He'd have come back here or headed for the nearest telephone. Or we'd have found him down there. No reason for him to crawl off and hide.'

'Yes,' she said, nodding slowly. 'I guess you're right. Unless neither one was able to get away through the machine and whoever it was kidnapped Tom.'

'You said you got down there pretty fast after you heard the shot, didn't you?' I asked.

'Yes.'

'Did you hear anyone leaving?'

'No, I didn't.'

I shrugged.

'Gee, that's gross—to eat raw hamburger that way.'

'I like it like this.'

'Hey! That's not dirt on your face. It's—'

We heard the front door open and close. Simultaneously, we both looked at the brown paper bag on the table.

But a moment later I heard a scream, and I knew that it was all right. It was not just any scream. It was a *kiai*, the kind of yell martial artists give when they attack.

I rushed out of the kitchen, heading for the front hall.

'It's all right, Barry!' I cried, just as another *kiai* sounded. 'Barry! It's okay!'

I reached the hall in time to see Barry kick Golly in the stomach. Of course nothing happened. I hadn't activated the system that would have caused him to fight back. Golly just stood there in the closet and absorbed the blow without stirring.

'Honest, it's okay,' I said. 'Your people must have a Golem back home.'

'That's a Golem?' he asked, stepping back and staring. 'I've heard them mention it, but I'd never seen the thing.'

'That's a Golem,' I said.

He picked a light jacket up off the floor.

'I was just going to hang this up,' he explained. 'He ... kind of surprised me. What's he doing in the closet, anyway?'

Barry is my height, but he's a lot heavier in the shoulders. His hair is straight and brown, a couple of shades lighter than mine, and his eyes are hazel. His movements are very graceful, almost like a dancer's, and I've seen him break bricks with his hands.

'We were waiting for the cleaning service to leave before I sent him in next door,' I said.

'I didn't see their truck when I came up,' he stated.

'Good,' I said. 'They're gone. In that case I'll do it now.'

I took Golly's hand and led him out of the closet, pausing to press PASS for Barry. Then I guided Golly to the metal door.

'What's going on?' Barry asked.

'Wait till I get this done and I'll tell you all about it,' I said.

I opened the door and took Golly inside. I led him back and around to the foot of the stairway. Then I opened the panel on his chest and pressed the PATROL button. My finger hesitated for a moment over the KILL button; I moved it and pressed SUBDUE. I stepped aside and watched him mount the stairs.

'Hey, you need a shave,' Barry said.

'Huh?' I asked, rubbing my chin. 'I just shaved last month.' It did feel kind of fuzzy. 'It's the full moon,' I said.

'So what are you sending that—thing—after?' he asked.

'Let's go back to the kitchen,' I said. 'I'll tell you while I finish eating. We've got a lot to do.'

We cut through the reception area on the way back. Another glance at the portrait hanging there set me to thinking. . . .

There was a time in the middle of the eighteenth century when French possessions blocked westward expansion of English colonies in America. If England had not won the Seven Years War, North America might well have been divided very differently than it is today, with a New England in the East, a New France in the middle, and a New Spain out West. Supposing England had not won the Seven Years War and that *somewhere* this situation prevails?

Supposing Cortés's tiny, lucky band of troops had not been quite so lucky and the Aztecs had not been conquered. . . .

Supposing the Russians had decided not to sell Alaska to the United States. . . .

Supposing Charles Martel had lost the Battle of Tours back in the eighth century, and Muslim troops had swept on up into Europe. Might we have a copy of the Koran rather than a Gideon Bible in hotel rooms today?

Supposing there had been an all-out atomic war and there were no humans left alive. . . .

Supposing the Crusades had not occurred, or had gone differently. . . .

Or go way back, and suppose the last Ice Age had lasted longer, or ended sooner. Or supposing humans had developed different abilities than those they have now and had learned magic rather than, say, calculus. . . .

Supposing that each of these possibilities were true, and many others as well, and that somewhere there is a world, a whole version of reality, where this is exactly the case. Supposing all of these worlds run together, side by side, parallel, as it were, emerging from their various decision points in history and pre-history. Supposing a transit device were possible, a means of tuning into and travelling among these versions of reality, these parallel worlds. If enough worlds existed, it would seem that there would be one or more where such a device was discovered.

Supposing it had happened here—say, back around the time of the Renaissance. And supposing it was realized that while full exposure to these other bands of reality would be disastrous to our entire civilization, a limited exposure could be of great benefit. . . .

Supposing only a few individuals existed on each such world—a family, perhaps—who possessed the means of transit and were responsible for the commerce among these bands of reality. Supposing a necessity for secrecy led them to assume the appearance of something other than what they were—say, perhaps, a think tank, a foundation. . . .

One might also suppose that these families would become related over the years, that there would be frequent visits and even something like a student exchange programme for the kids.

Just supposing, of course.

Barry comes from a pretty tough place. My sister Becky is a witch. My brother Dave currently lives in a castle. I also have an uncle named George who is a werewolf.

I've done a lot of visiting but I haven't done my hitch as an exchange student yet. I get my turn after Dave comes back.

CHAPTER 3

We call them 'bands,' these parallel worlds, after the areas on the transcomp's control indicator where we tune the transit field. The word transcomp, by the way, refers to the partnership of a transit machine with a computer—a situation which makes the work an awful lot easier than it was in the old days, back before computers were available. Of course, we had our computer several generations before anyone else did in this band, so we've been calling it a transcomp for a pretty long time.

Just as computers were developed in another band before they were developed here, Golly comes from yet another band, where they've long been expert at building androids—which is what he is, a soft robot.

There are a dozen-plus parallel worlds with which we do varying amounts of business. We call these the 'light-bands.' Then there are a number of bands that we know about, where we have observers in residence, but where we do nothing other than watch. For most of these—some of them recently discovered—we either do not know enough yet to try to be of help, or it has been determined that any interference on our part at this point in their development might do more harm than good. We call these the 'greybands.'

Then there are a few worlds where things went very wrong and there are no people left alive. These are the deadbands. We have learned a lot from them, though, just as we have from the greybands. And this makes us very careful about what we allow to cross from one band to another.

And there is one more category: the darkbands. There are three of them. Once there was only one. The inhabitants of that one have no scruples against interfering grossly in the normal development of other worlds, in exploiting their people, their resources, their technologies. They may well even be responsible for some of the deadbands. And that brings things full circle. For the lightbands were inadvertently responsible for the first darkband, a long time ago. In their zeal to help a developing world along, the lightbands had given too much of a good thing too soon to a promising civilization—including transit technology—with a disastrous effect upon its culture. We learned an expensive lesson from that darkband, and that is why we have been very, very careful in these matters ever since.

I have visited the greybands, the deadbands, and all but one of the lightbands. Seeing something of them all is considered a necessary part of one's education, in the families. We also study the histories of each of them, which is why I can be so glib when it comes to making up examples involving decision points and parallel worlds. Having to learn your own history is rough enough; having to learn a whole bunch of them is that much harder. The worst ones to learn are the ones which are the most similar to your own. But it does teach you a certain facility in playing games with the past.

I might add that I've never visited a darkband. But that's okay with me. I get the impression that we maintain covert agents in those places and that they do the same with us. But there is no normal commerce with them.

We talked about these matters in the kitchen after we'd filled Barry in on what had occurred. It seemed a reasonable conclusion that a darkband had to be behind what had happened, zeroing in on our equipment and waiting for it to be activated. Barry thought it possible that they had wanted to abduct a lightband transit operator in order to obtain some piece of technical information or other concerning our operations. He felt that Dad might well now be a darkband prisoner.

When I said that they couldn't have taken him away with the equipment damaged, he pointed out that whoever had come through could have brought a portable transit unit with him, smashed ours after subduing my father, and departed with him by means of his own gear—effectively isolating us and preventing us from notifying the other lightbands for a time. This thought had not occurred to me, and it depressed me even more than the guesses I had made so far.

I had assumed that whatever was going on was a part of something directed against our entire band rather than any particular individual. I thought this because of penetrations they had attempted in the past, elsewhere. Also, I found myself wanting to believe that Dad had escaped, because it gave us a chance of finding him, whereas I didn't know what we could do if he were a darkband prisoner.

I kept on eating while we talked. It sounds callous, but I couldn't help it. My metabolism just gets wild at certain times, and this was one of those occasions.

'Either he left by means of our equipment or he didn't,' I said.

Barry nodded.

'If he didn't, we can't be sure where he is,' I continued.

'If he did use our equipment, it should still be set at the transit band he went out on!' he said.

'Unless it got jiggled,' Becky added, 'when it was damaged. Weren't you just telling me the other day how sensitive that tuner is?'

I nodded.

'But not all of the bands are close together,' I said. 'If it's in the vicinity of one that's at a pretty isolated frequency, that will be enough.'

'But some of them *are* close together,' Barry said.

I put the empty plastic tray into the rubbish. My hunger was finally gone.

'It's kind of silly to talk about it,' I said, 'when we can go and look in a few minutes.'

'Let's go and look now,' he said, reaching for the paper bag in the middle of the table.

'Let Golly finish his search,' I told him.

'I'm not afraid to go in there.'

'I'm sure you're not,' I said, wondering whether he ever dropped that macho business. He'd been living with us for five months now, and he always seemed to have a bit of a chip on his shoulder. 'But it's his job, and I've got to go and call Mrs Dell anyway.' I rubbed my chin. 'I might even shave,' I added. 'Maybe you ought to eat something, too, while you're waiting. You might need some extra energy later.'

He thought a moment, smiled, and nodded again. 'You may be right,' he said. 'Okay. Go and call her. I'll grab some calories.'

I did that thing, and it turned out that she remembered the appointments list too, and said she'd call everybody.

When she asked how long we'd be shut down I didn't know what to tell her, though. So I said that we'd have to let her know. Of course, she realized that something unusual was afoot, and since she isn't in on family secrets I wasn't quite certain what to say when she asked, 'What's the matter, Jim? What's going on?'

'Well, it's . . . ' and I remembered the magic word ' . . . classified,' I said.

'Oh,' she replied. 'Well, I hope everything's all right.'

'It may be soon,' I said. 'I don't know yet.'

'Is there anything I can do to help?'

'No,' I told her. 'Thanks. We appreciate it. We'll call you as soon as things are straightened out. Goodbye.'

I hung up, hoping that that took care of the remaining loose ends, and I went upstairs and got out the electric razor Dad had given me for a birthday present. I'd only need to use it a few times, but when I looked in the mirror I could see that it was time to plug it in again. Funny. I hadn't noticed I'd looked all that fuzzy this morning when I was brushing my teeth, but the full moon effects had been getting stronger in recent months, and I'd a strong feeling it was tied in with this.

I had just finished and had opened a bottle of after-shave stuff I had also been given—deciding against using it, because it irritated my nose—when I heard a scream from next door. I ran the length of the hall and took the stairs like a mountain goat. It was a man's voice, and since Golems are voiceless it meant that Golly had just surprised someone and was in the process of doing the SUBDUE bit. And since the cleaning service had departed, it seemed to me that *this* could be our man, poking around, trying to get into the locked files or the safe, where some pretty sensitive materials might be found. Of course. It was the logical thing for a darkhand intruder to do try to steal our secrets to learn what it was that we wanted to introduce into this society at this time to strengthen it, increase its flexibility, make it too strong for them to be able to exploit.

So I ran. Not just because I was eager to see what he looked like, but because I wanted to get there before Barry did. Maybe I was misjudging him, but that warrior society in which he'd grown up had a pretty stern code in some life-and-death matters, and I was afraid if he got it into his head he was protecting Becky and me we might not get a chance to talk to the prisoner. On the other hand, the head of a household is a strong authority figure where he comes from, and with Dad and Dave gone, I was in charge. If I could just get there in time and remind him of this I'd a feeling things would be all right.

I heard another scream; also some interesting profanity. It sounded as if it came from upstairs next door and to the rear.

When I reached the downstairs hallway I saw that Barry was already at the door, opening it. And he carried the paper bag in his left hand. Becky was nowhere in sight. I raced towards him.

'Barry!" I called. 'Wait!'

But he'd already gone through the entrance.

I reached it and passed inside. I turned, then, and headed along the hallway to the rear. There came another outburst from upstairs, and the voice sounded vaguely familiar.

As I turned the corner into the rear hallway, I caught sight of Barry starting up the stairs, his right hand plunged into the bag.

'I'm in charge here, Barry, when my Dad is gone!' I yelled. 'And I said *stop!*'

He slowed and looked at me.

'Wait up, damn it!' I added.

He halted and sighed.

'I'm better fit to handle this thing, Jim,' he said.

'Probably so—if we do it your way,' I answered, finally reaching the foot of the stairs and turning. 'But don't. You'll blow our cover.'

'What do you mean?' he asked as I began climbing.

'I mean that the bird is flown,' I said softly. 'The smell is gone, and I recognize that voice. You might have, too, if you'd paid more attention. You keep that weapon in the bag and don't do anything that'll make this even harder for me to explain.'

'Uh, sure, Jim,' he said almost meekly. 'I didn't—'

I hurried past him and turned left when I reached the head of the stairs. I made for the library, then, which is also the main conference room, because that's where it seemed the sounds were coming from.

Through the open entrance I could see that the lights were turned on. The sounds of scuffling had ceased, but the voice I'd recognized was now pleading rather than cursing or shouting.

'Let me go, will you? That hurts. Why won't you answer me? I—'

I ran into the room and saw where Golly held a man sprawled face downward on a tabletop while he twisted his arm up behind his back with one hand and pushed on his shoulder with the other.

This was a very good position—for me, that is, not for the man who was in it. It was good because he couldn't see what I was doing as I unzipped the top of Golly's jumpsuit, opened the panel, pushed PASS, closed the panel, and drew the zipper closed again, setting some sort of speed record for the action.

Golly released him suddenly and I was at the man's side in an instant.

'Dr Wade,' I said. 'It's me, Jim Wiley. I'm very sorry for what just happened, but—'

'*Just what the devil is going on?*' he exclaimed, rising and turning towards me.

Then he saw Golly and he began to back away, edging along the table. He raised his arm and pointed.

'That man attacked me!' he announced.

'Yes, sir. He's a security guard,' I said. 'We had a problem here earlier, and he was sent over to keep an eye on things.'

'But I told him I'm a member of the foundation, that I have identification in my wallet. He paid no attention whatso—'

'He doesn't understand English,' I said, truthfully. 'He was the best we could get on short notice.'

'You should have done something,' he said, 'to prevent authorized people from being assaulted.'

'We did,' I answered, not realizing till after I said it that it might be taken as an impertinence. 'We hung out the CLOSED sign.'

'Not on the back door, you didn't,' he stated, 'and that's the one my key fits. If any other members were to show up that's the way they'd come in, too.'

'I'm sorry,' I said again. 'You're right, of course. I'll post a notice there as soon as I go downstairs. It's my fault. I should have thought of that. It never even occurred to me that anyone might come by at this hour.'

He adjusted his glasses and ran a hand through his wiry grey and brown hair. He was a tall, lanky man, a mathematician who worked at the lab. up in Los Alamos. He was also the head of one of the foundation-sponsored projects, and he did indeed have every right to be here any time he chose, should he need to go through the project files or something related.

'What sort of problem did you have earlier?' he asked.

'Someone tried to break in,' I said. 'It seems he got frightened off, though.'

He glanced past me at Barry, who was standing quietly beside the door.

'Why are you boys over here, then?' he wanted to know.

'My father got called away suddenly earlier in the evening,' I explained. 'I'm sure he would have thought to put the sign up out back.'

'I trust he'll be back soon,' Dr Wade said.

'I really hope so,' I replied.

'His absence is related to this—security matter?'

'Oh yes. Very much so,' I answered.

He smoothed his shirtfront and began picking up some scattered papers and placing them into a Manilla folder, from which they had fallen.

'Well, you seem to have done the right thing in calling a security person and closing the place down,' he said, 'though it was probably only your standard urban prowler, and I'm sure he's long gone. Look, I drove all the way down from the Hill because I only had my personal notes on a meeting we'd had last week, and I wanted to go over the whole file.'

He tapped the folder with his forefinger.

'I was planning on taking one of the bedrooms upstairs,' he went on, 'and staying over after I'd reviewed this stuff. I'm willing to take my chances. I doubt that whoever it was will come back, now you've been alerted. And even if he does,'—he glanced at Golly and smiled—'I'd feel safe.'

What could I say? I didn't like it, but I felt outranked.

'I guess that's your decision to make,' I began, but—'

'Good,' he said, squeezing my shoulder. 'It's a fair drive back, and falling asleep at the wheel is probably a bigger danger than anything going on down here.'

'Would you like us to make you a pot of coffee?'

'No, thanks. I brought a Thermos.'

I noticed as he glanced that way that an overnight bag rested on the chair beside the door.

'Funny,' he said, crossing the room and picking up the bag. 'There seems to be stuff about this meeting that I don't remember.' He waved the folder. 'I must have been dozing when someone circulated the equations.'

'Equations?' I said.

'Yes, there's a whole sheet of them I don't recall at all. Kind of fascinating, too. I'm looking forward to going over them. Good night, Jim. You too, Barry.'

He headed out the doorway and left us standing there with our Golem and a feeling that things had somehow grown even stranger.

CHAPTER 4

We made another sign there in the library, and we put it up on the back door when we went downstairs. We set Golly to continue his patrolling, since we knew he wouldn't bother Dr Wade any more. We also made sure that the mathematician was well settled in his room upstairs and, hopefully, unlikely to wander. When these things were done we returned next door to our kitchen, where Becky still waited.

The first thing that Barry said to me when we were back in our own quarters was, 'Are you sure that's really Dr Wade?'

'Yes,' I answered. 'I am.'

'Some of those darkbanders are shapeshifters, you know.'

'I know,' I said, 'and he's not one of them. They can't shift their smell. I know his. Also, the strange smell that was there earlier is just about gone now.'

'It's safe to go over, then?' Becky asked.

'I'm sure of it.'

'So what do we do now?' Barry asked.

'We all go back to the transcomp room.'

'Why?'

'There's something I want to see—a clue I missed, I think.'

'What kind of clue?' Becky wanted to know.

I turned and left the kitchen with both of them following.

'The more I think of it, the more I'm certain that Dad escaped through the transit field,' I said. 'Whoever he'd been fighting with didn't. That's why I smelled him all over the place earlier. But he's gone now too.'

'So?' Barry asked. 'We don't know where they went and we're stuck with a broken machine.'

'One thing at a time,' I said, as we passed back into the foundation hallway. 'The most important thing right now is to figure out where Dad went.'

Barry nodded.

'And if he did transit out, we ought to be able to tell where he is from the band setting.'

'Yeah,' Barry agreed, quickly. 'You may be right . . . ' he paused a moment and then added, ' . . . but what if the other guy changed the setting afterwards to confuse us?'

'Why should he have?' I answered. 'If he broke the machine and we can't use it, it doesn't matter. Besides, I get the impression he was in a hurry.'

We entered the storeroom, turned on the light, and advanced to the panel. In a moment I had it open and we were heading down the stairs.

We entered the transcomp room, which was unchanged, and I hurried forward and read the band setting. I found it puzzling, but I pulled the chart from the drawer to confirm what my memory was telling me. In the meantime, Barry had come up and was studying the dial.

'That's a darkband setting,' he stated. 'The third one, I think.'

He was right, and I nodded.

'Yes,' I said, 'but since our equipment doesn't penetrate there, there has to be another explanation. And I think I see it.' I reached out and tapped with my knuckles, hard, above the dial. The indicator dropped. 'See?' I said. 'It probably jumped when the equipment was struck.'

'But is it in a real band right now?' he asked. 'Or is it just out of tune?'

I waved the chart.

'This is a dense area,' I said. 'That's a bona fide band it fell to.'

'Which one is it?'

'Well, it's a deadband,' I said.

'Hmm.'

He reached forward and recalibrated the tuner to the original setting. Abruptly he struck the chassis beneath the dial. This time the needle jogged upward.

'Anything there?' he asked.

'Yes. A lightband.'

'Hmm.'

'I see what you mean,' I said. 'It could have jumped to the darkband from above or below.'

'Exactly,' he replied. 'Are there any others adjacent to these?'

'No.'

'I didn't think so. I thought I remembered that cluster.'

Becky came forward and studied the chart.

'I've visited both of those bands,' Barry said. 'You have, too, of course.'

'No,' I replied. 'Only the deadband.'

'I thought you'd been to all of the lightbands.'

'All but one,' I said, 'and that's the one.'

'How come you didn't go there?'

'Well, that's where my Uncle George lives.'

'So?'

'He's a shapeshifter, and I seem to take after him. Something about that place is particularly conducive to the phenomenon. He'd cautioned my folks not to bring me there until I was older and could gain conscious control of the process. Otherwise there was the possibility I might turn into a wolf and run off into the wilds.'

'So that's what this full moon business has been about with you?'

'Yep.'

He drummed his fingers on the tabletop for a moment, then said, 'And that might very well be the band he'd flee to, if he has a brother there.'

'Brother-in-law,' I corrected. 'It's Mum's folks. But yes, you're right. That could be it.'

'On the other hand,' Becky said suddenly, 'a deadband could be a very good hiding place.'

'There is that,' I said. 'But why?'

'Why what?'

'Why hide? All he really had to do was get away. They obviously wanted to penetrate here, and they succeeded. There's nothing really personal about something like that. He just happened to be in the way. They wouldn't be chasing after him now. They'd be about the business they'd come to take care of.'

'I wonder . . . ' she said.

'What?'

'Whether there might not be more to it than that,' she finished.

'Why should there be?'

'Just a feeling I have,' she said. 'Just a funny feeling.'

I shrugged. Nobody ever tells me anything.

'Your feeling doesn't matter if we can't go after him,' Barry said. 'And if we could, it still doesn't matter. He's safe from the darkbanders now—if they really came after him personally.'

She pointed at the dial.

'A darkbander could have looked at that and come to the same conclusion you did,' she said.

He chewed his lower lip for a moment.

'Okay, you've got a point,' he said then. 'There *might* be darkband agents after him, and we should be careful if we follow him. I don't think that's really the case, but it's better to be safe. Of course, all of this is academic,' he finished, 'if we can't transit out. Have you ever worked on the equipment, Jim?'

'Sometimes,' I said. 'Pretty standard maintenance stuff. But Dad always had me watch when he did any kind of real work on it, and he explained things as he went along.'

'It was the same with me back home,' he acknowledged. 'I guess we'd better check it out.'

I flipped on the power and showed him the one lit indicator.

'We could still probably receive,' I said. 'The damage is in transmission.'

'That doesn't do us any good.'

I killed the power again and unscrewed the damaged panel. When I pried it off he stared and shook his head.

'Uh-oh,' he said.

'Yeah.'

'There's a lot of work there . . . '

'How long will it take to fix it?' Becky asked.

'We're going to be working on it all night,' Barry said, 'even if we just replace everything.'

'Do you *have* replacements for everything?' she asked.

'I'm not sure,' I answered.

'If we've got to try repairing some of the parts as well, it's going to take a lot longer.'

'You're right,' I agreed. 'Then we're going to have to pull a lot of checks on it.'

'Has either of you ever done a job like that?' Becky asked.

'Not me,' I said.

Barry shook his head.

'Then it's too long and too uncertain,' she told us.

Barry laughed, without humour.

'If you've got a better idea, let us know,' he said.

'There might be another way for you to transit,' she said.

'Don't be silly,' Barry responded. 'Either you've got a functioning transcomp or you haven't.'

She gave him a long, hard stare. Finally, he looked away.

'Well, what do you know that we don't?' he said then.

She smiled, for the first time in a long while.

'That's the wrong question,' she told him, 'when time is so important. Supposing there is another way of getting you to those worlds? How would you go about finding Tom?'

'In the case of the lightband,' Barry said, 'we just ask the people on that side—the Kendalls—where he is. After all, he'd have come through on their equipment. For the deadband there'll be no people to ask, of course. But he'd be in the hidden station, or near it. You know that. You've been to those places yourself and—'

'That's not what I mean,' she said. 'If this works, I'm not

at all sure you'll arrive near the other transcomps. Probably not. I want to know whether you know your way well enough to get there on your own if I can transit you to the general vicinity.'

Barry studied her, his eyes narrowing.

'You're serious, aren't you?' he asked. Then, seeing her expression at that, he continued hurriedly, 'Well, yes. I think so. I mean, that's one of the reasons for all of the visiting we've done back and forth over the years, and for all the studying about each others' worlds, all the maps and histories. So we can find our way around in them if we have to. If you know a way of getting us there I think we could locate the proper places.'

He glanced at me and I nodded.

'I've no idea what you have in mind,' I said to her. 'But if you can send us, can you also bring us back?'

'No. I'd have to be there,' she said. 'I'll lose track of you once you're gone. But you said our transcomp can still receive. So turn it on, set it, leave it on, and have the people at that station send you back when you're ready.'

'We'd have to be sure that it *really* receives,' I said. 'Just because a light goes on and we get a humming sound doesn't mean everything's just right.'

She shrugged.

'That's your department,' she said. 'Find out.'

'You're right,' I agreed, 'and we will. But even so, I don't see how you can send us.'

She looked away.

'I don't *know* that I can,' she said. 'All I can do is try. It's the Old Way.'

'What do you mean?'

'How did they manage the transits before they had computers?' she asked.

'The computer isn't absolutely necessary. It just makes things a lot easier,' I said. 'In the old days you had to do a lot more pencil and paper work and manual adjustments for band drift and stuff like that.'

'That's not the old days,' she said. 'I mean the *real* old days. What did they do back before they could just push a plug into the wall and throw a switch?'

'They set up their own private power sources,' I said. 'Windmills, running water. Stuff like that. They learned the tricks from the more technologically advanced bands.'

'Uh-huh,' she said. 'How'd they get in touch with them to learn that stuff?'

'It must have been the other way around. They got in touch with us.'

'Just tuned in on our nonexistent machinery, huh?'

'Well, I'm not sure exactly how they reached the Founder and told him what to build—'

'You don't know.'

'No, I don't know.'

'There are other power sources than windmills and running water,' she said. 'We are going to do it the way it was done in the days before the Founder. The Old Way.'

Barry was staring at her, wide eyed, the fingers of his right hand tracing a strange design in the air. Becky ignored this entirely.

'So you guys check out the receiver,' she said, 'while I go and get some things together.'

She turned and left the room.

'She really *is* a witch!' Barry said softly.

I shrugged. I already knew that.

CHAPTER 5

As we checked over the machine I thought of the various bands and of what we all meant to each other. There are several bands about equivalent to ours technologically—ahead of us in a few ways, behind in a few others, on a par in most. Then there are a few that are definitely in advance of ours in most ways. Others are behind us, at various levels ranging from feudal through early industrial stages. The families study all of the time lines like mad, hoping to learn from mistakes in each other's development, trying to foresee the periodic crises through which every culture seems to pass, doing our best to make these transitions as smooth as possible.

Our commerce is mainly one of ideas, and our office has not always been located in the American Southwest. We have moved about from generation to generation, setting up in those centres where our influence will work the most benefit. After numerous family conferences, our ancestors in London actually brought in an associate from a high-tech band, coached him, and sent him to Dublin in the early nineteenth century. There he engaged in numerous drinking bouts with a troubled mathematician named Hamilton, with occasional talk of the symbolization of vectors in three-dimensional space. Years later Hamilton's work was ready and waiting when Heisenberg had need of it. It was rough on our associate's liver but proved useful in helping to understand the atomic age when it became necessary to do so.

Right now we run a foundation near Los Alamos, and some of the people from the lab, like Dr. Wade, are members. It is a genuine think tank, which accepts legitimate contracts on which our members can earn extra money by brainstorming ideas into reports and recommendations. And every now and then they may get fed an outside idea, something not always applicable to the problem at hand but which may well be recalled in another context, somewhere down the line.

All of this, of course, must be done very carefully and after considerable deliberation, in light of our knowledge of all our histories. For the wrong idea at the wrong time can be as dangerous as the right one can be useful. And according to family discussions, it seems that our band is passing through some fairly delicate times just now.

All of which makes everything sound very mechanistic and predictable, which is by no means really the case. A couple of the less developed lightbands seem to contain phenomena which do not lend themselves to easy explanation. Stories keep cropping up, for instance, of unusual people and magical-seeming happenings, which are very hard to investigate or explain.

Such as a band Dad and Mum visited about seven years ago. Feudal, agrarian, low tech. Castles, manor houses, nobles, serfs. Like that. It was being discussed whether improved methods of spinning and weaving wool, which would profoundly affect the economy of a large area there, should be introduced at about that time. (They weren't.)

At the time, their host came down with one of his migraine headaches and said that he wanted to visit an old woman who lived in the neighbourhood who had been successful in treating these in the past. She was nominally a midwife and herbalist, but he believed she possessed genuine paranormal abilities of a healing sort. So they rode out to her place. They discovered her to be dead when they got there, and foul play was involved, though nothing more was ever learned as to motives or guilty parties. But something more was discovered: a little girl was found hiding, crying, in the woods nearby. She called the old woman Granny, and neighbours told them that she'd lived with her for some time, though no one seemed to know whether they were actually related. And none of them knew of any other relatives of the girl's. Her name was Becky, and she hung on to my mother and cried. That's how I acquired a sister.

Becky doesn't talk to me about her early memories. But then, nobody believes in telling me anything important around here. Maybe she told Mum about things from when she was little. I just don't know. They seemed to have developed some sort of special bond early on. Becky's occasionally let something slip, though, and she does peculiar things and she seems to have ways of knowing things she shouldn't really know about.

Tonight was one of those times, with all that talk about Old Ways and of doing a transit without the machine. Becky does okay in school, but she doesn't really have that many friends. And maybe it isn't all that healthy that she spends all the time she does staring into flames and things like that. I don't know. But that's the sort of thing that made me kind of think of her as a witch. I never really doubted, though, that she had some peculiar secrets, and I'd a funny feeling that whatever she was about to do would be something I couldn't really understand. I shivered suddenly.

'The receiver seems okay,' Barry said. 'But you know, if we were to go away and leave it on, anybody who knows the proper frequency for our station could come through or send something.'

I nodded.

'If it's friends it doesn't matter,' I said. 'As for the dark-banders, I think they've already come and gone. I suppose we could leave Golly down here, though, to mind the store.'

'I think that would be a good idea,' he responded. 'Do you have any idea what Becky is going to do?'

'No.'

I checked over the receiver myself. It seemed that he was right about it.

'Well, I don't know what's going to happen or how long it's going to take,' I said. 'So I guess I'll go collect Golly and bring him down here to be a watchdog. You stay here, in case she gets back before I do. Okay?'

'Sure,' he said, jamming his hands into his pockets when I glanced at them. I'd only glanced at them because of the movement, and it had taken me seconds to realize that they were shaking. And it took me several seconds more to realize why.

Barry came from one of the bands where unusual people and happenings sometimes occur. But it had never occurred to me before that he might be sort of superstitious, or that he could actually be afraid of Becky.

I grinned, hoping to put him somewhat at ease, and I slapped him on the shoulder as I went by.

'Hold the fort,' I said, and I hurried on up the stairs.

As I passed through rooms and up more stairs, seeking

our silent, stalking Golem, I wondered whether there might actually be some basis for Barry's fears. Becky had seemed fairly sure of herself, reasonably confident about whatever it was that she was going to try. It seemed obvious that she knew something that we didn't know—or thought she did. Where could she have learned it? She had been too small when she had come to live with us to have had much in the way of complicated instruction from the old woman. The only alternative I could think of was that she might have learned some means of self-instruction. On those occasions when she sat in her room meditating, was she in communication with someone—or something—that taught her things of an unusual nature? The sudden thought of something like that going on up the hall from me for all these years was more than a little disturbing. If there was something more involved than Becky's own drifting mind, how was I to know whether it was something good, or—otherwise?

I snorted at this, and then I chuckled. I could see that I was overreacting to a series of guesses, and I knew that it had something to do with how upset I felt over Dad's disappearance. Becky had been my sister for most of my life—hers too, for that matter. She could get pretty mad at me on occasion, but I could never see her doing anything that would really hurt me. She just wasn't the sort to go around curdling milk, making dogs howl, and giving people the Evil Eye. If she did possess any sort of strange knowledge, she'd want to use it to help us. I knew that because I knew what she was like.

She's all right.

I caught a whiff of that faint, new car smell Golly exudes, and I followed it to the small records room up the hall from the library. Sure enough, I found him inside, moving in a slow circuit about the place, checking into every chink and cubby. I approached him, was recognized, opened his control panel, and changed his instructions. I took his hand in mine then and led him out the door.

'This way, Golly,' I said. 'I've got a new job for you.'

Becky had not yet returned when we got back to the transcomp room, but she showed up shortly after I had programmed Golly to guard the place and set him to stand sentry near the door. She came rushing in, a bulging pillowcase in her arms, screamed briefly when she saw Golly, let go, then grabbed at and recovered her bundle.

'I wish you'd let me know you'd brought that thing in here,' she said.

'I'm sorry,' I told her.

She frowned and moved away from the Golem.

'You could have slowed things down quite a bit if I'd broken any of this stuff,' she stated.

'I said I'm sorry.'

'Okay. Apology accepted,' she said. 'Is that receiver turned on?'

'Yes,' Barry answered, his back against the wall, his eyes following her every move.

'Good.' She cleared a space in the centre of the floor by removing a chair, a wastebasket, and a stack of periodicals to the room's far corner. She set the pillowcase in the clear area, knelt, and reached inside. She withdrew a candle and a candle holder, fitted them together, and set them on the floor before her. Then she took out a package of matches, lit the candle, and raised her head. 'Would one of you please turn out the lights?' she asked.

Barry nodded, crossed to a position beside the door, and flipped the switch.

'And close the door,' she said, 'so the light from the passage won't interfere.'

He pushed it shut.

Becky rummaged in the pillowcase again and withdrew more candles and more burnished holders. While she was fitting the candles in, she said, 'Okay, do you know what you are going to do if I am able to open the way for you to reach those two bands?'

'In the case of the deadband,' I said, 'I just have to search in the area of the transcomp. It's hidden in the basement of a ruined building. He could be holed up right there. If he isn't, he may have left a message. If there is no message, then a quick search of the area would probably turn up some sign if he'd been by. If I find any such indication I'll try following it. If I don't I'll come back, and we can scratch that one.'

'Same idea here,' Barry said. 'Only easier, since there'll be people around to ask. I'll just go through and check with the Kendalls as to whether he transitted in on their equipment. If he did, he's probably still with them.'

Becky pursed her lips and studied the flame as she slowly raised another taper and lit it from the first one. She set it aside and reached for another.

'No,' she said as she did this. 'It won't be quite that easy. As I said, I should be able to get you into the general vicinity of the stations, but I don't think that I can bring you in right on target. So you have to be ready to find your own ways from wherever you might arrive.'

She lit another taper. Their flickering light upon her face made her look stranger, older.

'How far?' Barry asked. 'I'd be in trouble if you set me on another continent or something like that.'

'No. Nothing like that,' she said. 'But I could be off twenty or thirty miles or so, something on that order. You'd still be in the general area.'

'I can manage that,' Barry answered. 'I spent over a month there once. I know the neighbourhood.'

I thought back over street maps I had memorized of the ruined city, over various topographical features I had had to learn, as well as the different places I could head to orient myself.

'I'll be okay,' I said.

She continued to light candles, lining them up to her left. Shadows danced upon the walls now, and across the surfaces of the equipment. Golly looked positively sinister in the gloom, like some figure in a wax museum. Even the faint drone of the transit receiver, hardly noticeable before, now seemed like the sound track of some film right before disaster hits.

'Okay, then,' she said. 'Gather round.' And she motioned us to sit in positions on the floor so that we formed a triangle, facing inward.

She withdrew three vanity mirrors from the pillowcase and set them up along the sides of the triangle, between us, so that each of us faced one mirror. Then she began placing the candles in a kind of zigzag array in the middle. There were seven of them, and we each faced their glowing reflections as well as the things themselves. The room suddenly seemed cooler, despite the flames.

'Uh, anything special we're supposed to do?' I asked.

'Just watch everything that I do,' she said softly, 'and when I tell you to do something later, just do it. It won't be anything hard.'

She reached back into the bundle and there followed a rattling, clicking sound. She withdrew a handful of brass rods. She placed these before her on the floor and then took out a pair of toothed wheels, apparently of the same material. They looked rather like fat, carefully sculptured gears, save that they were too wide and the teeth too small for them to have functioned in any sort of machine that I could think of.

Humming to herself, Becky began laying the rods among the candles in a different sort of pattern. There were nine rods, ranging in length from four to ten inches, about as thick around as pencils and engraved with serpentine patterns at each end. She set them in place very slowly, and she switched from humming to singing as she did so. Her voice remained too low, however, for me to distinguish any words.

I watched her hands as they moved among the flames. I watched the light sliding along the lengths of the rods as she adjusted them. I also watched the reflections across the way of her hands and the lights and the rods. Her low tune-less tune filled my mind.

She picked up one of the wheels in each hand, fitted them together, and turned them very slowly by pressing upon them and sliding her hands in opposite directions. Then back, then apart again. Back and apart. They made a gentle clicking sound in accompaniment to her strange tune. The lights seemed to flow together for a moment into a single bright smear. As this occurred I heard, briefly, a new sound—a high, keening note, almost a whine. It was gone in an instant, but it returned when the smear came again.

'What's happening?' Barry asked.

Becky glared at him and he shut up.

She continued for what seemed a long while after that, and the periods of brightness came closer and closer together. Finally, she set the two wheels, still touching, on the ground before her, and with her right hand she continued to roll them back and forth. With her left she began moving the rods into a new position.

Then, 'Barry,' she said, 'stand up,' and from the corner of my eye I saw him do it.

'Turn around,' she went on, 'and start walking.'

He moved, I heard a few footsteps, then nothing.

I continued to stare into the light, to listen to the clicking and the keening. There were moments when Becky seemed very far away.

Her left hand moved again, creating a new pattern with the rods. She sang again for a time, and my vision swam and was filled with light.

'Rise now,' she said, and her voice was faint, as from a great distance. I did as she directed, and then, 'Turn around,' she said.

I did an about-turn, and the air was filled with dancing motes before me, countless afterimages of the light into which I had been staring, blinking and darting like innumerable fireflies.

'Walk,' she said, and I did.

CHAPTER 6

I moved slowly, because I felt I should be running into something very soon. But after a time I realized that I had taken more steps than was possible, moving in a straight line in any direction in that room. Therefore, it would seem I was no longer in the room. And my vision had grown worse instead of better, the darting lights becoming brighter and more numerous—which just isn't the way afterimages usually behave. I noted, too, at about that time that the surface upon which I trod was no longer smooth. Therefore, it wasn't the floor.

Ahead of me was one big bright sheet of light, and I seemed to be advancing upon it. My feet and my hands tingled somewhat, and the entire experience was somehow not an unfamiliar one.

I still seemed to hear Becky singing, faintly, and I realized that it was important I keep moving, that I did not halt until I reached the light or stopped hearing her voice. My feelings were a bit disconcerting, as if I were somehow stuck at a point halfway between sleep and waking. I realized then that I had no idea how long I had been walking.

I realized something else, too, and I knew why the experience seemed familiar. All of the sensations I was feeling were a protracted version of the momentary tingling, swirling, flash-flecked sensation I'd known when doing a crossover by means of the transcomp.

So I kept walking and the light kept growing, and the only comforting thing about the whole business was Becky's fading tune. Soon the light came to dominate my field of vision. Then it seemed to grow even more rapidly, out of pace with my approach, until I felt that it was rushing towards me and then realized moments later that this was indeed the case. . . .

In one bright, frightening instant I passed through, and everything was changed.

I kept moving, automatically, discovering myself to be passing along a dirt trail, shadow-decked trees at either hand. All of the light now present had resolved itself into a sky full of stars and a larger glow somewhere off to my right, its source masked by dark boughs. There was a faint rustling of leaves and branches stirred by cool breezes. I heard the occasional cries and stridencies of birds and insects. The smells of damp soil, leaf mould, and fresh growing things came to me strongly; also, there were the scents of a number of animals, some of them familiar, some not so, against a hint of distant fresh water.

This was all wrong. I had expected nuclear winter, damaged buildings, rusting vehicles, dust, broken glass; in short, decades-old carnage. Instead, I found myself walking a quiet trail through an uncontaminated countryside. While this was certainly a more congenial place than the other, it was of no help to us whatsoever. It was wrong. Becky had somehow messed up. It—

No.

As I passed along the trail, and the treeline to my right dipped and retreated, I saw that the larger light from that direction came from the bright face of a full moon. Immediately, my hands began itching despite the cool breezes, and I felt perspiration break out upon my forehead. A jittery restlessness came over me, followed by a sudden shortness of breath, though I was not exerting myself particularly. And I knew then what had happened.

I had a mental image of Barry walking the broken streets of a blasted, deserted city. Obviously, Becky had sent Barry to the deadband rather than me, while I had been transported to the band I was supposed to avoid until I was older and, hopefully, better able to gain control of the process that even now seemed to be commencing. Not only had I been sent to the wrong place, I had arrived at the worst possible time.

I halted, panting, and raised my hands to my face. I could feel the stubble again in the places I had shaved earlier. I was suddenly aware of cramps in my legs, beginning in my calves and spreading up into the muscles of my thighs shortly thereafter. As I leaned over to massage them I felt pains in my shoulders.

I seemed to be cross-eyed, for my nose suddenly seemed longer and darker by moonlight. There came an audible creaking from my joints and a series of sharp lower back pains.

I tried to recall everything I knew about the phenomenon. For those of us who are susceptible to the change, there are supposed to be ways of resisting it and, ultimately, ways of controlling it. Unfortunately, I lacked particulars, having also been told that one had to experience the things first in order to realize how any controlling techniques should be applied. Great. I had hardly set out with a rite of passage in mind, but it looked as if my education was about to be furthered. It promised to be an interesting night.

I decided to try relaxing, going along with it, noting all of my reactions as well as I could for future reference.

Whether rubbing my legs helped them or whether the cramps went away by themselves, I do not know. I tried to straighten then, however, and discovered that I was unable to. It was as if I'd developed a permanent crick in my back. At least there was no pain associated with this. Realizing what was going on, though, I clawed hurriedly at my belt, noting that my hands seemed smaller and hairier, the fingers shorter. If I were going to transform I wanted to get undressed in a hurry. I did not want to find myself a big, doglike creature helplessly entangled in jeans, T-shirt, and tennis shoes.

I had to lie on my side to finish the job, and a steady series of aches rippled through my body as I thrashed about on the ground. My feet came out of my shoes looking suspiciously pawlike, and I'd a funny feeling I was developing something I could wag on my rear end. This could become extremely awkward, I realized, if I were separated from my garments when I retransformed, especially if there were ladies in the vicinity. I tried gathering my clothes up, with some idea of making a bundle of them that I could carry about in my mouth. But it was too late; my hands were no longer hands, and when I picked the loose garments up in my teeth I could see that they'd just drag and snag on things.

But I actually was trying to relax the entire time, to feel what each twinge did to me, as the fevers and chills alternated, my muscles spasmed, my bones seemed to shift about. There were times when it almost seemed I might be able to exert some control over the process, but I didn't dare. The last thing I needed was to mess things up and wind up some kind of freak. A crippled werewolf struck me as a pretty pathetic creature. So I just lay there and felt it and let it run its course. The one time I yelled, during a particularly painful twisting, it came out as a howl. Something in the genes, of course. I told myself that it had to be genetic.

Still, such considerations became more and more academic as the process continued. I knew that it affected my mind, though I could not have provided details at the time on everything that it did to my thinking. It seemed that my sense of the passage of time was somehow altered, though, for when the change had run its course I felt that the moon was higher in the heavens than it should be for the amount of time that seemed to have gone by. I didn't believe that this was just a matter of position, with me standing on all fours now—though my vision was no longer as good as it had been. On the other hand—or maybe I should say 'paw'— my hearing was enormously enhanced. Every tiny creak or rustle produced by the wind in its passage through the foliage, every little bug whistle, claw scrape, wing rustle, and fall of footpad came to me in full-fidelity stereo, some of the sounds almost painful. And my sense of smell, as highly developed as it was, had never been this good before. I knew from a few whiffs of the air exactly where the stream was located; I could tell where a rabbit had fled a little while ago, knew there was a fox in the vicinity, retreating now.

I took a slow step forward. Then another. It felt funny. I walked again, and I started thinking about my movements and I stumbled. I stood and tried again. I stumbled again. Frustrated, I raised my muzzle and howled. The sound frightened me a bit, as I hadn't planned on doing it. It just came out. But it made me realize that if I could howl without thinking I could probably walk without thinking, too—in fact, I might be better off not thinking about such things at all for now, and relying on reflex and instinct without letting my mind get in the way.

So I tried again with my mental machinery idling and this time I walked just fine. But there was more to come, and it was frightening. Apparently, the change was still going on, and not necessarily at a purely physical level. For when I put my thinking in abeyance and let my newly formed body take over, strange thoughts began to flit through my mind. They were not the sort of thoughts I had ever thought before. They were . . . hunting thoughts.

My head would drop low and move from side to side, and I would sniff the ground, seeking trails. Whenever I discovered one I realized that I knew what had passed there and how long ago the passing had occurred. Then I would raise my head high and sniff the breezes, seeking more distant scents. I passed among trees as I did these things, and images of fleeing game, myself pursuing it, passed through my mind. A part of me realized that I had had some destination in mind earlier. But that part, which I had put to rest to keep from stumbling, now seemed a very small part indeed. It was overwhelmed, more than half buried. Its objective was no longer of first importance. It would have to wait on the hunt.

It seemed as if a part of me were going to sleep, while another part, one I had not ever realized to be present, was waking up. To the drowsing me, everything that followed seemed somehow like a dream. I came later to wonder whether the me I had always been was like a dream to that sleeping other. . . .

Dreaming.

Running at a steady lope, the night alive with sounds and scents. Down hillside, along stream's dark bank. Pausing to drink the cold black water. All shapes are grey. The earth is signed with the smell of smaller game. I take a trail, follow for a time, lose it, try another. Moving quickly now, shadow amid shadows. Slipping ghostlike through brush and bramble. My senses extend me beyond my skull. I am become a piece of the night.

It is hunger, the rush of events, the heat of the hunt. Ahead, I hear movements. It knows I am coming. It flees. I taste the darkness, I hear the song the moon sings. . . .

There is no time, and as for space, it seems I move with such ease that the world rushes to meet me. I am suspended in the dark dream of the hunt, where reason sleeps as the scroll of sensation unwinds. I am dog-shaped death within the wood of the world, thing of fang and hunger. Beneath sky's eyes beast to feast blooding moon-turned hours. . . .

I was lost within the bitter dream of predator and prey, time without time, as night washed me and carried me far away. I know that I caught and I killed, and I ate, small furred things which sometimes squealed, but beyond this my waking consciousness censored much of the detail. I remember that at the time it had seemed the right thing to do—more than right, actually.

There was one point, well into the night's hunting, when my exuberance rose into a long, drawn out howl. Almost immediately, from across a great distance, I was answered by a similar voice. This reply drew me up short for a moment with a sort of tingling reaction I did not fully understand. The call was not repeated, however, and I was back on the track a short while later.

There are blurred spots and missing areas to that night, as there are in any dream or in any day of steady, repetitious activity. There were times when I slowed, times when I rested, times when I drank again from pool or stream. It seems that I was always alert, however, and that I still hunted with my mind even when my body was resting or otherwise engaged. Then, somewhere towards dawn, I began to tire, to slow. There were new scents in the air then, as of human habitation, but these were still sufficiently removed that I was not apprehensive.

I rested in a glade, tongue lolling, sides heaving, ears pricked and mobile. Had I been capable of speech at that time I would have said that nothing could have approached without my becoming aware of its presence. Just shows how wrong you can be. One night out does not give a novice werewolf a graduate degree in woodlore.

It had approached my resting place from downwind, with absolute silence. It would have been difficult to believe that anything that large could move with such stealth against a hypersensitive creature such as I had become, save for my own recent experience. I remember that the grasses had grown moist and the faintest spillage of dawn had begun in one corner of the sky when I received the first indication that I was not alone.

There came a single soft footfall from somewhere to my rear, and I was on my feet and turning even as I heard a low growled sound that seemed strangely like a word—my name. I beheld a wolf even larger than the one I had become, grey, and with large glinting yellow eyes. Flight would be useless, I decided, for I knew that it would catch me and have me at a disadvantage for my having fled, taking me from the rear. Fighting did not seem such a great idea either, but better here while I was rested than somewhere else when I was winded. There seemed no alternative, for why else would it have stalked me if not to do me harm?

With a snarl, I launched myself at the intruder, going for the throat with my teeth. But it turned quickly, its shoulder striking my shoulder, knocking me to the ground. In an instant, I felt teeth upon my throat—but they did not tighten. From my drowsing mind flashed a memory of something I had read concerning dominance and submission among wolves, that whole business about the loser exposing his throat to the victor, who then was bound to go no further with the attack. So I lay still. At some other level, also, it seemed the best thing to do. I just hoped this wolf had read the same book.

I lay there without moving, and the other's fangs exerted but the barest pressure upon my neck. This went on for what seemed a long while, and then the pressure was gone, the muzzle withdrawn. A growling followed, modulated so that it sounded like 'James'.

I stared, for the wolf began doing some very unwolflike things. It reared several times upon its hind legs, front paws extended high into the air. Then it commenced rolling about the ground, legs splayed at various odd angles. I realized what was going on moments later as its appearance grew more and more manlike, and even familiar. . . .

I tried growling and forming words within it, as he had done. I tried saying 'Uncle George!' though I couldn't be sure how it sounded to him. He did smile, though, as he nodded at me.

'I can see that you'll be needing some lessons in this

business,' he said. 'We'll start with one of the quick ways of changing back.'

I nodded my muzzle. It's always good to have an expert in the family.

CHAPTER 7

When I finished retransforming I realized that I was cold and very, very tired.

'Come on,' Uncle George said, taking hold of my arm. 'I've a cart not too far from here. We'll ride back to the manor.'

I followed him among the trees.

'I hope you brought a blanket or something,' I said, my teeth beginning to chatter. 'I don't feel too good.'

'I know all about it, boy, and I brought warm clothes for you.'

I found myself panting and I leaned on him as we walked, my feet grown wet from dew. When I stopped panting I began yawning, one after another. I couldn't stop.

'Oxygen,' he said as we trekked through the wood. 'You need a lot. It's partly because I hurried things to get you through the change fast. Even without hurrying it can be fatiguing.'

'You don't seem tired,' I managed.

'I know what I'm doing,' he told me. 'I can control it.'

'You've got to teach me more about it.'

'All in good time,' he said.

When we reached his cart, where a gentle-looking brown mare eyed us and snorted once, softly, from her position between the traces, I had to lean against the cart's side to stay standing while I drew on the trousers and the loose-fitting shirt Uncle George passed me. I stood wrapped in a dark blue cloak he had passed me, almost in a daze, while he dressed himself. He gave me a hand up into the cart. I'm not sure I could have made it on my own.

'You knew I'd be here tonight,' I managed, as I sprawled on the cart's bed and drew the cloak about me.

'Yep,' he said, as he took hold of the reins and shook them gently.

We moved forward, and I did not get to voice the rest of my questions because my mind fuzzed over and drifted, and talking was too much trouble. So was thinking. I felt myself going away. I slept.

I dreamed a bit—strange, disorganized things. There's a guy I know who got a summer job as a bank clerk. He told me that after he'd been at it for a while, he began having 'clerk dreams,' dreams of standing there at the window counting out money interminably. I guess any new, prolonged experience might impress itself on you that way. Mine was strange, though, because it wasn't all that visual, the way most dreams are. I was back in wolf form again, running through the woods, but seeing hadn't been all that important to me then and it wasn't now; my dreams were rushing sequences of smells and sounds, with me looking for something within them, and anything that I did see was mostly at a low angle and close up—roots, grasses, stones, the earth. Then a familiar scent came to me, and I realized that that was what I hunted, even though I did not really know what it represented, except ... moving, moving. Blurred images. Scent path grown stronger. And then I knew. I had entered a clearing and she was there, secured somehow to a tree. My mother. . . .

I woke up crying softly, wiping my eyes as the dream faded. Then I drifted back to sleep. This time there were no dreams that I could remember.

I became aware by degrees of the rattling of the cart, the plodding of the mare. For a long while I seemed to drift in that place halfway between sleep and wakefulness. Then I realized that I was no longer cold, and I opened my eyes and there was sunlight all about me. From the sun's position I guessed that I might have slept for a couple of hours. I saw, too, that we were on a much better road now than the rutted forest trail where we had started earlier. The trees had thinned out and were smaller at either hand. We seemed to have come to a higher elevation, also, because when I sat up, facing the rear, I was looking back and down over a great forested area. The shadows of a few drifting clouds to the east moved like dark islands across the bright, leaf green sea contoured of treetop, shrub, and glade. I turned around and saw that we were approaching a large manor house of stone and timber set upon a hilltop, surrounded by a stone wall. Our road led to its front gate. The gate was closed.

'We're almost home,' Uncle George said, not looking back. 'Thirsty?'

I realized that I was, as he passed me a water bottle without waiting for my answer. I took a long drink, replaced the top, and handed it back.

'Thanks,' I said, and I studied our destination. As we drew nearer I heard a low murmuring sound, as of many voices.

I moved into a more comfortable position and checked

myself over. My various aches and pains seemed to have vanished as I slept. Most of my fatigue seemed to have washed away also, and what remained seemed to be ebbing rapidly. I was surprised to discover that I was feeling fairly good.

When we finally came up to the gate Uncle George waved to two armed men, who opened it for us. 'Morning,' he said. 'Any word yet?'

'No,' the one on the left replied, but no trouble either.'

'Good.'

We rolled inside, and I beheld an armed camp. What had obviously recently been a large, parklike lawn was now well trampled, and there were men spread all over the place, many of them cleaning weapons, helmets, and chest and arm protectors. Fires burned here and there, and I could smell rich stews and strong teas. Off to the right, another group of men was eating; to the left, yet another group was being drilled in sword attacks. The three groups seemed to be of about equal size.

'Expecting trouble?' I asked.

'Yes and no,' he replied in his typical ambiguous fashion. Uncle George, on those occasions when he had come to visit us, had always been fairly quiet, and when he did talk I was not always certain what he'd said. But I also knew that he could make himself clear when he wanted to. Therefore, now just wasn't one of those times.

He turned on to a small cart trail, which led us to the rear of the manor. He drew rein before a stable, stepped down, and turned the cart over to a groom, who had emerged when he'd heard us coming. I jumped down from the rear and followed as he headed for a flagged walkway leading beneath some massive elms towards the rear of the house.

'Hungry?' he asked, as we entered.

I nodded. Actually, I was more than just hungry. I felt half starved.

'Me, too,' he said. 'I'll show you to a room where you can clean up while the cook finds us a meal. We'll meet in that side room with the big table,' he said, gesturing towards an open doorway to the right, 'in a bit.'

The room to which he conducted me was about the size of my room back home, though less cluttered. I opened the shutters and a cool breeze came in, along with a view of more ancient trees and a pair of outbuildings. After he had left, I filled a basin with water, pulled off my shirt, and began washing. I realized quickly that I needed it, so I undressed fully and gave myself a sponge bath. I decided on a shampoo too. Several basins and a good towelling later, I opened an armoire and located some fresh garments where Uncle George had told me they would be.

After I'd brushed my hair and rinsed my mouth and cleaned my nails, I left the room and made my way back to the little room off the kitchen. As I approached it I heard familiar voices. One of them was Aunt Maryl's. The other. . . .

'Barry!' I said as I entered.

He rose from the table, smiling faintly.

'I heard that it happened to you,' he said.

I nodded.

'You look okay,' he added.

'So do you,' I said, and he smiled, crookedly.

After I had embraced Aunt Maryl, a tall, dark-haired lady with a small scar above her left eyebrow, I seated myself and filled my plate. Then I glanced at everyone in turn. Barry lowered his fork and said, 'I got in last night. When I found myself walking through a wrecked city I realized that Becky must have got her signals crossed. It was dark, and it took me a while to figure out that I was across town from the place where the transcomp was hidden. Then it took me a couple of hours more to locate the station.'

'And?' I said. 'Was Dad . . . ?'

He shook his head.

'No sign at all that he'd been there,' he stated. 'I struck a light when I unlocked the bunker, and I saw that a fresh layer of dust had settled since the last time I'd been by. My footprints were the only ones, and there were no other indications of anyone's disturbing the place recently. So I set the comp and came through here to let them know you were somewhere in the area.'

Uncle George nodded.

'It was easy to figure what had happened,' he said. 'Also, it made it easy for me to find you, if she'd sent you as near to us as she'd sent Barry to that centre.'

'All right,' I said, 'I see. And if Dad didn't go through to the deadband that means he came here. Right? Is he okay?'

Uncle George looked away. After a few moments, Aunt Maryl shook her head.

'I'm afraid he didn't come here,' she said.

'What do you mean?' I asked. 'We figured the possible settings. It had to be that band or this one.'

'Well, no,' Barry said. 'The original setting seems to have been the right one.'

I frowned. 'I don't understand,' I said. 'It was set on a darkband, and they're blocked. You can't get through to them.'

He looked at Aunt Maryl.

'Actually, that is not entirely true,' she stated. 'With the proper tuning one can reach one of the bandit transcomps.'

'Bandit transcomps?' I said. 'I don't know what you're talking about.'

'Your food's getting cold,' Uncle George observed.

'I'm not hungry.'

'Yes, you are,' he said. 'Eat, and we'll explain things a bit.'

I began eating and my hunger took over. I kept going while they talked.

'The darkband your father transitted to was the third darkband,' Aunt Maryl began. 'It was formerly a lightband, but it had been successfully invaded several years ago.'

I nodded. I already knew this.

'But it was not completely conquered,' she continued.

'There was a resistance movement. The partisans have their own transcomps, and we've remained in communication with them. The lightbands have been supplying them with strategic materials and personnel since shortly after the conquest.'

'Dad knew about this?' I asked.

'Yes. He had been liaising with one such group for a long while. We believe that the darkbanders finally succeeded in tracing his signal. Obtaining the specific frequencies for the various lightband stations has been a top priority of theirs for years. They do have bandit stations of their own in all of the lightbands, but access to a station itself, which is also a field office, would give them the means for more subtle mischief than they could manage otherwise.'

'You've lost me,' I said.

'They've been trying to pick up your code for a long time,' she explained, 'and they finally succeeded. It sounds as if Tom fought with whoever came through and escaped by transitting to the bandit station in the darkband—'

'So if you know the frequency we can reach him from here,' I said.

'Not so simple,' she answered. 'They would have silenced

their unit and changed its settings almost immediately after Tom got there and told them what had happened. We're sure that's what occurred, because we've tried reaching them and we can no longer pick them up with the old setting.'

'That could mean they're all dead and the equipment wrecked!' I said. 'The darkbanders must have learned the partisans' code in order to be able to monitor them and pick up Dad's signal. After they'd sent someone through to take care of him, they probably attacked the partisans and wiped them out.'

'No,' Uncle George interrupted. 'It's not that hard to figure their frequency range and still not know the exact setting, if they're mainly receiving and not transmitting, which is normally the case. What they probably did was monitor a spectrum for incoming signals. You see, your station was not the only one that was hit—'

'Wait a minute,' I said, putting down my fork. 'You're making this sound like some kind of war.'

'It is,' my aunt said. 'There has been underground fighting going on ever since the takeover. All of the lightbands have been supporting the rebel forces from the beginning, but the actual conflict has been confined mainly to that band up until now.'

'Why is it suddenly spilling over?' I asked.

'The rebels have been growing steadily stronger,' she said. 'They're now in control of a number of large areas, which include some important cities and installations. It begins to look as if they might actually succeed in obtaining their objectives. So the first darkband is attempting to cut the links to all of their lightband supporters—and giving us problems of our own, to keep us occupied too.'

I studied Barry's face for several long moments. 'Did you know about all this stuff?' I asked him.

'Well, yes,' he answered.

'How come you never mentioned it to me?'

'I was told not to.'

'By whom?'

'My parents. Also your father.'

'Why shouldn't you have mentioned it?'

'I don't know. They never told me why.'

I looked back at Aunt Maryl.

'Well?' I asked. 'Why not? Why has everyone been keeping a thing like this from me?'

'Finish your lunch,' Uncle George said.

'I want to know now!'

'Finish your lunch,' he repeated. 'We'll talk more later.'

I studied all of their faces in turn, and I knew I wouldn't get any more out of them just then. I picked up my fork.

CHAPTER 8

It seems that I am destined always to be surrounded by secrets—and not to be in on most of them. I came to understand the reason behind some of this at a fairly early age, and I know that my position is hardly unique among the kids in the transit families. We go to school with kids in the towns where we make our homes, and we become good friends with some of them. We deal with other people in the community the same as anybody else. If, when I was very young, I'd known too much about the family's special business, there was the possibility I might have let something slip and created thereby an awkward situation. So I wasn't told too much when I was very young, but of course I knew that there was something a bit unusual going on. Kids always do, even if they don't understand. And this was probably the beginning of my paranoia about secrets.

All my life I seem to have been served up information about family affairs on a need-to-know basis. As I said, I could see the reason for it when I was much younger, but I sometimes wondered whether such treatment had simply become a habit with the families, practised even in matters where it was not strictly necessary. I can remember conversations between my parents that ended with a quick, whispered 'Later' or 'When he's not around' as I suddenly put in an appearance, or my mother's 'I don't want him to know about it'—one of the last things I ever heard her say, with no doubt at all as to whom the 'him' referred. Yes, I resent it when I'm treated as if I have no sense and no feelings. And since I was being treated that way again I resented it again. Obviously, something major was going on, with a small army camped on the Kendalls' front lawn. If they were willing to tell me about the darkband resistance and the fact that my father had crossed to one of its strongholds, why not finish the story? Why let the cat halfway out of the bag and stop it there?

We finished eating in silence. If someone had at least given me a reason I could have waited—maybe not patiently, but I would have waited until they were ready to tell me the rest. But nobody said a word till we were finished eating, when Uncle George remarked, 'Don't go too far off.'

'Okay,' I said. 'Why not?'

'Just don't.'

'I want to take a walk out back.'

He nodded.

I stamped out, departed through the rear door, and walked off among the trees. I wanted to be alone, which is what I told Barry when he'd tried to follow me. After a time, I came to a small stream, and I sat in the shade on its bank and tossed stones into the water. Not telling me things had to be more than just a habit. The fact that Barry's folks had told him about the fighting in the darkband, and that Dad had asked him not to tell me about it, proved that Barry's parents trusted him more than mine trusted me. If you want someone to be trustworthy it would seem you should try trusting him every now and then, to give him a little practice. I threw the next stone with considerable force. It struck a standing rock, bounced off, and hit against the side of a tree on the opposite bank.

I don't enjoy brooding and feeling sorry for myself. It's a bad way to spend an afternoon. I realized that I had felt some of these feelings and thought some of these thoughts before, but I had always shrugged them off, because I thought I understood the reasoning that lay behind my parents' attitude. But it was more than Barry's knowing things I didn't. The more I thought of how close Becky and Mum were, the more certain I was they shared secrets about which I knew nothing. Then there was Dave, off on exchange; I'd bet he knew all kinds of things I didn't.

I spent hours beside that stream in the small wood to the rear of the manor house, and nobody came for me, nobody called after me. Several times I got up and moved on along its course, because I'd used up all the stones in my immediate vicinity. The sky grew cloudier as the day advanced, and I half hoped it would rain on me to match my mood. But it didn't. The temperature did drop, though, and the breeze grew more chill. That was something, anyway.

Later—I don't know exactly how much later—as I was drawing back my arm to cast another stone, something caught my eye in among the trees on the other side of the stream. There was a stirring, and a whiteness where there had been no whiteness before. It took me a long stare to realize that a patch of mist had risen to hover between a pair of trees as if it were a curtain hung from their limbs. I didn't realize it had grown that damp, and I looked about for other foggy areas, but there were none that I could see. Peculiar. . . .

But perhaps it was particularly marshy over there. I watched the mist for a time, but though it was stirred, the breeze did not disperse it. Finally, I shied a stone through it but nothing happened.

At last, intrigued, I got to my feet and looked for a place where I could cross over. I located a series of exposed stones farther downstream, and I made it across there. After I'd climbed the bank and backtracked, I spotted the misty area again. It occurred to me that I was really grasping at straws to look for distraction in some will-o'-the-wispy patch of trapped moisture.

But I moved near and stood staring. It wasn't very big, but it was sufficiently dense to be opaque. I noted that the ground beneath my boots did not seem particularly damp, nor did I smell any odd gases. I extended my hand into it. It felt immediately cooler, though it was not masked from my sight. I waved it around a bit, but the fog did not disperse. I started to draw it back, but it seemed at that moment as if I heard a distant singing, and I froze as I tried to figure whether it was real, and where it was coming from if it was.

It faded and I stepped back, letting my hand fall to my side. Just as I did, though, it seemed another sound was beginning. It stopped the moment I lowered my hand.

I stood puzzled. I was certain now that I'd heard something, something which seemed to have its source directly ahead of me, though far removed. Also, it had sounded vaguely familiar. I remembered then, though, that this was one of the bands where magical goings-on were supposedly more likely to occur. Such being the case, it might be possible that I had stumbled upon something of this sort. If so, was this something good, bad, or neutral? Would I be enter-

ing a trap if I stepped inside, or might it be something useful or interesting?

The familiarity of the sound nagged, and that is what
decided me. I extended my hand again.

This time I heard the singing more clearly, and it
sounded so familiar that. . . .

'Becky!' I called as I moved forward. 'Becky! Is that
you? Where are you?'

I had entered a twilit place, pale to my right and left,
darker straight ahead. I had the impression that the dark
area led off for a great distance, rather than just a few feet
beyond the trees. I could not make out any particular forms
within the shadows. I took another step and called again.
This time my own voice sounded strange—muffled, flat.

Then, 'Jim?' I heard Becky's voice say. 'Is that you, Jim?'

'Yeah,' I called back. 'What's going on?'

'Where are you?'

'I just stepped into a patch of fog behind Aunt Maryl
and Uncle George's place,' I answered. 'I heard your voice.'

'Don't come any farther,' she said. 'But keep talking.'

'What should I talk about?'

'Anything. It doesn't matter. I've lost my way. I was
looking for you when I got lost. I must have come close,
anyway.'

'I think you came close,' I said.

'So talk, and I'll try to follow your voice.'

So I began telling her all of the things that had been
bothering me, just to make noise. I was sure she wasn't paying much attention, because she'd started singing again. *I*
wasn't even paying much attention. I knew it all too well.

Her singing grew louder, and after a time it seemed
fairly certain that she was approaching. I kept staring
ahead, and in a little while I saw a form coming towards me

through the mist. It seemed she was headed off a bit to my left, though, so I held out both hands and said, 'Becky! Over here!' She altered her course slightly and a moment later she caught hold of my hands.

'Just back up now,' she said, 'the way you came.'

I did, and after only a couple of steps I emerged into the place where I had stood earlier, facing the fog screen. She followed and threw herself into my arms, and I hugged her. Almost immediately, the fog began to disperse.

'I'm sorry,' she said. 'I'm sorry.'

'About what?' I asked.

'I mixed you and Barry up, sent you to the wrong places. I haven't had that much practice.'

'It's okay,' I told her. 'It worked out. We're both here at the Kendalls' now, and we're none the worse for it.'

'Did you—change?' she asked.

'Well, yes.'

'Was it bad?'

I thought about it for the first time in hours.

'It was kind of ... disconcerting,' I said, 'but I don't know that I'd call it *bad*. It was something I had to experience sooner or later, anyway. Besides, Uncle George says he can teach me how to control it. I should probably spend my exchange year here, learning the tricks of the trade.'

'Well, I'm glad I didn't get you into a lot of trouble.'

I shook my head. 'No real trouble. But neither one of us found Dad.'

'I know. He's in the darkband,' she said. 'The guy he had the fight with by the transcomp got away into our band, but Tom managed to shoot him—just a flesh wound, I think—before he transitted out. The darkbander damaged the unit then and—'

'Hold on! Hold on!' I said. 'How do you know all this?'

'The cleaning service,' she said. 'They came by after you left.'

'But they'd already been–' I began, and then I saw what she meant.

'The first man had to be the darkband agent,' she said, 'and it was his blood that you smelled. He must have had confederates in town–someone who's been studying us–to have come up with that story to cover his escape. Very thorough–that story was just in case we saw him leaving.'

'What did you do? And how did you know the other ones weren't the fakes?'

'I recognized the people in the second group. I'd looked out the window when I heard their truck pull up. It was the same one they always use. We'd never seen a truck for the first man, and I didn't recognize his name or his voice. I told the second ones the story you'd made up about the remodelling. And I remembered what you'd said about blood. So after they left I turned on the lights and looked around. I found some dried bloodstains on the back steps and a bloody handkerchief in the parking lot.'

'Why do you think he came through and attacked Dad?'

'I don't know,' she said. 'I have no idea exactly what he wanted. But I'll bet it has something to do with the war in the darkband. It could be that now things are more hectic there, the darkbanders are trying to stir up trouble in the other bands, to keep them from helping the partisans as much as they might.'

I pushed her out to arms' length and stared at her face. While I had complained to her a lot about not feeling trusted, as she was making her way towards me through the mist, going on about not being in on secrets that everyone else seemed to know, I had not mentioned every little detail—like the partisans. Now it appeared that she was yet another family member who was in on things that I wasn't.

My teeth made a gnashing noise as I brought them together.

'Jim, what's the matter?' she asked.

'*Everybody* knows stuff I don't!' I said. 'Even you! And you're a lot younger! How come Dad told you all this stuff when he didn't tell me?'

'He didn't!' she cried. 'I found out for myself! He didn't even know that I knew at first!'

'What do you mean "at first"?' I asked.

She hesitated, looking frightened. 'Later on, I did tell him some things I'd learned,' she said. 'That's what I meant.'

'So what did he do? What did he say?' I asked.

'He told me to keep them to myself.'

'That's all?'

'Uh-huh.'

'I don't think so,' I said. 'You've never been a good liar.'

'Well, maybe those weren't his exact words,' she replied. 'But that's what it amounted to.'

'Becky,' I said. 'Tell me *exactly* what he told you.'

She pulled away from me.

'Look, I don't want to talk about it,' she answered. 'I only mentioned the fighting because you told me how you heard about it when you were talking to me back in the fog. Let's drop it now. Okay?'

'Not okay,' I replied. 'I want to know. It's making me feel like an outcast. Why doesn't he trust me?'

'He *does* trust you,' she said.

'Okay, I'll guess what he said. He didn't just say keep your mouth shut. He said, "Don't tell Jim." '

She looked away.

'Didn't he?'

'All right. Yes, he did.'

'Why? If he trusts me why is he keeping me in the dark about all this stuff?'

'I can't say,' she replied.

'Why not?'

'He made me promise I wouldn't.'

I sighed. I slapped the side of a tree. A few guesses might have started tying themselves together in my mind about then.

'His present predicament involves all of this stuff, doesn't it?' I asked.

'Yes, it does,' she said.

'In that case,' I suggested, 'all bets are off. He's in trouble and he needs help. That would cancel any promises that got made back when he couldn't foresee this. I need the information if I'm going to be of any help to him.'

She thought about it, her face going through a whole series of contortions before she spoke.

'The reason he wouldn't tell you anything,' she finally said, 'is because Agatha's still alive.'

Agatha. That's my mother's name.

CHAPTER 9

Okay. Back up, Jim. . . . I thought hard and deeply about my mother—a thing I had not permitted myself to do for some time, because we had been very close, and thinking about it made it hurt all over again. She and Uncle George were brother and sister, though there was small resemblance, he being short, sandy-haired, stolid, while she was tall, slim, brunette; also, she was not a shapeshifter, and she lacked George's reticence. She talked more than he did, she touched more, she smiled more. Other relatives used to say that she had that generation's full share of extroversion and there'd been none left for George and Dalah. But she wasn't empty-headed or frail. She'd taught science and maths back home, and she shared her branch of the family's love for the out-doors. Her idea of a vacation involved camping, backpack-ing, rock climbing, canoeing; she was a very good archer and she was twice Women's Champion in the state pistol competition. I have to admit I was more than a little jealous when she brought Becky home and they grew close in ways I couldn't quite understand.

One day, almost a year ago, she'd gone off on one of those frequent family visits we pay among the bands—the things that really kept us current—and it dragged on for months, much longer than usual. Every time I'd ask about it, Dad would say something like 'Things keep coming up. Not to worry.' But of course, I did worry, because he seemed more and more troubled himself each time he said it. Then the last time I asked, he looked away and was silent for a while. I was almost about to repeat it when he finally spoke. 'There's been an accident. She won't be coming back.' Whenever I'd press for details he'd just say 'I don't want to talk about it,' or, 'There's nothing more to say,' or, 'Leave it at that.' When he didn't want to discuss something he could make Uncle George seem like the soul of loquacity.

So while I'd lacked details, I was given to believe that my mother was dead. Why would anybody create such an impression if it were untrue?

I stared at Becky, my rival, my partner in whatever loss or gain this brought our way, and thoughts and feelings flashed by too fast for me to categorize.

'I don't understand,' I said at last. 'It's bad enough not to tell me what's going on. But to deliberately mislead me. . . . How come you knew and I didn't?'

She started walking towards a fallen tree. I fell into step beside her.

'Tom tried telling me the same story he told you,' she said. 'But I discovered a bit later that it wasn't true, and I told him so. That's when he told me not to tell you.'

'Did he say why?'

'Yes. He felt you would figure the way to go to her to try to help, and that you would jeopardize the mission. He said this was the only way of handling the situation, and if everything worked out well you'd have a pleasant surprise.'

'And if it didn't I already believed the worst, huh? She's with the partisans, isn't she?'

'Yes. I don't think Tom liked the idea much more than we do, but I don't think he had any choice. She decided to go over while she was on that last trip.'

'Why?'

'A whole group of volunteers was going, from all of the lightbands. Most of them were specialists, possessing skills that would be useful.'

'Weapons,' I said.

'Well, yes. That too, I guess. But there was more. That darkband had been the place where she and her sister had done their exchange time. She speaks the language and she likes the place a lot, and her sister had married and stayed there, and—'

'I didn't make the connection,' I said. 'I knew the business about Dalah, but I didn't realize it was that band. She pointed it out to you, though, huh?'

'As part of something else,' she explained, coming up beside the fallen tree and seating herself on it. I only realized at that moment just how tired she looked. I sat down beside her and began breaking off twigs, snapping them into smaller and smaller pieces. 'It wasn't just her knowledge of weapons they needed,' she went on. 'That was really sort of secondary.'

'What, then?'

'Well . . . the reason she took me in. We're the same. You understand?'

I thought that I did; but I didn't quite know how to say it. In such cases simple and direct usually seems best, though. 'You mean, my mother's a witch?' I asked.

She shrugged.

'She never much liked that word,' Becky answered. 'It

has a special meaning in terms of membership in an early folk religion, and we're not really members. No. We're both sensitive to certain forces, though, which is why she was happy to find me. She wanted someone to pass the traditions along to.'

'What should I call you, then?'

'Anything you want, I guess. In some places they use the word "sorceress". Tom knows, of course. But we do have a tradition of secrecy, and it's especially important to keep the darkbanders from knowing where we all are. They'd try to get rid of us pretty quick if they found out, the way they did with Granny. They don't like us.'

'Why not?'

'Because they don't understand us and because we can hurt them. Almost all of us are on the lightbanders' side.'

We sat silent for a time; then she began again. 'Recently the partisans liberated several large areas, and the people there joined them. They've got a couple of armies now, and they're moving again. We think a turning point's been reached, that the fate of the band will be decided pretty soon.'

'Like I said, I've heard parts of this,' I told her, 'just today. But I didn't realize things were that close to some sort of resolution. I guess that explains the troops in the front yard. I suppose that even more could be on the way. I'll bet the lightbands are getting ready to send help.'

'They are,' she said, 'with special objectives.'

'Soon too, I'd guess.'

She nodded.

'Soon,' she agreed.

I threw away a final twig.

'How is it that you know so much?' I finally said.

'Agatha tells me these things,' she said, 'when I talk to

her. Some of the other things I can see for myself while they're happening—and sometimes before they happen.'

'So you've really been talking to Mum?'

'Uh-huh. There are ways we can sometimes reach each other.'

'That business with the candles?'

'Sort of,' she replied.

'When was the last time you were in touch with her?'

'During the night. I tried going to her first, but she wouldn't let me come through. She barred the path. Then I decided I'd better come here. But I was so tired I started to lose my way.'

'Was she . . . all right?'

'I think so. But they're in some kind of trouble. I can't tell exactly what it is yet, but I'm working on it. There's something they've got to do, but they're blocked.'

'Are they in danger?'

'I think so.'

'What should we do?'

'I don't know yet. I've got to learn the problem first.'

'I think we'd better go tell Uncle George and Aunt Maryl everything you've told me.'

'Not yet,' she said. 'They already know what to do when the time comes, but they can't do anything yet, because they're blocked. Of course!'

She looked up and smiled.

'What?' I asked.

'Blocks! Blocks!' she said. 'I think that might be what's the matter. But I've got to look and see.'

'You've lost me.'

'It's all right,' she said. 'Listen, Jim. I'm going to need some help.'

'What can I do?'

'Go and get me some food. I'm hungry. And bring me an empty bowl, too, a clean one.'

'Why don't you just come back to the house and eat?'

'No!' she said. 'Then we'd be in trouble. They might be able to stop us, because they know what I am.'

'Stop us? From doing what?'

'I'm not sure yet. I'll tell you later. But whatever you do, don't let anyone know I'm here.'

I glanced at the cloudy sky beyond the stirring tree limbs.

'Could rain,' I said.

'Then I'll get wet,' she stated. 'You won't tell, will you?'

'Why should I tell anybody anything?' I answered.

Uncle George found me while I was searching the pantry for some food and the bowl. When he asked me what I was doing I answered truthfully, 'Just looking for something to eat.'

'Well, when you finish I'd like to talk to you in the library,' he said.

This was it! I thought. He was finally going to fill me in as to what was going on. At last I was going to pick up those details I hadn't yet guessed or learned.

'Let's go now,' I said. 'I'll grab something to eat afterwards.'

He nodded and turned away. I followed him.

I was wrong. What followed was not at all a briefing on the darkband war or the fate of my parents. Instead, he had decided that it was time for my first full-scale lesson in werewolfery. Not that it wasn't fascinating. In fact, I got very engrossed in his explanation and demonstrations. I learned that a true shapeshifter can do it on purpose and does not need a full moon. I also learned that the wolf form, while easiest, is not exclusive; almost any shifting about is achievable, within the constraints of mass conservation, after a certain amount of practice. It was so interesting that I lost track of the time and did not realize that a couple of hours had passed, until he concluded and remarked, 'Maybe you'll want to skip that snack now, since it's so close to dinnertime.'

Instant guilt. I thought of poor Becky, half starved in the grove, waiting for her bowl and her scraps.

'Maybe just a small bite,' I said, backing towards the door.

He looked at me strangely, then said, 'I thought you'd have some other questions for me.'

'Would I have got answers to them?' I asked.

'Not yet,' he said.

I shrugged. 'Didn't think so,' I told him.

'Wait,' he said, as I began moving again. 'There's reasons.'

I nodded. 'I'm sure,' I said. 'See you later.'

He opened his mouth as if to speak again, apparently thought better of it, and nodded. I turned and ran from the room.

I wondered as I fled whether he had actually been considering telling me more than he'd originally intended. Maybe he felt sorry for me. Maybe. . . . What difference did it make? I already knew most of the important things, and I had to hurry. When I reached the pantry I quickly found Becky some bread and cheese and a couple of apples. I wrapped them in a napkin, and I picked up a small bowl, too. While I was doing this I heard a series of brief familiar cries from somewhere out back. I hid the food and the bowl inside my shirt and I departed.

When I stepped outside I saw him in a level area beyond

the stables. Barry had removed his shirt and boots and socks and was working his way through a *kata*, the punches and kicks punctuated by an occasional *kiai*. I had to admit that it was a rather pretty performance, but my thoughts were almost immediately elsewhere. That is, to tell him or not to tell him about Becky. On the one hand, I didn't know what she was up to or what it might lead to. On the other, he'd been in this from the beginning and had certainly acted as if he'd wanted to help. I just wasn't certain what I'd do if he decided it was his duty to tell the Kendalls that Becky was here and we were up to something.

What decided me? I sometimes wondered later. Was it that I trusted him? Or that I had to go past him to get to Becky, and he'd be curious where I was headed anyway?

CHAPTER 10

So I told Barry about Becky as we walked back to the wood, and about the things I had learned.

'I felt sorry for you,' he said, 'but Tom told me not to talk about it, and he's the boss.'

'I understand,' I said.

'He thought you'd fiddle with the darkband till you hit the right frequency,' he told me, 'and go to her . . . '

'He was probably right,' I said.

' . . . and screw things up royally for them.'

'Maybe that, too,' I agreed.

'Anyhow, I'm glad you know now.'

I nodded. We were nearing the place where I had left Becky and I was suddenly a bit nervous. I could see the fallen tree, but Becky was nowhere in sight. A moment later, however, I realized that what I had thought to be a rock or a stump was actually Becky, seated on the ground, not moving.

'I'm sorry,' I called to her. 'I couldn't get away and—'

'I figured that,' she said, raising her head. 'Bring me the food, and don't step on my design. Hi, Barry.'

As we drew nearer, I saw that she had surrounded her-self with an elaborate tracery of lines scratched into the earth. A damp-looking stick lay near her right hand, and there was a pile of dry ones off to her left. Barry halted and studied the markings suspiciously. I continued on, picking my way carefully amid the lines, avoiding stepping on any of them. She accepted the napkin of food but handed the bowl back to me.

'Go wash it in the stream,' she said. 'Then fill it about two-thirds of the way with water and bring it back.'

There were a few distant grumbles of thunder as I did this, but no rain followed. I came back with the bowl before Becky had finished eating, and I set it down in front of her, careful not to drip on her artwork. As I watched her eat whatever meal that was for her, I'd a funny feeling that I was going to miss my own dinner. I should probably have brought more.

She handed me the napkin and the apple cores when she had finished.

'Do something with these,' she said.

'Okay,' I agreed. 'Then what?'

'Then you wait,' she said. 'Over there.'

She gestured off in Barry's direction.

As I made my way back I tossed the cores into the woods and folded the napkin and put it in my pocket. I hun-kered beside Barry and waited.

'What's she doing?' he whispered.

'Looks like she's just staring into the bowl of water,' I said.

This went on for a long while, and finally—I'd known it would come sooner or later—I heard a bell, the dinner bell, ringing. Shortly thereafter I heard my name called, then Barry's. The voice was Aunt Maryl's.

Barry swore softly and glanced at me.

'We can't go,' I said.

'I know,' he replied. 'But what if they come looking for us?'

'We'll just have to wait and see.'

Several minutes later she called again. Again, we did not stir. But, 'Come here,' Becky said a little later.

We got to our feet and trod gently amid her drawings. She began speaking then, without standing, without looking at us.

'I see what's happened,' she said. 'It's a deadlock right now.'

'What do you mean?' Barry asked, when the next silence began to grow uncomfortable.

'They're pinned down near a key installation—some sort of power station,' she answered. 'If they can take control of the place it will be a turning point. They'll have the region. But there's a darkband force they can't get past, holding them in their position. Both sides know how important the situation is. Both sides are waiting for reinforcements. Whichever gets them first is going to win.'

The bell rang again. Our names were called again. This time there was a note of exasperation in Aunt Maryl's voice.

'Where are the darkbanders' reinforcements?' I asked.

'On the march, and they're bringing artillery.'

'Where are ours?'

'Waiting, in various places all over the lightbands,' she replied, and I immediately thought of the troops camped in front of the manor. 'But they can't get through to help the rebels.'

There came another rumble of thunder, and the wind stirred the trees and shrubs.

'Because the darkbanders are jamming the rebels'

transcomp,' she said, answering my unspoken question 'They've learned the rebels' frequencies, and they've a machine down in their camp that's blocking them.'

'So the darkbanders will win as soon as their help arrives,' Barry said.

'Unless their transmitter is destroyed,' she replied.

'And we can't transmit more people in to do that because the band is blocked,' I said. 'It's a Catch Twenty-two.'

'I can get us through,' she said softly, 'the same way I came here.'

'I thought Mum had blocked your way to the band,' I said.

'No, she just blocked my way to her. She can't keep me out of a whole damn band.'

'Say you can get us there,' Barry said. 'What good can three kids do against an armed camp? I don't see how we could get near the thing.'

'It's already night there,' she answered. 'I can cloak us in the dark, make us almost impossible to detect—for a while, anyway.'

The shrubbery rustled again, and this time there was no wind. Neither of them seemed to notice this and I said nothing. Something troubled me about her proposal, too, though it took me several moments to put my finger on what it was.

'Becky,' I said finally, 'you're not telling us everything.'

She looked up for the first time and met my gaze. I saw that her eyes were wet.

'I've told you everything that's important,' she answered. 'If I take us through and get us into their camp, and we break the transmitter, then the partisans' transcomp will start working again. They'll have reinforcements, high tech and low, pouring in. If that happens before the other side gets reinforced they'll break out and win the battle. Then they'll attack the station. It shouldn't be a hard thing to capture with all the extra help. There's other fighting going on elsewhere, but this battle is crucial. If they secure this area it might be the end of the war, except for the cleaning up.'

'I understand all of that,' I said, 'but it wasn't what I was talking about. Mum and Dad are with the rebels. . . . '

'Yes. Tom apparently got through right before the jamming began.'

'Well, if Mum's a sorceress with more experience than you, how come she didn't make a few people invisible and go after the transmitter herself?'

'They're jamming her, too,' she said.

'How the hell do you jam a sorceress, Becky?'

'You bring in one of your own to attack her,' she replied. 'Then she has to defend herself. They fight each other in their own ways then, and whoever slips up gets fried. They're too busy to do anything else. So you have a deadlock there too.'

'I thought the darkbanders didn't have any people like that.'

'They don't have too many, but they do have a few renegades working with them. They brought one along on this expedition because they knew this rebel group had one.'

'How long can a duel like that go on?' I asked.

'Till one of them slips up,' she said.

'I mean, how long can Mum keep something like that going?'

'I don't know,' she said. 'I've never done it. It depends on how strong they both are, and maybe how tricky.'

'What I'm getting at,' I said, 'is that you say you can cover us with some spell or other and get us into the darkband camp. But if they've got a sorceress in there, won't she be able to spot us sneaking in?'

'Sorcerer,' she corrected. 'Theirs is a man. From around here, I think. But I was counting on him being so distracted by his own problems with Agatha that he wouldn't feel us in the neighbourhood. If he does try anything he'll have to break his concentration to do it. Then she'll get him—and I could probably protect us in the meantime.'

'If you can take us through,' Barry asked, 'why can't you bring along all those troops in the front yard? If they were to flank the darkband camp or hit it from the rear the partisans would probably move in. We'd catch them between two forces.'

'No,' she said. 'I'm not that strong. It's a question of large masses as opposed to small ones. I can take a few people though, but not a big group.'

'One more question occurs to me,' I said. 'If you can get us into their camp and we break their machine, how do we, uh, get out again?'

She looked away.

'It will be a question of staying safe till the partisans attack,' she said. 'We either hide or we run for it, whichever seems the best idea.'

'I see,' I said, realizing that my mouth had become very dry. I had anticipated her answer some time back. Barry simply smiled and nodded. Mr. Cool. His people love that sort of business—coming back with their shields or on them. They even make up songs about it. As for me, it seemed pretty clear that even if we made it in and did the job, we were all going to die afterwards. On the other hand, my parents would probably die if we didn't try. I suppose I should have thought nobly and selflessly about how the fate of an entire band might hinge upon our action. But I'm not that noble and selfless. The place was just an abstraction to me. The only ones I really cared about were my folks. I'm not cut out for sainthood and I think most heroics are stupid.

So, 'I can't think of any better ideas,' I said.

'Then I think we'd better get going,' she answered, 'before the rain comes and ruins my keys.' She surveyed her designs once again.

'I wish there was some way we could leave a message for Aunt Maryl and Uncle George,' I said.

'If we succeed they'll know soon enough,' Barry said, producing a pocketknife. 'Before we go, though, I want to cut a good sapling and trim it. A staff is a great weapon.'

Becky glanced at the lowering clouds.

'Okay, but don't waste any time,' she said.

He headed back among the trees and I watched him go. I felt a drop of rain on my hand, another on my cheek. Across from me the shrubbery stirred slightly. Maybe just the wind.

'You're a tough kid, Becky,' I said, but she did not answer me. Instead, she began laying out the dry sticks on a nearby part of her pattern. Softly, very softly, she seemed to be singing as she did it.

I watched her for a time. The pattern of sticks she was creating seemed to bear some resemblance to the design she had made with the brass rods when she had sent me here. It wasn't identical, but there was some sort of coherence to the form which struck me as similar to that other one. When she was finished she rocked back on her heels and regarded her work, still voicing that nameless, airy tune. After a small while she began producing a soft clicking noise, and at first I wasn't sure how she was doing it.

A little later Barry came up, a staff in his hands, and

stood beside me. His face was even more expressionless than usual, and his gaze seemed a hard, flinty thing.

'All right,' he said. 'I'm ready.'

Becky did not reply at once, but her singing grew louder and the clicking began to occur more frequently, interspersed with a kind of rough, grating sound. I saw then that she was holding two small, smooth river pebbles in her left hand, rolling them back and forth against each other, occasionally clicking them together in counterpoint to her song. Then I became aware of something stirring, something blank and. . . .

I jerked my head up and to the left. Then I sighed. It was the fog. It had come back to the place it had occupied earlier, between the trees. Tenuous, drifting at first, it seemed to deepen, to grow more dense, to become more still.

It was only then that I realized that a part of Becky's design extended right on back into that area where the fog hung like some ghostly curtain, and that that part of her drawing seemed most like a path or trail. I felt more raindrops then, and a strong wind came up and blew about us, but the whiteness remained. Becky got to her feet and turned away, indicating that we should follow her and that we should pass through the same areas of her design that she did.

So I fell into step behind her, and Barry followed me. The thing wound around itself like a chambered nautilus, going in a counterclockwise direction. I heard the continued grating of the stones she rolled together, along with her singing, which rose and fell within the wind. The rain was coming down more heavily now, and when we made a final turn I saw that we had come on to that long last stretch which led into the fog. From the corner of my eye I thought

I saw something move off to my right. But three more steps and it didn't matter. We had entered the fog bank and the sounds of the storm were suddenly muffled and I no longer felt any raindrops. It was similar to my experience the other night. We had already come too far to be contained within that small wisp of mist, yet it seemed to stretch on and on for a great distance. The ground had a soft turfy feel to it. Becky's voice seemed somehow altered. I could hear no other sounds than the ones she was making, not even my own breathing.

Again it seemed we walked for a long while in a kind of pearly twilight, though I couldn't see for more than a few feet in any direction. I could see Becky ahead of me, and I followed her; I could sense, rather than hear, Barry's presence at my back. Somehow, I found this reassuring. It was far better to have their company than it had been walking off alone into the unknown, as I had the other night.

After a time the white walls receded and finally vanished. We were walking in a wood, and it was night. Becky kept going and we kept following until she finally raised her hand and halted.

'What is it?' I whispered.

'We're here,' she said.

CHAPTER 11

We crouched as Becky parted the foliage to give us a view of what lay before us. Directly ahead was a camp. There were tents and scattered lumps that looked like bedrolls, and a few fires and armed guards lurking about. Far behind it, to our left, was what I assumed to be the partisans' objective, though it didn't resemble any sort of power station with which I was familiar. It was a huge installation surrounded by a wire fence; it was filled with tall, fragile-looking towers, which wore halos of blue light. Lower boxlike structures were situated among the towers, and great dark cables coiled and stretched from one to another, seeming to tie the whole thing together. There seemed to be armed human figures patrolling among these forms.

Far off to our right, beyond the encampment we faced, rose a range of hills. Partly shielded campfires glowed here and there along its middle height. Again, I glimpsed some figures, possibly patrolling that area. Those would be the rebels, it seemed, my parents somewhere among them.

Becky made a small noise while Barry and I were studying the scene. I glanced at her and saw that she was staring far off to the left. I followed her gaze, but I could see nothing unusual at first.

Then, as my vision passed back and forth over that area to the rear of the camp, I spotted some small movements and several big outlines, which were being moved jerkily about.

'It must be their reinforcements,' I heard Barry whisper. 'It looks as if they're setting up artillery pieces back there.'

Becky made another small noise.

'We've got to go in soon,' she said.

'They may well save their ammo for daylight,' Barry remarked, 'when they can see better what they're shooting at.'

'Even so,' Becky answered, 'we can't wait till then. My spell works best at night, and the rebels are going to need reinforcements soon. It will take a while to bring them through and to tell them what they have to do.'

'Yeah,' Barry said. 'So what do we do now?'

'I'm going to need about ten minutes of silence,' she replied, 'to put our protection together. I'll let you know when it's ready, and then we'll go in.'

'Do you know which tent their machine's in?' I asked.

'No,' she said. 'We'll just have to look.'

'I'd guess it would be the one on highest ground,' Barry observed, 'which would be that big one towards the farther side.'

'All right, we'll head for it,' she said.

Then we backed away from the place where we had been kneeling until we came to a somewhat more open area. Becky seated herself on the ground. She appeared to be thinking. I sat down to her left, Barry to her right, and we waited. Nothing much happened for a long time, but then suddenly I felt it.

It was as if the woods were somehow more alive all about us, as if the trees were shedding something like gossamer on to us. But it was finer than any spiderweb; it was almost like a breeze with something of substance to it. But there were no real breezes blowing.

When Becky stood and said, 'Take my hands,' and we did, letting her lead us forward among the trees and out of them, it was almost as if we were wearing veils of some material that didn't quite register on the senses. But now I noted that every light source, like the distant campfires, seemed somehow muted, somehow slightly dimmed, yet in the dark spaces in between, everything seemed to be glistening slightly. It was almost like moonlight, though there was no moon risen.

We did not speak as we advanced upon the camp, but my heart was beating heavily and it seemed a real effort to keep my breathing silent and regular. When we neared the perimeter of the place I half expected some sentry to challenge us, but nothing happened. Surely as we passed the first tent someone would step out and. . . .

Nothing happened.

We kept going. We halted a couple of times to let people pass, but no one seemed to notice us. I'd no idea Becky could be that competently professional about anything. I resolved then never to tease her again. The cloaking spell was not a hundred percent effective, I'd gathered, and Becky took us far out of our way to avoid large concentrations of reclining troops. We did pass one man who seemed to be staring right at us. But he only shook his head and rubbed his eyes as we passed. Maybe he was a bit more sensitive than the others. We got out of his vicinity quickly, though.

It occurred to me as we passed along that if the tent we had made our goal was indeed the one we sought, our best chance of surviving after we wrecked the transmitter would be to keep going in the direction we were now headed, in that the tent lay near the farther perimeter of the camp. That area off to the place's left flank was open, and if we could cross it fast there were more trees in the distance.

There came an explosion from far off to the left, to the rear of the camp. Shortly, there was another. Even before the second detonation occurred, however, all three of us must have realized what it was, though we said nothing. They were letting loose some artillery rounds, lobbing shells over the camp and against the hillside. We hurried on. We had to find the thing now, and pretty quickly too.

As we neared the tent it seemed more and more likely that it was the one we sought. There appeared to be some sort of antenna affixed to the top of one of its main poles, and something that appeared to be a small generator stood humming behind the tent. Becky halted us and we studied the place for some time. There came more explosions from far to the left, and this time they continued fairly steadily. The first few must only have been trials, while this sounded like the beginning of a bombardment.

We discovered that it was impossible for us to communicate in whispers, and we didn't want to try shouting and possibly attracting local attention to ourselves, readily visible or not. There was a sentry leaning on a rifle in front of the tent flap in front. Barry nudged us both, pointed to the man, pointed to himself, and pointed to his staff. Becky and I looked at each other, then nodded. I couldn't think of any other way past the man, for if we went around to the side and cut a hole in the tent it would probably draw attention fast. Becky indicated by gesture that we should all advance together or we'd lose the protection of her spell. Barry nodded, and we moved forward again. The artillery barrage was still in progress and I could see clouds of smoke rising at various points along the hillside. How effective this might be in terms of actual damage I could not tell. From the rhythm of the firing and the sources of the flashes I could sometimes spot, it seemed that there were three field pieces in operation.

As we moved quietly but surely towards the tired-looking sentry, I thought ahead to what was going to happen. I did not doubt that Barry could knock him out quickly, relatively mercifully, and with a minimum of damage. He'd been training at that sort of thing all his life. But I was considering the moment when the man fell. We couldn't just leave him lying there as an advertisement that something was wrong. The only practical thing to do would be to drag him inside immediately. And that would commit us to fast action. Whether we were visible or not, it was going to put anybody on the inside on immediate alert when the trooper came crashing in. If it turned out we were in the wrong tent our entire mission would be messed up. And even if it were the right tent, there was no way of telling how many people might be inside.

Becky halted and put her hands on both of us, indicating pretty clearly that we should stop too. She pushed our heads together and moved so that her mouth was but a few inches from our ears. Then she spoke sharply, piercing the banging of the guns with her words:

'I don't like it! There's something very wrong in that tent!'

'What do you mean?' Barry said carefully.

'I don't know,' she answered. 'I'm sure it's the right place. But it's—like a trap. I've got this bad feeling of danger.'

Barry and I looked at each other. We already knew we were in danger, so it wasn't as if this was any special news. Besides. . . .

'What choice do we have?' Barry asked.

She was silent for several moments, then she nodded.

'But it's something special,' she added.

'I don't see how we can be more careful than we already are,' I said.

She nodded again and we resumed stalking the guard. Now I found myself wishing the artillery would continue just a little longer, to cover the sounds of the disturbance we were about to create.

As we drew near, the guard began shifting about, glancing in all directions. Several times his gaze slid right over us but did not falter. We continued our approach. Suddenly then, Barry moved. His staff cut an arc so quickly I barely saw it, striking the man behind his right ear. Barry was through the tent flap and inside then, almost before the guard began to fall.

I made a quick decision. Barry almost certainly didn't need any help I might give him, and as I'd decided earlier we had to dispose of the evidence. Therefore, I caught the guard under the armpits and dragged him back and through the tent's entrance—my job, as I saw it. Becky snatched up the rifle and followed. From behind me, within, I heard the sounds of a brief scuffle.

As soon as I had the soldier through the entrance, I lowered him, straightened, and turned to survey the interior. To the rear was a table supporting a unit that bore some resemblance to our transcomp back home. From the lights on its face it appeared to be turned on and functioning. Before it, a brown-shirted man—apparently its operator—was slumped unconscious. Towards the centre of the area Barry was attacking a second man, who was defending himself with a shovel. They circled and feinted several times, parrying each other's strikes. Suddenly Barry dropped and caught the man behind the knees with a sweeping movement of his staff. As he fell backwards, Barry was already striking again, for the stomach, the neck.

'Very impressive,' came a voice from the far side of the tent as the man sprawled and lay still, 'for one so young.'

Becky had just lowered the rifle to the floor and I was about to head for the machine. But we all turned in the direction of that assured, mocking voice. Its owner flowed to his feet from a cross-legged position atop a bedroll. He was barefoot, and he had on black trousers and a matching shirt open wide at the neck. I could see that some sort of medallion hung amid the hairs of his chest. He was not a large man, slim of build, and perhaps only a few inches taller than Barry. His dark hair was long and tied back in a ponytail, revealing a silver earring in his left ear. His eyes were very dark, and when he raised his hands I saw that he wore several rings on each.

Becky stifled a cry as Barry stepped forward, beginning to spin his staff.

'It's him,' she said softly, and I realized suddenly that the artillery had let up moments ago.

'Who?' I said.

'The one I saw. . . . '

Just then there came a splintering, cracking sound, and the staff fell apart in Barry's hands. The man stepped forward and Barry threw the two pieces he still held at him. The man brushed them aside with two almost casual gestures and continued to advance, and I realized what Becky had meant. This had to be the darkband sorcerer Mum had been fighting, the one Becky had assured me Mum would nail if his attention wavered. Only now his attention was entirely focused upon Barry and he seemed none the worse for it. This could only mean that Mum had lost, that she might well be dead now and that this man had done it. Suddenly, I wanted to attack him myself, but Barry was already there.

Barry spun suddenly into an attack I'd heard him refer to as a turning back kick. But even as he moved, the sorcerer was already stepping to the side, as if he'd read his mind. His hands seemed to move very slowly and to fall very lightly, but when they touched Barry's extended leg I saw him stiffen. Then Barry fell backward to the ground and lay still.

The man smiled and raised his head. He looked at Becky. He looked at me.

'...And his name is Crow,' Becky said. 'Smash the machine!'

Her hands were already drifting upwards as she spoke, and the man's gaze snapped back to her.

'What have we here?' he remarked, his own hands doing the same.

'What happened to Agatha?' she asked.

He looked for a moment as if he were considering whether the truth could hurt him in any way, then he said, 'I don't know. Our contact was broken when the firing started. Maybe she was hit. I haven't felt her presence since.'

I felt a tension beginning to build between them, as if at some level they were wrist wrestling, their arms swaying back and forth. I began to retreat towards the machine. The man she had named Crow glanced at me, as if he wished to do something to halt me. Almost immediately, however, he winced, and I continued on my way, feeling as if I had just avoided something nasty. My movements were slowed, however.

'You're strong, my dear,' he said. 'Becky, is it? But you're tired, very tired.'

'So are you,' she said.

'But I'm stronger, and I know more.'

He took a step forward. She retreated a pace. I could see that they were both sweating. I looked about for something to strike the machine with. There was the shovel, but it was too near Crow. Then I decided that the simplest thing to do would be to push it off the table. I set my hands on it and shoved. It didn't budge. Heavy.

All right. Becky was retreating again and Crow advancing as I caught hold of the edge of the table and tried lifting it. It moved a little, but not much. Barry moaned and stirred.

I turned my back on the table and caught hold of its edge again. I bent my knees and squatted. Then I began to straighten my legs.

Becky suddenly retreated all the way to the tent wall, covered her face with her hands and sobbed. Crow laughed.

'Not bad,' he said, stepping forward. 'But not good enough.'

My arms felt as if they were being wrenched out of their sockets as the table rose slowly above the ground. I felt the unit begin to slide along its surface. Crow must have caught the movement because he turned away from Becky immediately and faced me. I knew, somehow, at that moment, that he intended to kill me, and I lifted even harder. Barry was beginning to raise himself slowly from the ground, but he was in no shape to be of any help yet.

It was then that the tent flap moved and a great grey wolf entered and sprang. I thrust with my legs and the table rose and went over and the machine crashed to the ground. Crow was driven face forward into the earth, and I heard the snarls, saw the flash of Uncle George's fangs.

CHAPTER 12

I understand we all died that night and were later buried in the area. But I remember getting out through the opening Uncle George slashed in the far side of the tent and running with Barry's arm across my shoulders, half dragging him, Becky stumbling along to my left, as another artillery barrage let loose. I remember our making it to a place among some trees and collapsing there for a time before we were able to continue to a distant point where the hills began. It was almost morning before we'd climbed, turned to our right, and begun making our way in the direction of the partisans' position. Day broke before we reached it, though, and we saw the lines of attackers flow down the hillsides and begin their advance upon the darkband camp. There seemed to be an awful lot of them, and I detected gear from a number of different bands. The artillery ceased a little later, but all of the other sounds of combat now reached us with great clarity, despite the distance. I don't know how long we watched before the camp was secured, but our troops moved on then to attack the power installation, still dark and flickering, like some city of gnomes uncovered in day's light. The installation was surrendered without a struggle, however. Its defenders, who had been watching the battle, must have decided their cause was hopeless. It was only when I realized that the place was captured that I noticed how warm I had grown and looked up to regard the sun's position. It had moved considerably since daybreak. Several hours must have passed while we watched, though it felt as if we had been standing there for a much shorter time.

We continued on towards what had been the rebels' position the night before, avoiding craters and strewn debris more and more frequently as we came nearer. Uncle George had shifted back to his normal human form by then and appropriated some clothing from a wrecked shelter. I think he smelled my parents at about the same time I did. We raced forward and rounded a stand of stone. My father was seated on the ground, a bandage around his head, his back against a boulder; my mother was sleeping wrapped in a blanket nearby.

Becky and I rushed forward, dropping to the ground between them, reaching. . . . Barry followed more slowly, smiling.

Uncle George regarded his sister, then looked at my father.

'Busy night,' he said.

Neither Barry nor Becky had any after effects from their encounter with Crow; nor did my mother, other than a general fatigue, not all of which could be blamed on the sorcerer's duel. She told me very quietly why she had thought it best to deceive me as she had concerning her absence. I did not agree with her explanation, because I felt I was old enough to have handled the actual situation.

She nodded when I told her that. Uncle George had already explained to her what we had done.

'No more secrets,' she said. 'Promise.'

What could I say? That I was satisfied? It was a lesson in growing up, that's all.

'I'm just happy you're safe,' I told her.

Uncle George explained a bit later how he had suspected during our lesson that something was up, and that he'd resolved to investigate when we'd failed to respond to the summons to dinner. He had assumed his stealthier form and watched us. When we'd departed he had followed us through the design and the fog, having pretty much guessed what was going on when he'd seen that Becky was involved.

Dad grew concerned, though, when he'd heard Becky's story in its entirety. I'd thought he'd be upset about the darkbander getting away, but it was the part about Dr. Wade that really seemed to bother him.

'He definitely mentioned the presence of new material in that file?' he asked.

'Yes,' I said. 'He was very hot on studying it right away.'

Dad stared skyward and made the low growling humming noises he does when he's doing calculations in his head. Then he said to Mum, 'It's sometime in the morning back home. Could be he's still there, especially if he stayed up late.'

She nodded.

'I understand. I'm up to it,' she said.

They both got to their feet.

'Come on. We'd better hurry.'

They hunted up the transcomp machine, and Uncle George agreed to act as operator and see if ours was still receiving. After a few signal tests he claimed that it was. Before I transitted out, he squeezed my shoulder.

'I'll be seeing you for some more lessons one of these days,' he remarked.

'I'm sure,' I said. 'Thanks for everything.'

He smiled—the first time I'd ever seen him do that.

We needn't have rushed. Dr Wade was still asleep when we returned home. This gave us time to clean up—I even shaved again—and to begin preparing a heavy breakfast.

Our timing was pretty good. Dr Wade was up and about before we were finished. I got sent upstairs next door to invite him to join us. He agreed readily. He seemed to be in an awfully good mood.

'This has been an unusually fruitful visit,' he said.

'Oh. Great. See you downstairs,' I replied.

He was beaming all over the place during breakfast, and, having bought Dad's explanation involving an accident for the neater but still obvious head dressing he wore (or, at least, pretended to), he tried to get Dad into a discussion about the equations he'd turned up, and something he'd just named a 'particlemosaic', which he claimed the formulas justified. I couldn't actually tell whether he was talking about some theoretical concept involving energy levels in particle physics, or whether he was saying that it had some immediate application in either weapons systems or pure energy systems. Becky, Barry, and I ate fast and cleared out quickly, leaving him there having coffee with Dad and Mum.

Later, when I wandered—all right, I was curious—near the doorway, I saw that Dr. Wade was leaning back in his chair with his eyes closed while Mum spoke to him softly and steadily. A little later Dad purged all of the new material from the file.

I still remember the man's words as he departed: 'I keep feeling I've forgotten something, but I just can't think what it could be.'

'Must not have been very important, then,' Dad told him.

The darkband invader had, as I had already guessed, been attempting to sabotage our band by introducing a radical and sophisticated physical concept we were not likely to come up with for a long while yet, just at a time perfect to do maximum damage. It was the timing game again. Perhaps nothing bad would have come of it, but we operated our social engineering programme by the same rules as the darkbanders—rules of thumb, in a way, derived from experiences in other bands.

Other bands. . . . Like the one we died in.

Parallel worlds seem to be created when a certain key turning point in a band's history is reached. There are some theoreticians who say that every decision that is made results in the creation of a parallel world, that every either-or situation goes both ways, with a resultant infinity of universes. They say, though, that the minor variations produce changes too subtle to be detectable with any equipment we have today. Whatever the truth of the matter, there is only a limited number of bands we have detected and that we are able to tune in, and things have worked themselves out in a variety of ways in these different places. The principles which determine just what constitutes a major turning point in a band's history are profoundly obscure things. We have very little idea as to how they operate.

But we were there when it happened. It was the first time in memory when a new band was activated.

There is now an additional lightband—the one where the partisans captured the power installation, won the war, and drove the darkbanders out.

But there is still a third darkband. There, according to intelligence reports, the rebels' transcomp was destroyed by artillery fire and no relief got through to them. My parents died during that barrage, having been near the machine. Becky, Barry, and I died in the enemy camp, along with Uncle George. Whether it was all Crow's doing or whether he'd had help from the troops could not be discovered. Personally, I think he would've had to have had help.

It is a very strange feeling to know that there is a band where I died. But supposing I hadn't? I'm sure I'd be getting ready to go to my rescue.

And if I succeeded? It would be an even stranger feeling, I suppose, meeting me. What would I say to myself? And which of us would really own my stereo tapes?

Or Becky? What would we do with another Becky? Or Barry? Or if we had two Mums and Dads?

People are not duplicated this way among the other bands we can tune in. The bands all parted from wherever they came, a long, long time ago, and slowly, subtly, they changed as they went their own ways. Our theoreticians tell us that there would have been full sets of duplicates initially, as happened here, but that gradually, over the centuries, these would have been smoothed away.

But I wonder about all of the people in the new lightband who know that they have twins living in a conquered country. They will be among the first in the new attempts to free the third darkband, I am certain, and there will doubtless be some very interesting impersonations and encounters. One day I hope to go to it as a lightband and to visit my grave, our graves, with flowers.

I could philosophize, I suppose, about some cosmic balancing of good and evil or some such. But there are more lightbands than darkbands, and philosophical concepts—especially ones involving morality—always get too fuzzy for me too soon. Like I said, I want to be a scientist, and I want to work in those areas of discovery where, in the long run, the facts are always stronger than the guesses.

Speaking of long runs. . . .

It's a beautiful night out there, and the moon will be rising soon.

I think I'll go and sing to it.